S0-BDH-537

WITHDRAWN FOR
$16⁰⁰

SLJ 01/07

WITHDRAWN
Media Center
UPTON MIDDLE SCHOOL
800 Maiden Lane
St. Joseph, MI 49085

WITHDRAWN

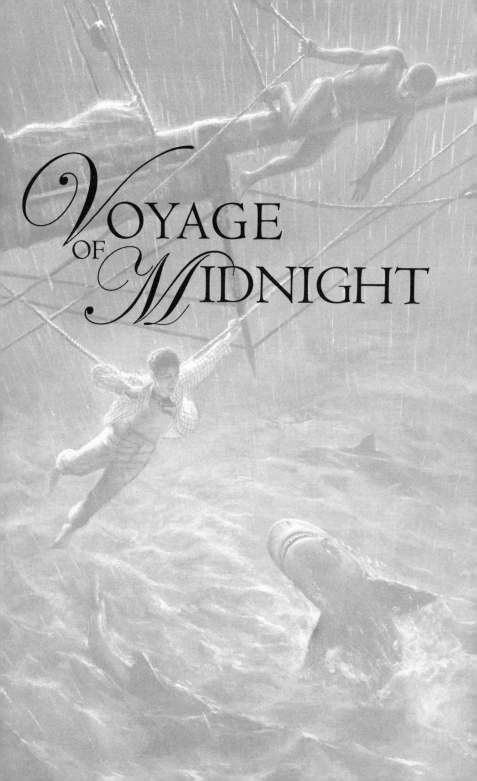

VOYAGE OF MIDNIGHT

MICHELE TORREY

VOYAGE OF MIDNIGHT

CHRONICLES OF COURAGE

Alfred A. Knopf
New York

Voyage of Midnight

Being the true story of my, Philip

Arthur Higgins', misfortunate childhood,

of my subsequent voyage from Africa

with a cargo of slaves, of the frightful

sufferings endured during that middle passage,

and of what happened afterward.

As told to
MICHELE TORREY

Once again, a hearty thank-you goes to Ron Wanttaja, my fellow writer and Washingtonian, for his assistance with all things nautical. His keen sensibilities and sharp "weather eye" kept me from going too far adrift (or so he thinks!). Also, my heartfelt appreciation goes to Susan Marlow of Washington and Erick Cordero of Costa Rica for their help with the Spanish. ¡*Gracias!* As in all my previous books, if there are any remaining errors or exaggerations, whether nautical or otherwise, they remain my responsibility alone, as to write a story of this nature it is often necessary to perform a balancing act between "fact" and "fiction."

THIS IS A BORZOI BOOK PUBLISHED BY ALFRED A. KNOPF

This is a work of fiction. Names, characters, places, and incidents either are the product of the author's imagination or are used fictitiously. Any resemblance to actual persons, living or dead, events, or locales is entirely coincidental.

Copyright © 2006 by Michele Torrey
All rights reserved.

Published in the United States by Alfred A. Knopf, an imprint of Random House Children's Books, a division of Random House, Inc., New York.

KNOPF, BORZOI BOOKS, and the colophon are registered trademarks of Random House, Inc.

www.randomhouse.com/kids

Educators and librarians, for a variety of teaching tools, visit us at
www.randomhouse.com/teachers

Library of Congress Cataloging-in-Publication Data
Torrey, Michele.
Voyage of midnight / Michele Torrey. — 1st ed.
    p.   cm.
SUMMARY: In the early nineteenth century, when his sea-captain uncle invites him to assist the ship's surgeon on his next voyage, orphaned fourteen-and-a-half-year-old Philip, eager to be with family, accepts, only to find out that his uncle is a slave trader.
ISBN-13: 978-0-375-82382-4 (trade) — ISBN-13: 978-0-375-92382-1 (lib. bdg.)
ISBN-10: 0-375-82382-4 (trade) — ISBN-10: 0-375-92382-9 (lib. bdg.)
[1. Orphans—Fiction. 2. Physicians—Fiction. 3. Slave trade—Fiction.
4. Voyages and travels—Fiction. 5. Uncles—Fiction.] I. Title.
PZ7.T645725Voo 2006
[Fic]—dc22   2005036269

Printed in the United States of America

November 2006

10 9 8 7 6 5 4 3 2 1

First Edition

To my father,
who sowed the seeds
of equality,
justice,
and human rights
in my heart

And to those
who have died
without a voice

Amazing Grace! How sweet the sound,
that saved a wretch, like me!
I once was lost but now am found,
was blind but now I see!

—John Newton,
former slave trader, 1779

I never saw my father. He was a sea-faring man and died before I was born, lost overboard in the middle of an Atlantic gale.

My mother and I lived together for four and a half years at our cottage in Magford, England, before she fell ill and breathed her last, leaving me with nothing but her cold hand pressed against my cheek and the pound of rain against the shutters.

Thus, in the year 1811, I became an orphan and a ward of the parish.

I needn't relate in detail my life in the Magford workhouse—the watery gruel and hard bread; the scowling face and long cane of Master Crump; the nights, the years, spent shivering beneath my moth-eaten blanket—no, for it's the story of many an orphan and so holds no uniqueness other than that it happened to me. It's enough to say that I was miserable, praying each night to God Almighty that I might join my father and mother in heaven. For what, indeed, was the purpose of living if I was only to suffer?

When I reached the age of ten, I was sent to work for a cushion maker. I'd have thought it impossible for my suffering to increase, but increase it did. Already I was a sickly lad, pale, scrawny, no larger than a child of seven or eight years old. I was placed in a confined, hot shed where it was my task to pick the sticks from piled moss before feeding it into enormous, clattery, steam-powered rollers with teeth that looked as if they'd fancy nothing better than to devour the arm of an orphan. Clouds of dust constantly swirled about the room, into my nostrils, my mouth, my lungs. My eyes swelled and smarted, red and itchy. Each evening, I was let off from work to eat my supper of black bread and thin beer, after which I curled up in the shed loft on a pile of dirty cushions stuffed with moss.

Oh, Father in heaven, I'd ask, coughing, already knowing the answer, *does nobody love me? Me, Philip Arthur Higgins, who once had a mother who kissed his cheek and a father who promised to return from the sea to see his first son born? Does nobody love me anymore?*

After endless months of working for the cushion maker, one day my hand caught in the roller. Pain raced up my arm, and I shrieked and fainted as the rollers mercifully shuddered to a halt.

"Philip Higgins? Come, lad, wake up. Look sharp, I say. There's someone here to see you."

I opened my eyes, my hand smarting, my body raging with fever. I lay in a bed in the workhouse infirmary. Master Crump towered over me, scowling, reeking of camphor. He poked my ribs with his cane. Once he saw I'd awakened, he stepped aside and another man took his place. A stranger whose blue eyes glittered with curiosity as he peered at me and I at him.

I blinked the sleep away and sat up.

He was handsome, about thirty years of age, swarthy, his skin weathered and darkened by the sun, his hair dark brown and curly. Two gold hoops dangled from his ears. His shirt was striped red and white, his trousers made of tarred canvas, wide-legged and chopped off just below the knee. Stockings covered his muscular calves, silver-buckled shoes his feet.

I made a pitiful object compared to him.

"I'm your uncle," he growled, not unkindly. "Your mother's elder brother. Isaac Smythe is my name." He smiled then, his teeth glinting of gold, shining, to my eyes, like heaven's glory.

I burst into tears.

I'm no longer alone. I've an uncle. . . . Dear God, an uncle . . .

"Come now, lad, stop your blubbering and dry your eyes." Uncle produced a handkerchief and I blew heartily into it, wiping my eyes and staring at him as if he'd disappear were I to blink.

"But how . . . but why . . . ?" The words twisted in my throat and I blubbered again, the pain of so many years of hardship making it impossible for me to speak.

Uncle laid a hand upon my shoulder, a strong hand that near collapsed me with its weight. "When I was your age, or a bit older perhaps, I ran away to sea. I've only just come home to find my sister long dead, with her child living like a pauper." He fell silent then while I blubbered on and my head clogged with happiness.

An uncle! An uncle!

When I finally composed myself enough to dry my eyes again, Uncle dropped a few halfpence into my uninjured hand. They clinked together, making a jolly sound. "See that you're a good lad, Philip, and that you get well. Pray, try to be a man, and maybe you'll find your tongue."

I'd always believed the thin-lipped scowl upon Master Crump's face to be a permanent fixture, but when Uncle placed two quid into his hand, the scowl vanished. "I'll be sending money for his upkeep. Mind his hand and his health or it'll go poorly for you." Turning to me, he said, "Take care, Nephew, for I shall return someday."

And with a wave, Uncle was gone.

The next few months were the happiest of my life, at least since before the day my mother had died. My hand healed—though I'd carry the mark of the accident to my grave—and my health improved. But more than that, I knew somebody loved me and that I was no longer alone.

Scarce a moment went by when I didn't recall Uncle's kindness, his glinting teeth of gold, his jaunty air of adventure, his dropping the coins into my hand, and, best of all, his warning Master Crump to look after me or it'd go poorly for him. I knew that someday Uncle would return as he'd promised and we'd live together as a family, and I'd never have to smell the moldy stench of the workhouse nor eat pauper gruel again. I imagined a home, warm and smelling of meat pies, with a roaring hearth and real beds with posts and pillows. I imagined attending a regular school, for though I'd received some basic reading and writing, and of course my catechism, from the parish fathers, they seemed more interested in how fast and long I could work before I fell ill once again.

Six months passed, and my memory of Uncle's face began to dim.

I was certain too that Master Crump was pocketing Uncle's money without any benefit to me. The one time I dared to ask Master Crump about it—and couldn't he afford to feed me more than gruel?—I felt the sting of his cane and was told that impertinence was a sin. I was then locked in a dark cupboard until the next evening, a frequent punishment in which Master Crump took pleasure and which I feared more than death.

On nights when the wind rattled the roof and rainwater sluiced down the windows, nights when I shivered under my blanket, staring at the single burning candle that the night warden secretly allowed me, I worried for Uncle. Perhaps, like my father, he'd been lost at sea, swallowed by an Atlantic gale.

After a year, to my bitter disappointment, I was let out to work once again. Upon my leaving, Master Crump presented me with a catechism in blue paper covers. It smelled of camphor. "Mind your catechism, lad," Master Crump pronounced. "You're not long for this world anyhow, but while you are spared, you must work sharp and mind your catechism."

As usual, I cowered under his presence, wishing that I'd my uncle's strength and force of character. "Th-thank you," I muttered, wondering if it was a sin to thank someone for making your life a misery.

Finally, standing on the stoop with my hand on the latch, I summoned the courage to speak. "Master Crump, please, m-must I truly go out to work? Is—isn't my uncle providing for my welfare?"

I hardly took another breath before he grabbed my arm. I heard the whoosh of the cane. Felt it crack against my back.

"Why, you ungrateful wretch!" Master Crump was yelling, loud enough for everyone in the workhouse to hear.

Whack!

"There are necessary evils—"

Whack!

"—in this life—"

Whack!

Whack!

"—and we must all do—"

Whack!

"—our part—"

Whack!

"—by enduring what—"

Whack!

"—must be—"

Whack!

"—endured!"

Whack!

Whack!

This time I worked in the cotton mill. I was forced to stand on a crate for sixteen to eighteen hours every day, and if I sagged from exhaustion, I was quickly roused by a sharp box on the ears or a savage kick on my backside. It was difficult to tie up the threads while my eyes were blinded by tears, while I breathed in lint dust, and while my head swirled with dizziness. Finally my legs gave way and I collapsed into such a state that no amount of kicking could rouse me. Back I went to the workhouse, where I nearly died of fever.

By the time I recovered, I'd reached my twelfth year and it was time that the parish authorities were relieved of my charge. Unfortunately, no one wanted me. I was known among the townsfolk as a "luckless lad," not very useful and so chronically ill that I'd soon be at heaven's gate. I was summoned before the parish board, where three stout, red-faced, bewigged gentlemen peered at me over their spectacles.

"Do you wish to go live with your uncle?" one of them asked me.

I gasped. "He's alive?"

"Of course he's alive, lad."

"Oh yes! Please, I want to live with my uncle!"

And so, to my profound relief and joy, it was arranged. I, Philip Arthur Higgins, would board a ship in Liverpool and sail to a city called New Orleans, in America, where my uncle lived.

CHAPTER 2

On a crisp September day in 1818, I gladly left my native soil.

I stepped aboard the ship *Hope,* firmly believing that her name represented my new status—that of a lucky lad, on his way to a relative who joyously awaited his arrival. I clutched my blue catechism to my chest (the book now worn and dog-eared), my spare clothing and a letter from the parish authorities stuffed inside a large knotted handkerchief. (Though I'd not read the contents of the wax-sealed letter, I imagined it stated Uncle's desire that I reside with him, granting him custody.)

With a shilling in hand, dressed in my new corduroy breeches, a new shirt, a new red leather hat, and new leather brogans that squeaked when I walked, I stood on the deck and peered through the crowd, wondering who'd been appointed as my guardian during the long voyage over. After the *Hope* cast off, I wandered a bit, knocked about by sailors and shoved aside by rough passengers. But after both dinner and supper had come and gone and no one had yet to appear as guardian, I made my way down to steerage and squeezed into a corner of the bulkhead where a dim light fell. There I collapsed into a fitful sleep, my head on my bundle, my stomach squalling louder than a baby.

For the entire night, I lay, scarce able to breathe as the ship rocked and lurched. The air was stifling and smelled like a privy. I believed I might die as my stomach turned inside out again and again. By morning I could hardly raise a finger from weakness. About me I saw throngs of people, some ill like me, some laughing, quarreling, talking. Children played. Men smoked pipes. Women cooked meals and greasy smells fattened the suffocating air. Throughout the day I heard cursing and moaning. Feet tramped constantly past my little nook, and no one gave me a second glance. In this position I passed a second night, and a third, until fever raged once again and my mouth hung open, parched with thirst.

I'd have died, I suppose, had not a family noticed my condition. By their brogue I knew them to be Irish. Their clothing was patched and thin, their faces pinched with hunger. Though they'd nothing to spare, they fed and nursed me throughout that long voyage.

"Thank you," I'd whisper.

"Think nothing of it, child," they'd reply.

The *Hope* was beaten by storms and tossed about like a cork while hundreds of souls moaned and cried. Halfway through our voyage many of us became ill with typhus, and bodies were being cast overboard daily. Sharks followed so closely that sometimes families saw their dead relations torn to shreds before the bodies could sink. Upon our arrival in Baltimore seventy-seven days later, over forty of the four hundred fifty passengers had died. That I wasn't among their number was a miracle.

My Irish family bade me farewell after a period of quarantine. They gave me a few shriveled potatoes to keep me until I reached New Orleans but refused the shilling I offered, saying I'd have need of it. By this time I was well enough to stand by the rail. My heart beat fiercely as I waved goodbye. I wished I could go with them, even though my uncle waited for me in New Orleans.

I'd thought New Orleans was just a few days' sail away. But I was to spend eleven more weeks aboard the *Hope.* My potatoes and shilling long gone, I'd no choice but to beg for food and drink. Ashamed, I roamed the decks, a mere skeleton, my new clothes turned to rags long ago.

"Please, mister, can you spare a crumb?"

"Please, ma'am, can you help a poor orphan?"

"Please, mister, I'm quite hungry."

I hated my words. I hated my condition.

Then and there, I vowed to never be hungry again. *Never.* Once I arrived in New Orleans, that is.

I wondered what Master Crump was eating for dinner, and whether it was hot, and whether he had to pick the mouse droppings out of it first. I hoped it was cold, moldy, weevily gruel. And whatever the nourishment, God forgive me, I prayed he'd choke to death.

When the *Hope* finally arrived in New Orleans, I clambered over many ships to reach the wharf. There were so many that they moored five, six deep, with wooden planks placed from gangway to gangway for crossing.

The wharf was a frightening place. It was a quarter of a mile broad and stretched in both directions forever. Bales of cotton lay stacked about, walls of white. Shouts and cries came from every angle—merchants hawking oranges, oysters, and fish. A never-ending stream of half-naked Indians, coarse riverboatmen, immigrant families, and gangs of slaves flowed by. Though I'd heard of slaves, I'd never seen one before. I gawked at the color of their skin, some so dark it shone like blacklead polish. They shuffled past and I shrank back, looking up and down the wharf. How would I ever find Uncle? How would he ever find me?

Panting, I scrambled atop a cotton bale, dragging my grimy clothes-filled handkerchief, in which I still carried the sealed letter. "Uncle?" I called, searching the crowd. "Uncle?"

I tried different cotton bales along the wharf, each time calling for him and straining my eyes for that jaunty walk, those gold earrings. . . . Many times I ran after someone as he strode away, calling "Uncle! Uncle!" only to find a stranger's face staring back at me once he turned about.

Where was Uncle? Had he forgotten I was coming?

Toward evening I found myself back in front of the *Hope* (or very near to her, considering she was moored six deep). I pulled the letter from the parish authorities out of my handkerchief. It was crumpled, water-stained, the wax seal still intact. On the front was written "Isaac Smythe, New Orleans, United States."

I studied the passersby and waited until a kindly-looking gentleman came my way. I approached him, holding out my letter. "Please, sir, I'm an orphan child. Do you know where I can find my uncle?"

But he shoved past me, his boot treading on the toe of my brogan as he mumbled something about wharf-rat urchins and filthy smells.

The next chap frowned, and his nose crinkled as if he were disgusted by my stink, but he took my letter and gave it a glance. The hair beneath his hat shone silver in the waning light. "He is your uncle?" He spoke with a slight brogue.

"Yes. Isaac Smythe's his name, and he was to meet me here. He's a sailor."

"May I?" the man asked, his gloved hand poised over the green wax seal.

I nodded, wondering if I was violating the law by letting someone not in authority break the seal.

"Hmm," he said. "All it says here is that Isaac Smythe's last known address was in New Orleans, and that he is hereby given custody of his nephew, one Philip Arthur Higgins."

I blinked. "That's all it says?"

"I'm afraid so." He handed the letter back to me. "Tell me, you didn't by any chance arrive on the *Hope* this afternoon out of Baltimore, I suppose?"

"Yes." Tears burned my eyes. For all these weeks I'd assumed that the important letter with the green wax seal acknowledged Uncle's desire for the custody of his nephew. But it contained nothing of the sort. *Doesn't Uncle know I'm here? Did the parish authorities just send me away to be rid of me, not knowing where Uncle was? Am I to try to find him in this great, frightening city?*

The man was saying, "Perhaps you can help me. I'm looking for my nephew who was aboard, about your age. Paddy O'Brien. Did you know him?"

"I—I don't know. A good many lads died aboard the ship— more'n ten, I should think."

The man frowned and, without another word, stepped aboard one of the ships and disappeared in the direction of the *Hope*. By this time it was dark enough that whale-oil lanterns were being lighted all along the waterfront. The bustle of the wharf had slowed. I swallowed my hunger and settled beside one of the cotton bales. My lip quivered. I was adrift in this foreign city, with no one who cared whether I lived or died.

A while later I watched as the kind man with the brogue meandered his way back across the ships and deposited himself once again on the wharf. His face now shadowed with dusk, he looked about, saw me curled in my nook, nodded, then turned and strode away. I watched as he disappeared into the crowd.

I was dreaming of roast beef with gravy when someone shook me awake.

It was the man again.

"Would you like to come home with me?" he asked. "The purser of the *Hope* says my nephew died," his voice choked, "and, well, it seems to me that, well . . . Would you?"

Had he spread mutton and chops before me and said I was the long-lost son of King George, I couldn't have been more surprised. My chest swelled. My throat thickened. I found my voice, quavery with relief. "Yes, please. You're quite kind, Mr. uh—"

"Gallagher."

"—Mr. Gallagher, sir. The kindest fellow I've ever known."

He took my hand then, helped me to my feet, and off we went into the big city.

"Why, bless me," Mrs. Gallagher said, putting down her sewing and rising from a chair by the window. "If he don't blow away in the first stiff breeze, it'll be a miracle."

And though I'd never seen her before in my life, and though I was dirty and no doubt as smelly as the water-filled ditches that lined the narrow streets, she kissed both my cheeks and wrapped her ample arms about me as if I were her own beloved nephew, Paddy O'Brien, who'd died at sea and was eaten by sharks. She smelled of rose water and talc, and, like Mr. Gallagher, she'd a crown of silver hair and a kindly look. "You poor, poor lad. Mr. Gallagher told me. Such a hardship." And so saying, she released me, her eyes moistened, and she turned away to dab her tears.

Mr. Gallagher put a hand on my shoulder. "His name's Philip. Philip Arthur Higgins, isn't that right, lad?" He looked at me. "He says he's twelve."

For a while no one said anything. Then, fearing perhaps that Mrs. Gallagher had changed her mind, especially as I was so dirty, I said, "I'll do anything, ma'am. I'll clean, I'll work sharp, I'll run errands—"

But Mrs. Gallagher was turning back around, hushing me. "My, my, my, but there'll be plenty of time for that later. My heart alive! Where are my manners? First things first. Let's get you scrubbed clean and dressed proper. And I'm sure you're hungry as if it were the last day of Lent. Mr. Gallagher, fetch some water on to boil while I see to dinner. . . ."

And off Mr. Gallagher whisked me, to a copper tub set in front of the fireplace, where steam presently curled to the ceiling, where bubbles slopped over the rim, and where I soon slipped my body into the hot water, gasping, for it smarted. Once I was scrubbed clean and decently covered with bubbles, Mrs. Gallagher brought a tray of food—ham, bread, eggs, and potatoes. Then the two of them left me alone as I ate the most glorious meal of my life, never having known before that food could taste so scrumptious.

If ever there were two angels on earth, they were Mr. and Mrs. Gallagher.

My new clothes smelled of soap. I was allowed to keep a candle burning all night. They *tsk*ed and shook their heads when I told them the story of my life. "Such a shame," they said, their foreheads creased with sympathy.

I gladly went to work in their chemist's shop on Rue du Dauphine in the French Quarter. The shop was below and the living quarters above, and so it was a cozy arrangement. Every day (except for the Sabbath, of course, when we attended Mass), I ground powders with a mortar and pestle as my body grew strong (owing to Mrs. Gallagher's fine and generous cooking). I labeled bottles and made deliveries. I even learned to help customers, for Mr. and Mrs. Gallagher said that I was a polite and pleasant-looking lad, and therefore well suited for customer service. After a while, I knew enough to be able to compound simple prescriptions.

Mrs. Gallagher doted upon me, calling me her "little English boy."

Meanwhile, Mr. Gallagher tried to locate my uncle, but no one seemed to have heard of a Mr. Isaac Smythe, a sailor by trade.

Months passed, and though all should've been well, though to complain would've made me an ungrateful wretch, still, as I lay awake at night, covers kicked off in the New Orleans summer, a part of me was unsettled. Where on this vast planet was my only living relative, the only family left to me? For wherever Uncle was, that's where I longed to be.

I leaned across the counter and handed the customer his parcel. "Stir half a teaspoonful of the wine of antimony into a tumbler of flaxseed tea," I told him. "Drink it often. Should loosen the congestion straightaway."

The customer thanked me, paid his bill, and left the shop to the jangle of bells.

Mr. Gallagher had been standing beside the scales, deciphering a prescription. Now he removed his spectacles and mopped his forehead with his handkerchief. The day was hot as scorched gruel. Flies buzzed, landing on soaps, bins of dried herbs, and bottles filled with vinegar, wine of tar, and iodine. "Philip? A moment, please, if you will."

I put the coins in the till, then stood beside him, expecting him to give me a prescription to fill, a powder to weigh, or a delivery to make.

Instead, he replaced his spectacles and said, "Mrs. Gallagher and I have noticed you've been downcast of late." I must've flushed a brilliant red and looked dreadfully guilty, for he hastened to add, "No, no, don't misunderstand me, lad. We've no complaints, certainly; we love you like a son, indeed we do." He smiled and patted my shoulder. "And you've a home with us so long as you need it or want it, you know that."

"Thank you," I replied, wondering where this was leading. "You've been quite generous. You saved my life, surely, you and Mrs. Gallagher both." Though I'd lived with them for months, though they'd invited me more than once to call them by their Christian names, Sean and Mary, (Mrs. Gallagher had even asked me at times to address her as "Mother"), still I'd never been able to call them anything other than Mr. and Mrs. Gallagher. Anything else seemed odd, as if I'd be telling a lie. "I'm forever in your debt, Mr. Gallagher. When my uncle finds me, or when I find him, I'm sure he'll pay you for your troubles. He's quite well-off."

"Uh, no need for that. You've repaid us tenfold just by being here. Don't know how we got along without you before. Well, my point is, we've given it a lot of thought, Mrs. Gallagher and I; you're a bright lad, and it seems to us that a lad such as yourself needs some proper schooling—"

I gasped. My eyes flew open. My knees went a bit shaky. "School!"

He mistook my reaction, saying quickly, "It won't be so bad, really, and you'll still get to work in the shop after school, and I'm certain you'll make friends. You'll learn sums and multiplication, and, well, a sharp lad like yourself really should have a proper education so he can move up in the world—"

But he could say no more, for I'd flung my arms about him. "Oh yes!" I cried, jumping up and down, knocking his spectacles loose. "Yes, yes, yes!" And presently we were both laughing so hard that it took us a few moments to realize the bells had jangled and we'd another customer in the shop.

It was a deliciously happy moment. The kind which one remembers sorrowfully once life has returned to misery. Like a bright light one sees above as one lies below, mired in a horrible, blood-soaked pit.

CHAPTER 3

$\mathcal{M}$r. and Mrs. Gallagher enrolled me in Catholic school. They gave me a crisp new catechism as well. Mrs. Gallagher kissed me each morning before sending me off, saying I must tell her all about my day the moment I returned. When I wasn't working in the shop, I did my schoolwork. I learned French, Greek, and Latin. I learned my arithmetic tables, geometry, grammar, and geography. I became known as a keen scholar. Mr. and Mrs. Gallagher were quite proud.

During all this time, Mr. Gallagher and I continued searching for my uncle. I even spent six months' allowance on an advertisement in the *Orleans Gazette*. For weeks afterward, every time the shop bells jangled

I rushed to see who it was, crestfallen when it was not my uncle. Eventually Mr. Gallagher took me aside.

"Philip, you'd rather not hear this, I suppose, but it's time you faced the possibility that something has happened to your relative." I must've looked as woebegone as I felt, for he murmured sympathetically and wrapped an arm about my shoulder. He smelled of sulfur and aloe. "You must look to your future, lad. Leave the past where it belongs."

For a while I said nothing, hardly able to realize that all my dreams of Uncle, of having a family to call my own, were simply that. Dreams. Nothing more. I picked a thread off my apron. "Do—do you think he was lost at sea? Drowned? And maybe that's why he can't find me?"

Mr. Gallagher squeezed my shoulder, and I knew he hesitated to answer. "Perhaps" was all he said.

A pain wrenched my heart, as horrible as the day my mother had died and left me an orphan. "But Uncle was *family. My* family. He was all I had."

Mr. Gallagher looked sympathetic. "Yes, lad. I know."

After that, the days, weeks, and months were a blur. I threw myself into my studies and my work at the chemist's shop, trying to fill the empty hole inside me.

Then, one day, everything changed. Nearly two years had passed from the time I'd first arrived in New Orleans. I was fourteen and a half years of age and still, as Mr. Gallagher liked to say, "hardly bigger than a turnip."

I was on my way to make a delivery of pills to a patron at a hotel located on the city side of the wharf. Walking along the banquette, I happened to glance through the doorway of a tavern. A man was sitting at a table, smoking a cigar and reading a newspaper, a rattan cane by his side. He was dressed in a black silk frock coat, with a tall black beaver hat resting jauntily upon his curly head. A gold watch hung from the fob on his waistcoat. He was a fine, handsome man, wealthy-looking, swarthy, with small gold earrings.

I knew him immediately.

He was my uncle.

For a moment, I stood rooted.

Then I cried "Uncle!" and rushed inside.

His face registered surprise. He scowled and drew back, saying, "What the devil is the matter with you? Get away from me."

"It's me, Uncle. It's me—Philip Arthur Higgins. Only I've grown up now."

"The deuce you are. I'd know my own nephew should I run across him."

"But it *is* me. You came to visit me at the Magford workhouse when I was ill, when I'd injured my hand. You've custody of me now. I came to New Orleans to find—"

Uncle held up a hand, stopping me. "Hold on there, lad. Quiet now." He looked me up and down and turned me about, all the while puffing on his cigar, the smoke billowing from him as from a coal fire. "I declare," he finally said with a half grin. "Never thought to see you again. You've grown and put meat on your bones, I'd say."

I grinned so wide my cheeks smarted.

Uncle clapped me on the back, barked with laughter, then snapped his fingers and hollered to the tavern keeper, "A beer for my nephew!" Then, to me: "Why, it's grand to see you again, Philip. Grand indeed."

Over the next hour, I sat and sipped my beer and answered his questions about where I'd been and what had happened to me, and what I'd learned both at the Catholic school and at the chemist's. I discovered that the reason we'd been unable to locate him was because his name was actually Isaac Towne; he'd given the parish authorities a false name because, as he said with a wink, he didn't like the cut of their jib. He was captain of his own ship now, and had done quite well for himself.

"I'm leaving on a voyage come early next week. I'll be needing a surgeon's mate. Would you fancy the job, Philip, lad? Your knowledge of pills and plasters will come in handy."

I felt my eyes widen. My heart skipped a beat or two.

A voyage with Uncle! Even in my wildest dreams . . . "Yes, of course!"

"Then it's arranged. I'll make it my business to rig you out."

"I'll—I'll have to tell Mr. and Mrs. Gallagher."

"Naturally."

We agreed to meet the following morning at the crack of dawn, no later, whereupon I'd begin my duties. I shook Uncle's strong hand, then skipped down the banquette to complete my delivery, a shiny silver dollar Uncle had given me tucked in the pocket of my waistcoat.

I'd thought telling them would be easy.

Just a simple *Oh, by the way . . .*

But that evening at supper I picked at my food, my appetite blown away as if caught in a hurricane and drowned in a whirlpool.

"Philip," inquired Mrs. Gallagher, her forehead creased, "is something the matter? I've cooked your favorite—corned beef and cabbage—and you've hardly touched it, my dear. A mouse eats more than you."

I shifted uncomfortably. Heard the tick of the mantel clock. And though I was staring at my plate, I knew Mr. Gallagher had set down his fork and was studying me. Today he smelled sweetly of yellow jessamine. (Just before supper, he'd mixed the flower petals with black snakeroot and other herbs for Mademoiselle Dupré, who suffered from headaches and restlessness at night.)

"Philip?" he asked after I'd said nothing.

I looked at them miserably. They'd been so kind. . . .

"I—I found my uncle."

Mrs. Gallagher gasped. "How wonderful for you, my dear!"

Mr. Gallagher said nothing, but still looked at me, as if knowing there was more to the story.

"He's captain of his own ship now, done quite well for himself."

"Why, bless me, that's delightful!" exclaimed Mrs. Gallagher. "Isn't that delightful, dear?"

I said, "He's off early next week on another voyage."

"Is he now? Well, again, that's wonderful." Mrs. Gallagher laid her hand atop Mr. Gallagher's. "Don't you think that's wonderful news, dear?"

Mr. Gallagher sighed deeply. "And?"

"He's hired me as the surgeon's mate. I've agreed. I start come morning."

There followed a long silence. I stared at my plate again. At the corned beef, no longer steaming. The cabbage, beginning to dry at the edges. Outside a dog barked, small and yippy. From next door, I heard the clink of silverware and someone laughing.

"Oh dear," Mrs. Gallagher finally said.

"Never mind your supper, then," said Mr. Gallagher. "You'd best hurry along and pack your things."

I gladly escaped to my room, relieved that the hard part was over.

In the morning I stood by the door, canvas bag propped against my leg.

"Oh blessed Mother Mary, look after my little English boy," whispered Mrs. Gallagher as she kissed both my cheeks. She smelled, as always, of rose water and talc.

"Come, Mrs. Gallagher, don't cry," I said, my throat tightening. "I'll come back someday, I will."

"But what do we know of him, this uncle of yours?" asked Mr. Gallagher, cleaning his spectacles with a handkerchief.

I shrugged, wishing I didn't have to hurt them so, wishing I didn't have to say goodbye, as goodbyes could be, I was learning, very hard indeed. But I'd done a lot of thinking during the night. My bags were packed and I'd a vessel to board and an important position as surgeon's mate. "I don't know. But he's my uncle. He's *family.*"

"Why, dear, of course he is."

Mr. Gallagher replaced his spectacles and looked serious. "You always have a home with us, you know that."

Again my throat tightened. I clenched my jaw, refusing to cry. *Surgeon's mates don't cry.*

"Yes, of course you do, dear." Mrs. Gallagher enfolded me in her ample arms until talc tickled my nose and I sneezed.

I pulled away. "Well, thank you. Both of you. You—you've been most kind to me. I'll not forget." My voice cracked. "I'll bring you something from . . . from wherever I'm going. I'll . . ."

Mrs. Gallagher tried to smile and failed. "Do you promise, *absolutely promise,* to come home and see us again, my little English boy?"

"I promise."

Mr. Gallagher pressed five dollars into my hand. "Keep it. You've earned it, you have."

I thanked them both again and picked up my canvas bag, filled with clothes, books, toothbrush, tooth powder, comb, and such. I opened the door to the shop. Bells jangled. The morning air was cool.

"Well, goodbye, then," I said, looking back once more.

"Goodbye, dear. Mind your manners, now. Study your catechism."

"Farewell, Philip."

And off I went, my brogans clipping the banquette, off to my new life, my new adventure.

CHAPTER 4

I didn't like the look of Uncle's crew. They appeared hard-eyed and shifty-looking. When I mentioned this to Uncle, he laughed and tousled my hair, saying there was no need to worry, that he knew what he was doing. He had sailed with some of these men before and knew them to be crack sailors. I still had my doubts but bit my tongue, not wanting to sound like a child.

The ship, however, was glorious. The *Formidable* was its name. Uncle said it was a Baltimore clipper and had been a privateer just a few years back, from 1812 to 1814, during America's Second War of Independence. Even knowing little about ships, I could tell she was sleek and fast, her two green masts rakish and daring. The deck was flush and clean. Her hull was painted black, and she'd two carronades plus twelve long guns, six on either side, each capable of throwing 9-pound shot, according to Uncle.

"But who will we be firing at?" I asked as I followed him about the brig. The sun was just peeping over the horizon, casting the sky in purple hues. A light breeze carried the scent of frying fish, brine, and damp timbers. "The war ended in 1814."

"All in good time, my lad, I'll answer your questions all in good time. For now we must attend to matters at hand." Uncle made his way past one of the inboard boats, turned upside down; past sailors going about their business; and stopped midships, where a man was digging through a box filled with what appeared to be medicines. "Jonas?"

The man stood and turned abruptly. I stepped back. He was old—sixty, maybe—with protruding eyes. The whites of his eyes weren't white at all, but yellow. Truth was, all of him seemed to be yellow. Pockmarks pitted his sallow skin. Yellowish gray hair hung in lank strings.

Uncle laughed and clasped the man's hand in both his own, pumping it vigorously. "Jonas Drinkwater, my good friend, well met once again!"

"Captain Towne," replied Jonas, fixing him with a yellow eye. "Good to see you."

"Wasn't sure if you were still alive, you looking like something that died in the gutter." Uncle winked at Jonas, then at me, before pushing me forward. "Jonas, this is my nephew, Philip Higgins. It's well you look surprised! Didn't think a scoundrel like me had a family, eh? Ha! Not only is he family, he's a sharp fellow. Been to school and everything. Proud to call him my own. And you'll be happy to know he'll be your assistant and charge during the voyage." And with a thunderous clap on each of our backs and a hearty laugh, Uncle left me with Jonas.

I felt color flush my cheeks and dropped my gaze to the

deck, realizing I'd been staring. *This* man was a surgeon? I was to work under *this* man for the entire voyage? I felt a shiver of misgiving, but quickly dismissed it. *Uncle knows what he's doing,* I told myself.

Jonas stepped about me, inspecting me from head to foot. "How old are you, boy?"

"Fourteen. And a half."

"You look no more than eleven. Maybe twelve. And what do you know about medicine?"

"I—I can fill simple prescriptions, sir—"

"Don't call me 'sir.' "

"No, sir. I mean, yes, sir. What I mean is, sir, I can mix compounds and—"

"How many grains make one scruple?"

"Wh-what?"

"You heard me. How many grains make one scruple?"

"Twenty."

"How many scruples to one dram?"

"Three."

He grunted. "What's paregoric used for?"

"It quiets the cough and calms the nerves."

"Dosage?"

"A tablespoon for adults."

Again he grunted. "You'll do. Now organize this medicine chest so I can find what I need."

When he turned away, I took a deep breath and steadied myself. "Dr.—Dr. Drinkwater?"

"Name's Jonas."

"Please, Jonas, where are we off to? Where's the ship headed?"

He turned back. A frown creased his yellow face. "Didn't the captain tell you?"

"No."

Then Jonas erupted with laughter, suddenly not looking so frightening or ugly anymore. He thumped me on the back as had Uncle, smiling a great, yellow-toothed smile, but said nothing.

Jonas and I shared a whitewashed cabin next to the captain's quarters. There were two bunks—berths, in sailor's language—stacked against one wall, with only three by seven feet square of walking space. Lodged between the bunks and the wall opposite was a desk piled with medical books. Across from the desk was a cupboard for our belongings. To my relief, Jonas agreed to allow me a candle at night, but only after I promised him my every share of grog for the entire voyage.

That first night, gazing at the candle flame, a solitary glow, I reviewed the events of the day, concluding, *My uncle's the handsomest man and I'm the luckiest lad in all the world. I think we'll get along pleasantly.* I then recited my prayers and fell asleep.

Once the ship was in a smart condition and watertight, her hatches fitted with sound and doubled tarpaulins, all things well secured and caulked, the *Formidable* left New Orleans on the eighth day of January, 1821, in fine weather, the wind at the southwest. Five days later we crossed the bar at the mouth of the Mississippi, with the wind from the north-northeast, and set a course to sea.

There were forty-six of us, including the captain. There were the gunner and his mates, who looked after the ammunition and the long guns. There was the cook, whose galley was on the forward deck, and who could be heard mumbling to himself even over a high wind. There were two mates; then there were the steward, the cabin boy, the bo'sun, the carpenter, the sailmaster, and the cooper, and all the other sailors.

Everyone had tasks to do. As for me, once the medicine chest was organized, I didn't have much in the way of regular tasks and wondered why Uncle felt he needed both a surgeon and a surgeon's mate on a voyage where there wasn't much of anything happening. I was so delighted, though, to finally be with Uncle after all these years that if he needed both a surgeon and a surgeon's mate, that was jolly fine with me. It just meant Uncle wanted me near him.

As it was, I followed him about like a puppy, asking endless questions. After all, he was family. My only family.

"Uncle, weren't you lonely for your family when you first left for sea?"

"Uncle, have you ever fallen overboard?"

"Uncle, have you ever been to India?"

"Uncle, will you ever get married, do you think?"

"Uncle, can you teach me navigation?"

"Uncle, where are we off to?"

"Uncle, have you ever gone to school?"

"Uncle, do you think I might make a good sea captain someday?"

Some questions he answered; some made him crack with laughter and clap me on the back (nearly jarring my teeth loose), repeating, "All in good time, my lad, all in good time." Finally, perhaps in an effort to batten my hatches, he agreed to teach me navigation.

So, beginning on our fifth day at sea, each day at noon we stood on the quarterdeck and took the sighting with a sextant. Then we went below and consulted the almanac and studied the charts, plotting our course from one penciled X to the next.

"So we're headed to Havana, on Spanish Cuba," I said one day, tracing our route with my finger. I stood with my legs braced as the *Formidable* rolled and tossed through the ocean swells. Above, it was a fine, vigorous day, and my hair smelled of wind. "If the weather holds true, we should arrive sometime tomorrow."

Uncle's blue eyes glinted. "Aye, you're a sharp lad."

"Then we're returning home?"

Uncle gave me a hard look, seeming to weigh something in his mind, then shrugged. "I suppose it's time you knew." He produced another chart and unrolled it atop the first, leaning over the table and caressing the chart with his hand. I stood next to him, hearing the breath whistling through his nostrils, looking to where he pointed. "After Havana, we're headed to Africa."

Africa . . . I peered at the African continent, my breath catching with the promise of adventure. "What's in Africa besides jungles?"

At this, Uncle straightened and placed a strong, square hand on my shoulder. His expression was solemn. "Philip, lad, have you ever wanted to be rich?"

I remembered my vow to never be hungry again. And since arriving in New Orleans, I'd kept that vow. Money was the answer. Money and family. "Yes, I want to be rich." *More than anything*, I realized.

Uncle's lips curled up in a smile. "There's black gold in Africa."

"Black gold?"

"Slaves, lad. *Slaves,*" he hissed.

The word hung in the air. Visible, touchable, vibrating like a plucked string. My scalp prickled and I became aware of Uncle's excitement. It flowed warmly from his hand, through my shoulder, into my being. As if he *wanted* my approval. Me, little Philip Arthur Higgins, onetime orphan and ward of the parish workhouse. And in that moment I'd have given my approval to anything—taking half the world, even.

Uncle's eyes met mine.

I smiled. "Yes, Uncle. That would be quite nice, I think."

The house was set among the palm trees, a wide veranda stretching across the front, shady and inviting. As we climbed the last step onto the varnished expanse, the door opened and a man emerged. "Ah! Captain Towne!" he said in a broad American accent. "At last you've arrived!" Dressed in loose white cotton pantaloons and a linen shirt, he was a red-faced fellow of enormous girth. Sweat beaded on his forehead and dampened his clothing. He dabbed himself with a handkerchief.

"Emmanuel Fitch! Jolly good to see you again," said Uncle, slipping his rattan cane under his arm and shaking Mr. Fitch's hand.

Jonas muttered a pleasantry while I stood by awkwardly.

"Emmanuel, may I introduce my nephew, Philip," said Uncle.

The man's hands were hot and sticky. I said, "Good to meet you, sir," and he ordered cool drinks all about.

Presently we sat upon the rattan chairs on the veranda, surrounded by slaves who served drinks and aired us with fans. My first sight of slaves had been on the day I'd arrived in New Orleans. Since then I'd seen many members of the dusky-hued race, most especially when I'd fill a prescription for their masters. As I relaxed on the veranda, I admitted to myself that these slaves both frightened and fascinated me. They were well formed, silent, padding about on their bare feet and serving all our wishes before we even asked. I wondered what they thought of their fat, sweating master; of my swarthy, earringed uncle; of pop-eyed, yellow-faced Jonas; and of me, pale little Philip.

Truthfully, I'd never given slavery much thought (being much too busy with my own life), believing only that rich people owned slaves, while poor people didn't.

For the next hour, Mr. Fitch and Uncle discussed business. The loading of the equipment. The goods and trinkets for trade—colored cottons, glazed beads, brass bracelets, tobacco, bells, kegs of gunpowder and rum. The necessary provisions and supplies. Where the best cargoes were to be found. Places to avoid—African rivers where there was bound to be trouble of one kind or another. The top bargaining price allowed per slave. The expected date of return . . .

Flies droned about my sweet drink. The breeze from the bird-feather fan ruffled my hair, cooling my sweating scalp. The slave boy operating the fan shifted from one foot to the other. My eyelids drooped.

"Do you like him?"

It took me a moment to realize someone was talking to me. It was Mr. Fitch. "I said, do you like him?"

I cleared my throat. "Like whom?"

"The slave boy. His name's Pea Soup. He's your age."

Well formed and muscular, Pea Soup was staring at the floor, his face impassive, still moving the fan. Up. Down. Up. Down. "Well, yes, I suppose I do. I like him very much," I said, wondering what Mr. Fitch meant by this.

"Would you like to have him?"

The astonishment must've shown in my face, because he chuckled, along with Jonas, whose now-familiar laugh sounded like the braying of a donkey. Uncle watched me sharply.

"I'm serious, young fellow," continued Mr. Fitch, once he'd caught his breath. "If you like him, you can have him. Consider him my gift to you, in gratefulness for your uncle's friendship and business acumen."

"Well, I—"

"Go ahead," urged Uncle. "It's a valued gift. You should be honored."

"Then I accept," I said, breaking into a smile, touched by Mr. Fitch's generosity. Surely he was a very rich man! "And I *am* honored."

"Excellent!" cried Mr. Fitch. "Fresh drinks all around!"

And soon we were clinking our glasses together, toasting one another's health. I glanced at Pea Soup, wondering if he understood what had just occurred—that he belonged to me now. But he still stared at the same place on the floor, his face unchanged, moving the fan.

Up. Down. Up. Down.

CHAPTER
5

*T*hroughout that long voyage across the Atlantic from Cuba to Africa, I liked to stand at the bow, with spray dashing over the cutwater, our sails full and tight, and imagine the fortunes I'd gather.

I was no longer the poor orphan boy without a halfpenny to his name and with just a mouthful of food in his belly, wearing only rags. I no longer toiled eighteen hours a day doing someone else's bidding, coughing up moss dust while someone else became rich and laid a cane across my back.

No, I was *Master* Philip Arthur Higgins now. I had a family and owned a personal servant. I was on my way to ship a cargo of slaves and become rich. And for the first time in my life, I'd receive payment for my own labor, sail the world as I fancied, and answer to no one but myself. Me, Philip Arthur Higgins, master, speculator, and entrepreneur, just like my uncle.

I imagined the day I'd return to the Gallaghers for a visit, telling tales of my adventures. I'd leave them with so much gold that they'd never have to work again, sorry they'd ever doubted Uncle.

It took me a few days to teach Pea Soup his duties. At first I tried telling him, but he just stared at his feet, his face blank. Without a common language, I had to act out his duties, from laundering my clothes to serving my meals to cleaning my quarters. Jonas laughed, telling me I looked a fool. That it wasn't difficult to tell who was master and who was slave with Pea Soup just standing there while I scrubbed my dirty pants.

"You could whip him, you know," suggested Billy Dorsett, the cabin boy.

I'd been showing Pea Soup how to replace the candle in my lantern when Billy appeared at the door of my cabin. I didn't like Billy. About a year younger than I, he seemed a dull boy—dull wits, dull eyes, dull hair—and he had a vulgar fascination with bodily excretions and emissions.

"Everybody knows a darkie don't do what he's supposed to without a whipping to show him how," he was saying. "Everybody knows that."

"I'll do things my own way, thank you very much." I hoped that the snap to my voice would dismiss Billy, but he lingered in the doorway. I returned to my task. "Anyhow, Pea Soup, you take a candle, like so—I've a ready supply in the drawer at all times— then you open the lantern door; there's a latch here, mind you don't pinch your fingers—"

Billy said, "He's probably stupid, that's why he don't do what you tell him."

I frowned at him. "And how would you know?"

He shrugged and started to pick at a place in the wall where the whitewash was peeling. "I could teach him if you want, if you don't got time."

"Thank you, but no," I said with a sigh, thinking, *Bother it all!* Pea Soup was staring at the floor, his arms dangling limply. With Billy here, my hopes of teaching Pea Soup to keep a candle lighted in my lantern at all times were dashed. "Well," I said to Pea Soup, speaking English to him, though I knew he couldn't understand, "looks like we're finished. Let's go on deck, where the air is fresher."

Billy moved into my room as I pushed past him, Pea Soup padding softly behind me. I turned. "Clear off, Billy."

He looked at me blankly, as if he couldn't fathom why I didn't want him in my quarters, riffling through my belongings. Pulling him by the sleeve into the passageway, I shut my door. "Stay out of my cabin."

I let go of him then, but to my irritation Billy followed us to the upper deck and pestered me for the next half hour. I finally dismissed Pea Soup and locked myself in my cabin, away from Billy Dorsett.

Despite Billy's pestering and despite Jonas' braying, soon Pea Soup was performing his duties. And though Pea Soup moved like a tortoise, not finding a reason to hurry for anything, I couldn't complain. Even the little he accomplished left me more time to study my catechism, study medicine with Jonas, and learn navigation from Uncle.

Several times during the voyage, Uncle invited me to dine at his table, where he asked after my studies and my health. Besides eating better food (for the captain's larder was more generous and varied than that of the crew), we chatted happily, with me doing most of the chatting. I told him how I'd recently charted the course of my life. Never again would I drift according to the desires of others, for I'd be a slave trader, just like him. Upon my announcement, a smile creased Uncle's face and his pale blue eyes glittered as if he'd just opened a chest brimming with treasure.

At our next supper, he presented me with a pair of gold hoop earrings, the Book of Common Prayer, two volumes of Shakespeare, and a Spanish learner. He said Spanish was a language I must master if I wanted to one day fill his shoes. I thanked him in Greek, Latin, and French, adding that an aptitude for languages was my gift from God.

The air in Uncle's cabin smelled of chicken and dumplings and fried potatoes. My stomach was full and tight, and I thought what with the gifts from Uncle, all the food that I wanted, and the course of my life charted, I'd never been happier. Smiling, I let out a contented sigh.

Uncle leaned back in his chair and paused to light one of his new Cuban cigars before saying, "You do know that it's illegal, don't you, lad?"

"Really? Learning Spanish is illegal?"

"No, but the slave trade is."

My smile faded. I was silent as the ship creaked and moaned, not certain what Uncle meant. Hadn't I seen hundreds of slaves in New Orleans? How, then, could it be illegal?

As if he'd read my mind, Uncle said, "Oh, it's still all right to *own* slaves." He waved his cigar about. A cloud of blue smoke hovered above us, smelling strong and sweet. "Probably always will be, as it's the natural order of things, the way God intended, written plain as day in the Holy Bible."

"Then what do you mean? How is it against the law?"

He squinted at me through the smoke. "What I mean is, a few years ago our beloved British government decided that it was illegal to *export* slaves, to take them from Africa and sell them elsewhere. Slaves now have to propagate themselves, for there will no longer be any fresh ones from Africa, not if England has her way." He paused to cough. "Ridiculous law. Now, because the slave trade is illegal, what used to be a respectable occupation has become one of smuggling."

Smuggling? "You—you mean . . ." My voice trailed off. Some of my excitement over the gifts he'd just given me blew away like cigar smoke. It'd never entered my mind that I'd be disobeying the law. So far as I knew, I'd never disobeyed the law, or any person, in my lifetime. Such a prospect filled me with dreadful fright. "But—but *why* is it illegal?"

Uncle put his cigar to his lips. The end glowed with fire. Over the orange tip, he watched me intently. "Why? Because some half-wit somewhere in some bloody parliamentary hall thinks that somehow he can stop the natural order of the universe. They sit there with their wigs and ink stains and think they know the way of the world. It's a ridiculous law, this prohibition of the slave trade. Total rubbish. Misty-eyed nonsense is the sum of it. Violates man's free will and his desire to engage in enterprise."

I picked at the binding of my Spanish learner. "Then what will happen if we're caught by the Royal Navy?"

"Nothing." Leaning back in his chair, he belched, absently patting his stomach.

"Nothing?"

"Because, Philip, my lad, Britain has no authority over the Stars and Stripes." He smiled, his gold teeth lighting up his swarthy face. "We're an *American* vessel, owned by Yanks. And while the slave trade is illegal in the United States as well, the American government doesn't seem to care too much. Oh, they have a few gunboats here and there, but mostly the politicians pat Britain's hand and tell her what she wants to hear, meanwhile looking the other way as the American slave traders ply their trade and make the United States rich. Ha! How I love America!" He shook his head, chuckling. "And Britain doesn't dare illegally board an American or French ship, as to do so might start another war."

"Then why am I learning Spanish?" I asked, and rushed to add, "Not that I don't want to, Uncle—"

"Simple. In case we should run across an American cruiser—highly unlikely, by the way—Yanks have no authority over Spanish vessels. And lucky for us, the ship's name, the *Formidable*"—except Uncle pronounced it *For-mi-DAH-blay*—"is the same, whether in Spanish or English. If worse comes to worst, I become Don Pedro, while you become Don Felipe. It's simpler that way. Of course the ruse will only be believable if we speak tolerable Spanish. Even my ship's papers are in Spanish."

"Your papers?"

"*Sí*, Don Felipe. The ship's logs and certificate of ownership." Again he laughed, motioning to the captain's desk with his cigar. "You can check my papers if you want. All is in order for a Spanish vessel. They're fake, of course. The real papers I keep inside here." He patted his corn-husk mattress. "Trust me, no one will find them."

"No one?"

Uncle winked. "Not unless you tell them."

"Then nothing will happen?"

"Trust me, Philip. Nothing will happen."

I did trust Uncle, more than I'd trusted anyone in my life. If Uncle said nothing would happen, then nothing would happen. If Uncle said that anti-slave-trading laws were ridiculous, then they were ridiculous. *After all,* I told myself, *Master Crump made all sorts of rules—eat your gruel, no pillows, only one blanket per child—but that didn't make them right. Just because something is a rule or a law doesn't mean it's right or good.*

I licked my lips, weighing my words. "I do trust you, Uncle, more'n anyone I've ever known."

He clenched his cigar in his teeth, reached over, and patted my shoulder. "That's my Philip."

Later that night, under the light of a lantern hanging from the mainmast, Jonas pierced my ears.

"This will smart," he warned me, and I could tell by the slur in his voice that he was half-seas over.

"Just keep the needle steady, will you?"

He grabbed my earlobe with a filthy hand and stabbed it.

I was unprepared for the wave of pain that quickly drained the blood from my head, turning my bones and the stool beneath me to rubber.

Jonas moved to the other side. "Brace yourself, boy, here comes the other one."

I bit my lip. My heart fluttered. My eyes watered. But within minutes, to my pride, two gold earrings were dangling from my earlobes.

Jonas bent close. His breath smelled like the bilge. "Well, I'll be. Never knew till now how much you look like Captain Towne."

"Do I?"

"Aye. Both of you look like right scoundrels, you do." He burst into his donkey-bray laugh and placed the needle back in its pouch.

I held up a mirror.

Do I truly look like Uncle?

Indeed, I saw the same blue eyes, the same mouth, the same nose, the same dark brown hair. And no longer was I the pale, wan lad of yesteryear. During the weeks of life at sea, my skin had weathered. Under my curly hair, a dab of blood trickled down each side of my neck. But peering closely into the mirror at my earrings and at the fresh wounds behind them, I became aware that I wasn't the only figure reflected. Over my shoulder, staring at me from behind my back, was Pea Soup. And simmering in his eyes and written upon his face, I saw it clearly—an emotion so intense, so naked, that the hair on the back of my neck stood on end.

Hatred.

I whirled about.

But Pea Soup merely stared at the deck, his face blank, sweeping with his broom.

Back and forth. Back and forth.

During the first part of April, we sailed along the coast of the Gulf of Guinea. It was the beginning of the rainy season, and the rain fell in torrents. The wind, punctuated by squalls, gusted from our port quarter, pushing us along at a furious rate.

Africa . . .

I could scarcely wait to arrive. The very name of that dark, mysterious continent stirred my soul and promised excitement and wealth, despite the fact that I was now a smuggler as well as a master, speculator, and entrepreneur.

The whole crew seemed on edge. Tempers rose. Fights erupted. On account of the rains, those not on duty were confined to the lower deck, where the men sweated and stank like old cheese. Jonas and I took refuge in our cabin. I took to wearing white cotton pantaloons and a loose linen shirt, having received several of each as parting gifts from Mr. Emmanuel Fitch. Still, I sweated in the claustrophobic heat. Billy Dorsett asked if I'd an extra set of cottons he could borrow, but I fibbed and said it was my only one, and didn't he have something important to do?

On the morning of the seventh day, the rains abruptly ceased. I emerged onto a steaming deck, blinking like a sewer rat, the sun piercing the backs of my eyes. A sweltering, damp breeze blew over the *Formidable,* smelling of wet wood, salted sea, and earth. On the horizon, still miles away, a line of land stretched as far east and west as the eye could see. It appeared flat, and without feature.

"Africa," announced my uncle. He stood beside me and placed an arm companionably about my shoulder.

"The delta of the river Bonny," I replied, for although the weather had been rotten, I'd continued to assist my uncle with navigation and knew our destination.

"Beware, beware the Bight of Benin: One comes out, where fifty went in. . . ."

"Excuse me?" I stared at my uncle.

He burst out laughing. "Just an old saying," he said jovially, thumping me between the shoulder blades. Then he turned and began issuing orders as the crew scurried about, flinging themselves up and down the shrouds and across the yards like monkeys. He posted lookouts, ordering them to keep a weather eye out for any distant sail.

"But we're safe, right?" I said to Jonas, who'd joined me at the rail. "If it's a British warship, we fly the Stars and Stripes. If it's an American warship, we fly the Spanish flag. Right, Jonas? We're safe, aren't we?"

Jonas shrugged. "Safe enough. The law says they have to catch you with slaves aboard, otherwise they have to let you go." His yellow, protruding eyes gazed sharply out to sea, this way, that way; his fingers drummed the rail. "All the same, boy, best just to steer clear and avoid trouble altogether. Don't want them even knowing we're in the neighborhood."

We thankfully saw no sign of sail, and the *Formidable* made good course for the outermost shoals, which extended miles seaward of the delta, creating a frightful surf. Here we navigated a channel that led to the great estuary, all the while with the sounding lead in hand to measure the depths, for the estuary was very shallow and dangerous.

After anxiously waiting for the flood tide, our clipper-brig *Formidable* scraped over the bar and sailed up the waters of the Bonny, a river half as broad and deep as the Mississippi. We sailed past Bonny Town, shaded by coconut palms and plantain and banana trees, and past a dozen legitimate traders anchored in the waterway. As we sailed, a number of Africans paddled out in a large canoe and boarded our vessel. They seemed pleased to see Uncle, and he likewise to see them. (He was a very important man, I was learning.) For a price, they'd pilot us upriver to our destination.

Two hours later we cautiously worked our way under easy sail into one of the many creeks that fed the Bonny.

Dense forests of mangroves lined the water's edge. Birds took to flight as our tall masts skimmed by. Finally, when the sounding lead revealed only three and a half fathoms of water, we put down the helm and dropped anchor.

CHAPTER

6

The next morning, my uncle, Jonas, eight sailors armed with muskets, and I set off up the creek in the big canoe, with the Africans paddling.

Heat rose in sultry waves. Insects chorused, and clouds of mosquitoes droned about me. I swatted them away, grateful that one of the Africans had suggested I rub my body with palm oil to prevent their bites. But the palm oil had other effects. My clothes, freshly laundered the night before, were now oily and clinging to me. I wished I could bathe in the creek, but Uncle told me to beware: the creek teemed with crocodiles and man-eating sharks. Put one toe in the water and they'd eat you alive.

I clutched the gunwale and peered into the murky water. A snake swam by. And deeper, a blackish gray shape, seven feet or longer, kept pace with our canoe. I saw another. And another. *Blimey! Sharks?* I glanced at Jonas, who was sitting beside me. Sweat was trickling into his eyes. He blinked and wiped his face on his sleeve, panting a bit. He didn't look so well. Come to think of it, I didn't feel so well either. I sat rigidly, sweating like a beast, and prayed that our canoe was stout.

The noon sky was clouded over and my stomach was growling by the time we pulled up onto a clearing nestled between mangrove swamps. Two buildings constructed of cane poles wrapped in vines and daubed with mud stood in the center.

The Africans who were guarding the buildings greeted us, and we disembarked. One of the Africans from Bonny Town served as interpreter.

"We've come to buy slaves," my uncle told the leader.

"We have plenty of slaves for you," he was informed. "I am the king's representative. First you make generous gift to King Pepple and then we bring slaves out so you can have a look."

After gifts of handkerchiefs, chintz fabric, silk, cotton, beer, and brandy were ceremoniously presented, the afternoon was a parade of human flesh. My uncle, in shirt and duck trousers, with a palm-leaf hat and his rattan cane, walked up and down the fettered queues, smoking his cigar. Men, women, boys, and girls—hundreds of them—stood stark naked before him. "Look here," Uncle said as I tagged along behind him. "You must open their mouths and look at their teeth and smell their breath. Rotted teeth and fetid breath are signs of ill health. We want only healthy negroes."

And as we peered into this mouth and that mouth—Jonas too—a hard knot formed in my stomach and a queasiness stole over me like a thief.

What's wrong with me? I wondered. *Something I ate?*

"See this one?" Uncle was saying, poking the slave of interest with his rattan cane. "See the gray hair, both on the head and the privy parts? He's quite old. Won't survive the journey over, and I daresay no one would buy him even if he did." With a snap of his fingers, he ordered the man removed from the queue. "The children? They're like little trout. If they don't come up to here in height, we don't want them. No babies."

First Jonas, then Uncle, pinched and slapped each one's flesh, squeezing their muscles and buttocks and probing their armpits. They ordered them to raise their arms, to jump, to dance, to turn about, to speak, to breathe deeply, and to cough. "See that one?" said Uncle to me. "Weak leg. Don't want him. And this one? She's coughing. She'll need treatment before we can accept her. Generally speaking, though, they're prime stock. Yes, prime stock indeed. Should make the passage without too much bother." Here, as Jonas moved on, Uncle paused and pierced me with his blue-eyed gaze. "Something the matter, Nephew?"

"I—I don't know, really. I feel ill. Must've eaten something rotten." I covered my stomach with my hand and grimaced, suddenly wishing Uncle would order me back to the *Formidable*.

Uncle studied me a while longer before he sighed and clasped an arm about my shoulder. We began to stroll past the rows of slaves. "Maybe it's indigestion; maybe it's not," he was saying. "I won't lie to you, Philip. Slaving isn't easy. I started in the business when I was twelve—"

"You were only *twelve*?" I looked at my uncle with new eyes, feeling an even greater bond between us.

"Yes indeed. I was hardly taller than your shoe strap. Didn't know anything more about it than you do now. Took me a couple of years to harden up to it, to become a man. It's a man's business, no doubt about it, a business no one with sensibility

46

should attend, but it must be done just the same. A necessary evil, so to speak."

"A necessary evil?" I blinked, confused.

"You see, Philip, slavery is a way of life here in Africa. Natural order of their society. Been going on for thousands of years. The tribes continually fight among themselves, taking prisoners of war and forcing them into slavery. All these people you see in front of you? They're prisoners of war. It's a sad situation, to be sure. So, if you follow my reasoning, if *we* didn't take the slaves, then the Africans would just enslave the prisoners—or, more likely, dispatch them as surplus population."

"Dispatch them?"

"Kill them."

"Oh."

"They've only so much food and water to go about, you know. So really, we're doing the slaves a favor."

"A favor?"

"Saving their lives, in a way." He gestured about him with his cane. "Look at the conditions these people live in—the swamps, the mosquitoes, even sharks in their bloody rivers. They're savages. Ignorant, naked savages. Half of them are cannibals. Believe me, once they reach civilization, they'll be better off and thank us."

I chewed my lip, pondering. "Do you really think so?"

"I know so." Uncle smiled. Again he gestured about him, cigar smoke trailing his arm in a gray plume. "Would *you* want to live like this?"

"No," I answered truthfully.

"Then you agree we're doing them a favor?"

Eyeing the rows of slaves, naked, dusted with dirt, living out their lives in a godforsaken savage land, I thought how different they'd look once they took up life in America. They'd have clothes, learn to speak English, attend Mass at Saint Louis Cathedral, perhaps even go to Mr. Gallagher's shop to have a prescription filled for their master or mistress. It was a comforting thought. And then they wouldn't be enslaved in Africa, or killed as surplus population. "Yes, Uncle, we're doing them a favor."

"Then it's settled." Uncle took one more puff from his cigar, then flicked it onto the sand, where it lay smoking. "Feeling better?"

I smiled, realizing that, indeed, my queasiness was gone. "Much."

"That's my lad," he said, releasing me.

Just then a gust of wind blew through the mangroves and rustled the buildings' palm-leaf roofs. Uncle clamped a hand on his hat to keep it from blowing away as he recommenced moving down the queue. I hastened after, but not before a heavy rain, with droplets fat as shillings, began to fall, putting out Uncle's cigar with a smoky sizzle.

For the next few days, as rainwater turned the ground to mud, Uncle carried out his negotiations.

More trade goods from the *Formidable* began to arrive— hogsheads, crates, and bales, stacked on cane pallets and covered with tarpaulins. Some of the crates were broken open and the contents examined as carefully by the Africans as we examined our cargo of slaves. Were it not for the rain and the sense of secrecy regarding our illegal task, the entire event would've had the air of a marketplace, bustling and commercial.

Under the shelter of a tarpaulin strung between the two buildings, Jonas and I kept busy attending to the slaves. Pills for pains, plasters and poultices for coughs and congested lungs, bandages and salves for wounds, bitters for disruptive bowels, tonics and elixirs poured down unwilling throats as a cure for every other ailment. (Though the slaves were, on the whole, a healthy lot, and while much of our treatment was preventive, Jonas told me that many of them had been marched hundreds of miles from their homes in the interior, where they then spent weeks in the barracoon awaiting our arrival. Few of them were without some kind of ailment.) Then we shaved their heads and clipped their fingernails and toenails so they'd be less likely to cause damage if they had a fight.

Assigned the nasty task of inspecting the privy parts of each individual for any signs of the pox, it became quite necessary for me to put on the air of a surgeon's mate, which I was; else all I could think of was the fact that I was still just a lad, only fourteen, who daily examined the mirror in hopes of finding his first whisker. It was an immodest task, and I breathed a sigh of relief when it was finished. No sign of pox among the lot. I was beginning to realize that education wasn't only found within the pages of a book.

The day before we were to load the slaves aboard the *Formidable,* they were branded. Rain pounded the tarpaulin, spattering off the edges like a waterfall before flowing in cool, muddy rivers about our feet. Under the tarpaulin we built a fire, set atop a sandbox to keep it from getting wet; it was a small fire of green mango wood, billowing a bitter-tasting smoke that stung and swelled my eyes. Jonas was free with his curses. His eyes looked as if they might pop from his head.

Several iron brands with the name of the ship lay in the hot coals. Once branded, the slaves became the property of the *Formidable* and her owners. Jonas placed a pot of palm oil in the sand next to the fire. Outside the tarpaulin stretched a queue of Africans, the queue so long the black bodies disappeared into the gray, pounding rain. I swiped my brow with my sleeve, dreading the task of branding over three hundred slaves.

Jonas motioned for the two burly African guards to bring in the first slave—a lad, fifteen years or so, iron collar about his neck, eyes wide, breath coming in gasps. As the two guards tossed him onto his stomach, pinning him in the mud, Jonas took one of the irons out of the fire. Through the dusting of ash, the iron's end glowed as orange as Jonas' eyes.

My pulse quickened. The air stank of hot iron, mud, and fear.

"Dip the end in palm oil, like so," Jonas wheezed, "and press it firmly between the shoulder blades." Flesh sizzled. The boy squirmed. A moan escaped his lips. "Keep it there for a few seconds, release, and it's done. Simple." Jonas waved his hand, indicating he was finished with the slave. The two guards hauled the boy from the mud and back out into the rain.

"Why the oil?" I asked Jonas, watching as the boy stumbled to find his feet and feeling those familiar gripes in my belly, as if I'd swallowed something rotten.

"So the flesh won't stick to the hot iron." Jonas coughed the woodsmoke from his lungs, then said, "Makes a nice clean brand. Now you try."

The two guards brought in another slave—this time an older woman—and forced her to the mud. I reached for the iron, blinking back the smoke, seeing the sudden, unsettling image of the Gallaghers watching me. A wave of nausea rolled through me like an ocean swell and I clenched my jaw, thinking, *You'll just have to harden up to it. Become a man. Like Uncle.*

"Go on," prompted Jonas. "Dip it in the oil."

Pushing all thought away, mouth dry as bones, I dipped the iron into the oil and pressed the brand between the slave's shoulder blades. She threw her head back and screamed.

"Harder," said Jonas. "You're barely touching her. There, that's it. That'll do."

As the woman was led away, her cries vanishing into the pounding rain, Jonas cuffed my arm and laughed. "See? You lived through it. And believe me, it gets easier."

I managed a smile.

And so the morning continued as one slave after another was branded, some crying dreadfully, others enduring silently, and all sorts in between.

It was some relief to discover that Jonas was right. For a while the task *did* become easier—only one more step in the procedure, like forcing medicine down their throats or measuring their height. But then, come early afternoon, as I sat on my chair and pressed the iron onto the back of a comely female who howled and writhed, I'd a peculiar, unsettling memory. One of Master Crump laying his dreaded cane across my bare back while I begged and pleaded for mercy, my nose clogged with the stench of camphor. Again and again and again he whipped me, deaf to my cries.

No, Master Crump, please, no, no, nooooo!

My breath caught. A lump grew in my throat as a gust of wind whistled through the tent and my vision blurred.

"What's the matter with you, boy? You're shaking like a leaf. Gimme that iron." Jonas grabbed it from me while I wiped my eyes, coughed, and cursed the fire.

Must be the smoke.

The next slave was a fine specimen of manhood. Tall, broad-shouldered, and muscular, he didn't look away as did the other slaves. Instead, he stared defiantly at Jonas and me, a roaring fire of hatred in his eyes. I'd my doubts as to whether the two African guards could hold him should the man decide to fight. They yanked the chain attached to the iron collar about the man's neck and forced him to his knees in the mud. Then they began to push him onto his stomach.

I retrieved an iron from the coals and prepared to dip it in the pot of palm oil.

Next thing I knew, there was an animal-like roar, two black bodies went flying through the air, and the iron was yanked from my hand.

Then, suddenly, the monster of a slave lowered his face to mine. For an instant only, I stared at him—saw that fiery hatred; the visage of murder; his sharpened, pointed teeth—before he thrust the red-hot brand onto the flesh of my chest, just below my throat, holding me by the shoulder to press it all the harder.

My skin fried. Popped.

Pain seared through my body.

I shrieked. The world spun round.

Oh God, it hurts! It hurts!

Jonas hit the man's arm, loosening his grip.

I must've fallen off my chair, for suddenly I was in the mud and mud was in my ears.

I smelled flesh burning—my own.

All about me echoed screams. The crack of a whip. The retort of muskets. Jonas cursing. The bellowing of the giant. My uncle shouting orders.

And then, except for the rain, the moaning and weeping of the slaves, and my own stifled cries, it was silent.

I lay for a while, my chest throbbing and burning, until my uncle came and stood under the tarpaulin. "Philip, get up." When I didn't move, he said it again.

Slowly, I sat up in the mud. My chair lay overturned beside me, along with the branding iron. Stuck to its end I saw shriveled, blackened flesh. "Is he dead?" I asked, remembering the slave's look of murder, the gunshots.

Jonas picked up the iron and returned it to the embers. The fire snapped, sending a plume of sparks upward. Outside the tarpaulin, rain roared. Water streamed off the canvas.

"Stand up," said Uncle. His face was hard, his eyes slitted. He held a whip coiled in his hand.

I did as Uncle told me. I wiped the mud off my face.

Uncle motioned to someone behind him. "Bring the slave here."

Five sailors brought the giant, two on each side, one with a musket jammed into the slave's spine. Mud caked the slave. Mixed with the mud, I saw blood. Again the slave stared defiantly.

Uncle looked at me and pointed at the slave. "Brand him."

I stood rooted, unable to move, my chest afire.

"Put him on his face," said Uncle to the sailors. Then, again to me: "I said, brand him."

Still I stood, watching as the slave gave no resistance, staring at me all the way down as the sailors shoved him onto his belly in the mud.

"Go," whispered Jonas, pushing me from behind. "It's got to be done."

I reached for a branding iron. My hand shook. The end of the iron glowed red. I started to dip it in the oil.

"No oil," ordered Uncle.

And so I branded the murderous savage. Pressed the iron deep into his flesh, just as he'd done to me. His flesh quivered and smoked, but he made no sound.

A great well of rage boiled up inside me, and after the branding was over I bellowed and hurled the iron into the fire, scattering embers. I stormed from the tent into the rain, glad my chest hurt, glad it burned, glad I'd be scarred forever.

I fell to my knees in the mud, hair hanging in soggy strings, and vomited.

Uncle was there, his hand on my shoulder. "Nothing to be ashamed of. I was sick plenty of times when I was your age. Have Jonas see to your wound." He walked away, boots sucking in the muck.

CHAPTER 7

*U*nder a cloudy yet rainless sky, we loaded 368 slaves aboard the *Formidable:* 244 men and 124 women and children. I'd have doubted the vessel's capacity had I not seen it with my own eyes.

While we'd been gone up the creek, the rest of the sailors, under the supervision of the carpenter, had built double decks in the hold. The decks were like shelves, with two feet between each deck. Arriving in canoe loads of fifty or so, the slaves were herded into the hold and onto the narrow-spaced tiers, shackled together two by two, while a pair of mounted carronades swept the hold in the event of an uprising. With the exception of some screaming and fainting, all went smoothly. The females and children were placed together in the aft hold (there was no need to shackle them), separated by a reinforced bulk-head from the men in the main hold. They were packed together tightly—too tightly, in my opinion, for they were like spoons in a drawer. How would they even roll over?

I mentioned this to Uncle, but he reassured me that all the negroes would take exercise twice daily—stretch their limbs, dance, and enjoy themselves. That they'd have two meals a day of boiled rice, beans, and yams, and that the men would be given a pipe and tobacco once daily to share about. "So don't let it trouble you," he said, in as pleasant a mood as I'd ever seen him. "They'll have many opportunities for comfort."

Uncle's mood was infectious, sweeping all my doubts away. *See? The arrangements are excellent,* I told myself. *While the slave trade is a necessary evil, it's not such a rotten thing after all. You've seen the worst of it, and it'll get better from here. As Uncle said, they'll have many opportunities for comfort.*

The night before we were to weigh anchor, I lay curled in my berth. Jonas slept above me, snoring. A candle burned in the lantern hanging on its peg above the desk. Cries and moans issued from the hold, seeming to permeate the air, the very timbers of the deck above me, the whitewashed boards of my cabin. A sudden irritation grabbed hold of me, and I thought, *Why don't they just calm down and have it over with?*—whereupon I fell into a fitful sleep, dreaming of the time when Master Crump dragged me by the ear, the arm, the ear, from the cotton mill back to the workhouse; me burning with fever, barely able to stand; him saying, *Why must you always be so difficult? Why can't you just do your job like all the other good lads?*

Reprovisioned with wood, water, yams, and rice, with our fine ship well tallowed, every seam caulked within and without, and her standing rigging tarred black as a crow, we heaved up anchor to the tune of "The Maid of Amsterdam," set our fore topsail, and headed down the creek toward the river Bonny. I offered to help Uncle navigate the shallow waters, but he chased me off. Said he'd important work to do for the moment, else we might ground on a sandbar and lose our ship and precious cargo altogether.

So I sat on deck, under the shade of one of the spare boats hanging above, studying languages and sweating like a coal miner. Chains rattled and cries came from below, but I was beginning to understand that the racket was a constant bother I'd have to tolerate. Until we were safe at sea and out of sight of land, none of the slaves would be allowed on deck; otherwise, I was told, they'd try to jump overboard and swim back to shore. It was an unhappy arrangement, but would soon right itself. The faster, the better, in my opinion. I felt rotten for them, remembering my time aboard the *Hope,* and the horror of steerage.

While I'd been upriver, Uncle had encouraged me to begin a journal of African words and phrases, seeing as I'd a gift for languages. It was this journal I studied now, determined to be able to talk to the slaves and African slave traders directly on future voyages.

I was scratching a mosquito bite when the cabin boy, Billy Dorsett, approached me.

Up until now I'd distanced myself from the crew, not wanting to become too friendly with such a shifty-eyed, foulmouthed bunch—although, I admitted, it was quite lonesome with just Jonas and Uncle to talk to. Frankly, there were many nights I lay awake wishing I'd a friend, begging God for a *real* friend, someone my own age, someone who liked my company— a companionship I'd never experienced before. But Billy Dorsett wasn't my friend of choice, nor would he ever be, not if I'd anything to say about it. I hoped God hadn't sent Billy as the answer to my prayer. He was about as pleasing as a horsefly in the eye.

"What is it, Billy?" I asked, not looking up from my journal.

"My head aches."

"Go talk to Jonas. He's the surgeon."

"He said he's feeling out of sorts and to come talk to you."
Billy sat cross-legged beside me, as if we were old chums.

I stifled the urge to groan and tell him to clear off. Instead, I
set aside my journal, hoping my businesslike manner would rid
his mind of any ideas of friendship. "Right, then, I'll fetch you
some medicine."

Returning, I handed him a pewter tankard filled with water
and tartaric acid—good for headaches. "Drink it down." I picked
up my journal, waved away mosquitoes, and within seconds was
sounding out African words: "*Ọkọchì . . . ǹsala . . .*"

"How long does it take?" Billy asked.

I blinked at him, pretending I'd forgotten he was there.
"What the devil are you on about? How long does *what* take?"

"The medicine. To work. How long do I gotta wait?"

"Until your headache's gone."

"Oh."

I returned to my journal, fanning myself a bit with my palm-
leaf hat before setting it back on my head.

"Does it hurt?" he asked.

"Does *what* hurt?"

"That." And he poked my chest wound with a grubby finger.

"Bugger and blast, Billy! Keep your hands off me! Of course
it hurts, you dolt!"

"Sorry. Just wondering, is all."

"Don't you have something to do?"

Billy shrugged. "Not really. What are you reading?"

I sighed, pulling my journal away from his prying eyes. "You
know, Billy, it's helpful after drinking medicine to rest awhile. Es-

pecially if you've a headache. Apply a wet rag to your forehead and shut your eyes. Two to three hours should do it."

"My headache's gone now."

"Oh." I suspected that there had been no such thing as a headache in the first place.

"I wish I coulda been there."

"Been *where*? Billy, can't you see I'm busy?"

"I wish I coulda seen it when you branded him."

I turned away, disgusted, and gazed off into the distant sky, the clouds heavy and promising rain, my wound throbbing. I was trying to forget that dreadful day. . . . The fire of hatred in his eyes. His teeth, filed to points. The stink of burning flesh. My own shrieks of pain . . . To forget the shame I felt over the rage that had consumed me and the pain that I'd inflicted upon him. Him—a helpless slave.

"They say you branded him hard, like you was trying to reach his backbone."

"Clear off, Billy."

"They say he's a mighty warrior. Or *was* a mighty warrior, anyways."

A warrior? I admitted a grudging admiration toward the slave who'd defied us. Who stared directly at his captors with un-abashed hatred. Who refused to make a sound even as I inflicted horrible pain upon him. Certainly the slave possessed a courage I could never hope to have.

"They say he's meek as a lamb now, all 'cause of you," Billy was saying. "That you could poke him with a sharp stick and he won't do nothing."

"Who says he was a warrior?"

Billy shrugged again. "Everyone. They say his name's Ikoro, which means 'warlike,' and that he hates us white folk." And here Billy raised his bum and released some wind with a loud honk, grinning. This display of bodily functions seemed to distract him, however, as for a while afterward he appeared at a loss for words.

"Well," I prompted him, after scooting away several feet, "what else do they say? Exactly why does Ikoro despise us?"

Billy moved closer. "They say it's 'cause we make his people into slaves."

I frowned, thinking. "But Uncle said—I mean Captain Towne said—that if *we* didn't take the slaves, then the Africans would just enslave them or kill them as surplus population, as prisoners of war. Captain Towne says slavery's been happening in Africa for thousands of years. Natural order of their society. We're saving their lives and doing them a favor."

Billy slapped a mosquito on his neck. "I don't know about all that stuff."

Just then Pea Soup approached from nowhere, his face blank as usual, and handed me a tankard of liquid. I took a sip, pleased to find that it was sweetened lime juice. It was the first time he'd shown me such a kindness, and I hoped it was the beginning of an industrious relationship. I'd come to believe that the look of hatred I'd seen reflected on Pea Soup's face that night had only been a trick of the light, for I'd seen nothing of the sort since. "Why, thank you, Pea Soup," I said, smiling. "It's jolly good." Then Pea Soup began to fan us with a piece of canvas he'd had tucked in his loincloth.

"Anyways," Billy continued, "so a while back Ikoro got together this big army of savages and laid ambushes and slaughtered white folks everywhere like they was dinner. Chopped 'em to pieces. Ate their livers and hearts. Cooked their gizzards."

"Sounds awful."

"Slaughtered Africans too, if they was into helping white folk capture slaves and suchlike."

A breeze gusted over the deck. Overhead, the yards creaked. I took a gulp of lime drink. "Sounds like a monster."

"Would have chopped you to pieces too, if you hadn't gotten him first."

I wiped my mouth and stared at him. "You know, Billy—"

He leaned in close, as if we were conspirators. "What."

"You're revolting."

He smiled. "Thanks." And, seeming pleased, Billy stood up and ambled away, leaving me with my tankard of lime juice, my journal of African words, and Pea Soup stirring up the breeze.

"*Ǹgàjì,*" I said. "Pea Soup, do you understand? *Ǹgàjì.*"

It was an hour later, and Pea Soup still fanned the air, chasing off the mosquitoes. It'd occurred to me that Pea Soup would be a grand resource if he happened to know the language. I repeated the word, but he only glanced at me briefly, blankly, and then stared at his usual spot, somewhere close to his feet. "The interpreter said it means 'spoon,' and so if you speak this particular African language, then you must know its meaning. *Ǹgàjì.* Have you heard this before?"

Up went the canvas, down went the canvas.

I frowned. "You know how to talk, don't you, Pea Soup? Come to think of it, I've never heard you speak at all. Perhaps you're a mute. Are you a mute?"

I shaded my eyes and gazed at him, knowing he couldn't understand a word of English. And, as usual, he didn't say anything. I decided he really wasn't disagreeable to look at. Fact was, I wished my own frail body would find a form of masculinity as had Pea Soup's, though I wouldn't care to be black as midnight, nor have coarse, woolly hair. I'd never seen him smile, and wondered if he'd good teeth. As his owner and master, I was responsible for his teeth.

"Well," I said, sighing and returning to my journal, "perhaps you just don't know *that* word. Perhaps, as a savage, you've always eaten with your fingers. How about *ezē*? It means 'tooth.'" I tapped my front tooth. Still nothing. I pointed to myself. "Philip." Then I pointed to him. "Pea Soup. Can you say 'Pea Soup'? That's your name. Probably not God-given, but it's your name nonetheless. 'Pea Soup,' can you say it?" I said it again, slowly: *"Peea Soooup."*

I might've pursued this had I sensed any understanding from Pea Soup. Instead, his monotonous blankness left me yawning, and I wondered if it was even possible to guide him out of savagery. After trying a dozen words on him and receiving no response, I set down my journal and nodded off, thankful nonetheless for the breeze.

For the rest of the day, amid thunderous squalls, we made our way to the mouth of the river Bonny, where we anchored for the night. Then, in the pale light of dawn, we up-anchored and navigated between the numerous sandbanks with the high tide, carried over the final bar by the moist land breeze.

Once we'd left the river Bonny, a calm settled, along with a pouring rain. We anchored and waited for the sea breeze. This was the most dangerous leg of our journey, for, as Jonas told me, the patrol squadron liked to lie in wait for slavers leaving the mouths of rivers, when the ships were filled to the gunwales with slaves. Unable to get rid of their cargo, the traders would be caught red-handed with the illegal goods.

Keeping a sharp lookout during the lull, we ate our breakfast. Afterward I studied my journal of languages and my catechism until Jonas called me to my medical station, for we'd several complaints of fever among the crew. Normally, we diagnosed and treated the crew where they lay in their hammocks, but today, because of the heat belowdecks, we'd set up a temporary infirmary for the crew on the deck, under an awning.

As I opened the medicine chest, the rain stopped. A minute later the cry "Sail ho!" resounded from the masthead.

Those of us gathered under the medical awning ducked our heads out and gazed upward. The lookout was peering through his spyglass directly out to sea.

"Where away?" came Uncle's voice from aft.

"Four points off the port bow."

"What flag?"

"Can't tell. Wait . . . weather's clearing off." A minute later: "It's the Union Jack. Britain."

I heard Uncle say, "Run up the Stars and Stripes! What kind of vessel?"

"Uh—she appears to be a warship, Captain. She's picked up the sea breeze and is headed straight for us."

Uncle ran up the rigging, nimble as a lad. But before he could arrive at the masthead, the lookout cried again, his voice cracking with panic. "Sail ho! *Two* warships, Captain! One behind the other one! And this one appears to be American!"

CHAPTER
8

"*All* hands! All hands!"

The entire crew of the *Formidable*, save for those who lay groaning in their hammocks with fever, erupted into pandemonium. Like bees in a hive.

A clot of men circled the capstan, raising the anchor inch by blasted inch, cursing and praying aloud. Men slammed gunports open. Rolled out the long guns. Dumped ammunition, muskets, daggers, and swords on deck. Loaded and primed small arms, and jammed them into belts. Sailors swarmed the rigging, waiting for the signal to set sail.

"Jonas, pray tell me, what's going to happen?" I kept asking, hurrying to take down the awning covering our medical supplies. "Are they going to sink us? Are they going to kill us? Are we going to have to fight?"

Jonas paused and clutched the pinrail, panting. "Blood and thunder, don't ask so many questions, boy," he finally gasped. "Of course they're not going to sink us if they think we've got slaves aboard. Just know that if we get *caught* with a boatload of slaves, we'll lose everything and have to face trial. Or worse, your uncle could be hanged as a pirate. You too. United States law."

I stared at Jonas as if this were a jolly joke and he was about to burst into his donkey laugh and slap me on the back. "Did you say *hanged*?"

"Indeed I did."

"But—but—can't we just raise the Spanish flag?"

"Too late for that, boy. And besides, British ships have permission from the Spanish government to board Spanish vessels. Either way, they've got us pinched." He shoved me aside and began tugging on one of the awning's knots. "Now shut your trap and do your duty or it'll be an early end to your fine career."

"Pea Soup!" I screamed, seeing him lounging against the bulwarks, watching everything with a keen interest. "Help us! For the love of God, help us!"

By the time our anchor was raised and every canvas set and spread, the pursuing vessels were only a half mile distant. Their bows slicing through the water, spray flying over them in dashes of white, they looked like greyhounds in full sprint. The wind that blew them along finally, thankfully, caught up with us, and we turned and scurried back into the mouth of the Bonny, navigating the channels under a cloud of sail in water hardly deeper than we drew, dashing over the bar, spray flying over our low bulwarks as we hurried on through wind and surf into deeper water.

"Steady, men! Steady!" cried Uncle. "Ready the main topgallant stays'l!"

In a short time we came upon Bonny Town and ran between the merchant ships at anchor, meanwhile setting every stays'l we owned as Uncle variously called "Haul taut!" "Sheet home!" "Hoist away!"

Crowds of sailors lined the rails of the merchant ships. Colorful pennants flew from halyards. And when one of the pursuing vessels fired a warning shot from its bow gun, though it fell far short, the merchant sailors cheered and waved their caps at the naval ships. At the same time, screams echoed and thuds pounded from the hold beneath us.

"Prepare to receive the wounded." Jonas flung open the medical chest. His hands shook as he handed me a leg saw, a tourniquet, the surgeon's kit, bandages.

"But, Jonas, are we truly going to go into action? Because I've—I've never yet cut off a leg. What if some poor fellow's hit with a cannonball? Jonas, what about the slaves? Who'll know if they're in need of assistance? Jonas, should I have a weapon to defend myself? Jonas—"

"For pity's sake, pipe down and hand me a drink, will you? Brandy."

At half past four, miles past Bonny Town, just as the vessels were almost upon us, sharpshooters firing their muskets from the shrouds, the wind fell light and Uncle hauled out into a branch of the Bonny running eastward.

Immediately it split into two tributaries, with a narrow spit of brush-covered sand, a quarter mile broad, running between. For a heart-stopping moment we scraped sand with our bottom, but were soon into the northernmost fork, still flying with every scrap of sail. The Royal Navy vessel veered into the south fork and was now almost abreast of us, mastheads towering over the jungled sandspit between. To our dismay, the American warship, a two-masted schooner, followed us into the north fork, scraping bottom as well. We held our collective breath, desperately hoping she'd founder, but on she came, tenacious as a bulldog.

"I'll go to the devil, I will, rather than let them have us or our cargo!" roared Uncle. "Ready the carronades for firing! We'll sink these self-righteous upstarts."

Soon the gaping mouths of two carronades, shiny black, short-barreled, and wicked-looking, poked through our stern gunports. The gun crews clustered about the carronades like moths about a lantern.

"Three fathoms, Captain!" cried the second mate, who sounded the depths. "And getting shallower!"

"Keep a foot of water under her keel," was Uncle's response. "And fire as you bear."

No sooner had he said so than both carronades blasted with a will. A wave of air concussed the ship like a giant hammer, shaking timbers and rattling teeth. Jonas slopped his brandy. Pea Soup screamed, sank to the deck, and covered his ears. My own ears rang as I fetched a pistol from the pile of small arms. The acrid stink of gunpowder swirled through the air.

"You stupid fool," Jonas slurred, slouched against the medicine chest. "You don't know how to use that. Put it away."

I looked at it, realizing that he was right, that I didn't even know how to fire it, much less load it properly. Tossing it away, I picked up a cutlass instead.

Right, then. Should be easy enough. Aim and stab.

"What are you going to do?" Jonas was saying. "Hack off someone's leg instead of sawing it off? You're half anyone's size, plus you're a surgeon's mate, boy, not a soldier. Besides, we're doomed. We're *all* doomed. They'll either catch us or kill us, and either way we're doomed."

I sank down beside Jonas, feeling as dour and helpless as he looked, hearing Pea Soup scream and scream as the carronades blasted their 32-pound shot over and over again and the *Formidable* shuddered with the strain. Just how did I get into this predicament? Me, Philip Arthur Higgins, a hardworking, law-abiding lad who some said had the makings of a good scholar. Me, Philip Arthur Higgins, master, speculator, and entrepreneur, whose short career was about to end in bleak failure, perhaps even at the end of a rope.

"Two and a half fathoms, Captain! We're going to ground!"

"Prepare to jettison the cargo!"

I blinked, wondering what Uncle meant.

But before I could figure it out, a cheer began with the sailors at the stern and spread throughout the ship. All about me, sailors tossed their caps in the air or waved them to and fro. Everyone was grinning. "They've grounded! Captain, they've grounded! And we shot a hole right through her bows!"

I jumped to my feet and stared aft at the American warship. Indeed, she'd settled on a sandbar. She was listing to the side, yardarms reaching toward the muddy bank, sails bulging with the strain. And as I watched, sheets snapped. A sail ripped asunder with a sound like a cannon blast. Men darted about like ants on an anthill.

"She's stuck hard," said Jonas with a yellow grin.

Onward we sailed, up the creek, reducing and trimming sail, the jeers and taunts from our crew fading into silence once the American vessel was lost from view. The masts of the British ship were gone as well. Again we were surrounded by nothing but chattering birds, mangrove swamps, and clouds of mosquitoes.

We cast anchor, watching and listening as the sun sank— a blood-red fireball beneath the mangroves—and darkness fell.

We had a plan.

In the wee morning hours, when the tide was favorable, the *Formidable* would slip past the American vessel.

All light would be extinguished.

Men would be posted throughout the hold to keep the slaves quiet.

Fourteen men in our longboat would tow our ship.

All sails would be furled, for sails blocked out the night sky, and a lookout on the American vessel—supposing he could see the sky at all—might wonder why it'd suddenly disappeared as we floated silently past.

Gunners would be ready to open fire, if necessary.

If we slipped by successfully, then we'd sail like the dickens toward the mouth of the Bonny, leaving the American cruiser stranded miles back in the creek, wondering and wondering where the devil we'd gone.

As surgeon's mate, I was beginning to realize that the only action in which I'd ever be likely to participate would be the aftereffects of action. The bloody effects. In other words, I was to wait. To stand in readiness and wait. This satisfied me, for as I was small for my age and well suited for scholarly pursuits, I decided I'd take Jonas' advice and leave the combat to others.

At half past two in the morning, when all was securely battened, we left our anchorage. We'd gone no more than a quarter mile when a heavy rain began to fall and a lucky breeze blew from astern. We dared not set an awning for shelter, as we didn't want anything flapping in the wind. So, sticky as molasses, I stood under the shelter of one of the spare boats hoisted high above, trying to see more than just vague shapes in the darkness.

At least the mosquitoes don't pester us when it's raining, I thought, attempting to cheer myself up. At the same time, I realized I was a bit queasy. *And where's that Pea Soup when I need him? I could use a bit of sailor's biscuit to calm my stomach.*

A half hour passed . . .

An hour . . .

Rain pounded the boat above me, sluicing off the gunwales,

spattering the deck. Despite my shelter, I was drenched—at least from the waist down. I'd been caught in a downpour once in New Orleans, on my way back from a delivery clear across town. I'd opened the shop door, shivering. Bells jangled. Then Mrs. Gallagher was there, tut-tutting, whisking me upstairs, and drying my hair with a towel, meanwhile drawing me a bubbly bath that steamed the windows.

I miss you, Mrs. Gallagher, I realized. It wasn't the first time I'd thought of the Gallaghers since embarking upon my voyage, but it *was* the first time I did so while an ache grew in my belly— quite apart from the usual sickness. Rather like a cold, heavy stone settling deep inside.

The sky rumbled.

The wind intensified.

I was thinking about corned beef and cabbage just like what Mrs. Gallagher often cooked—thinking I could actually smell it, taste it, perhaps—when suddenly a bone-jarring bolt of lightning ripped the sky asunder. And in that split second I saw a ship, almost abreast with the *Formidable*. And even after the light vanished, the images remained, seared onto my eyeballs. Our gunners, crouched like tigers beside the long guns. A young man aboard the American vessel, blond and mustached, staring openmouthed at us. Hat upon his head. Rain pouring off the hat's gunwales. The American warship no longer listing to its side, but level in the water. Gunports black and gaping. Sharpshooters positioned in the shrouds.

An earsplitting crack of thunder pounded the darkness that followed.

My hair stood on end.

Uncle screamed, "Blast them to hell!"

The *Formidable* discharged her cannon just as lightning

blazed and thunder roared. At the same time, musket balls punched the deck like hail. I dove for cover behind the mainmast, the blood surging to my head.

Beneath me, the hold erupted with banging and screams of terror. Again lightning flashed and thunder crackled. The air sizzled with a burning stench.

By the deuce, I'm about to be killed!

And suddenly Jonas was there, wheezing, a bottle of brandy in his hand. "They must've been waiting for us!"

In the next flash of light, to my horror, men leaped from the other vessel onto our ship. "They're boarding us, Jonas! Do—do they hang us now or later?"

Jonas didn't answer, instead tipping back his bottle and guzzling.

I closed my eyes and pressed back against the mainmast alongside Jonas, ignoring the splinters and dampness, the chills racing up my spine, the clatter of my teeth. In the darkness I heard the clash of cutlasses. A grunt. Pistols fired. Thunder crashed.

"Fire at will!" The timbers of the *Formidable* shook again.

Someone screamed in agony. I peered about the mainmast, swiping the rain from my eyes. In the thunderous flashes of light, I saw one of our crew clutching his belly. Crimson mushroomed on his shirt. He sank to his knees, then fell to his face. "One of our men is down!" I cried.

Except for his coughing and wheezing, Jonas didn't move.

I shook him. "I said, one of our men is down! He could be dying!"

Jonas stirred. "Then what are you waiting for, you stupid boy? Go and fetch him. Do your duty."

Me? Fetch him? Under enemy fire? But what if I'm hit?

These were my thoughts even as I shoved away from Jonas and dashed through the darkness toward where I'd last seen the wounded fellow. Forward, near the foremast.

Lightning branded the sky. In that instant my breath caught. A sword glittered in its sweep toward my neck. Behind the sword was a man, his face hard and murderous. I ducked and dropped to the deck just as darkness swallowed us, just as the sword swished through nothingness. I crawled away, knees thumping, water sloshing, hearing someone's frightened panting and realizing it was my own.

Oh God! Save me!

Crawling, crawling, expecting at any second to have my head parted forever from my body, I bumped into something. Something warm, wet, and hairy. And with the next eerie flash, eyes stared out at me from a doughy face. Pale. Sightless. Dead.

It was the man I'd been after.

I stood, muscles tensed, wanting to run, shrieking, back to Jonas.

But at the next stroke of lightning, all thoughts of the dead man vanished. For I spied Pea Soup at the bow, dagger clamped between his teeth, climbing out onto the bowsprit. He glanced back. And in his eyes I saw it again.

It . . .

That dreadful, murderous hatred.

CHAPTER 9

*W*ith a clarity as searing as lightning, I knew there was only one reason Pea Soup would be crawling out on the bowsprit with a dagger.

Sabotage.

No doubt he was off to sever the towline that stretched from the end of the jibboom to the longboat. And if it was severed, the *Formidable* would be dead in the water. We'd be finished in minutes.

I understood this in the time it took me to leap over the dead man and dart to the bowsprit, heart pounding.

I had to stop him.

Lightning flashed every couple of seconds, illuminating Pea Soup in an eerie light display.

Already he was several feet out over the

water, crawling like a caterpillar atop the gigantic wooden spar that thrust outward and upward from the bow of the *Formidable* like a sword.

Light . . .

Darkness . . .

Light . . .

Darkness . . .

"Pea Soup!"

He hesitated, then looked back, the shock of discovery registering on his face.

"Pea Soup! I order you to return! Now!"

Light . . .

Darkness . . .

"Now! Do you hear me? I—I demand you obey me! I'm your master!" I heard my voice, shrill, hysterical almost, punctuated by earsplitting cracks of thunder.

Narrowed, hate-filled eyes glared back at me. Rain pounded and ran in rivulets down both our faces. Then Pea Soup took the dagger from his mouth, turned away from me, and continued to crawl into the darkness.

I peered at the water below, remembering what lurked beneath.

But I'd no choice. Not if I wished to save Uncle. Not if I wished to save myself and the *Formidable*.

Taking a shaky breath, I climbed out on the bowsprit. My hands grasped and pulled, slipping on the smooth, wet surface. Water streamed into my eyes. And every few seconds, total darkness surrounded me, except for the images seared into my brain as with a hot iron.

Images of a jutting bowsprit. Pea Soup in front of me, naked except for a loincloth, black as tar, inching along, dagger in hand.

The myriad of ropes and lines arced beneath me, sweeping like evil grins—footropes, sheets, and stays, attached at both ends. Creek water, black with night, seeming to roil with shapes beneath. Dreadful, hungry shapes.

By the devil, whatever you do, Philip Arthur Higgins, don't fall now.

On I struggled.

Desperate, I took a conciliatory tone, though I knew he couldn't understand a word. "Pea Soup, come back, please. I promise I'm not angry. And if I've ever done anything to hurt you, I'm sorry. Tell you what, I'll give you some extra food—I will, really I will—if you'll just turn round. All right, several extra portions. Cook's got some fine jam. You can have bread and jam. Really, I swear I'm not angry. I'm not even angry that you've a knife. A gigantic, bloody knife. Just please, *please,* come back. Pea Soup, Pea Soup, don't *do* this."

And then he stopped. Or rather, he *was* stopped, by the tangle of spars, lines, and blocks, all coming together at the juncture of the bowsprit with the jibboom—the extra spar that stretched even farther from the ship, maybe forty feet, all told.

I caught his heel.

He kicked me away.

I inched forward and seized his ankle.

He grunted and flailed his leg, catching me in the teeth.

I let go, tasting blood.

Thunder cracked like a musket blast in my ear.

On he crawled.

No!

I lunged for him, grabbing both his ankles.

He kicked. And kicked.

He's strong, I realized. *Far stronger than me.*

And with that realization, a brilliant bolt of lightning dazzled my eyeballs and sizzled my spine, and Pea Soup bashed me in the nose with his foot.

Stars exploded.

Off the bowsprit I slid.

Down I went, heart lurching.

Flailing, screaming, I caught one of the arced ropes under the bowsprit with a hand. I dangled over the water. Indeed, there *were* shapes below. The water boiled with activity. I gasped. "Help me! Pea Soup, help me! For pity's sake!"

Pea Soup peered down at me.

"Save me! Please! There are sharks in the water!"

And in the stark white light, his eyes hardened. As if they'd suddenly turned to stones.

Then he spoke, the first words I'd ever heard him say. His words, like a stab through my heart. Spoken through wickedly pointed teeth, each word seethed with hatred. "Tonight you will die!"

I saw the flash of steel an instant before he swiped the knife through the air, severing one end of my rope. At that very instant, three things happened. The *Formidable* shuddered with the firing of her long guns. Pea Soup lost his grip on the knife and it tumbled out of his hands as he bellowed with rage. And I plummeted down before I jerked to a stop, toes skimming the water, desperately clinging to what was left of the rope, wet hemp burning my hands.

I raised my legs, but not before something scraped my foot. Something rough and wet and alive.

"No!" I shrieked.

I don't want to die! Not like this!

I looked up. Pea Soup had turned about and was crawling back toward the ship. Probably to fetch another knife.

"Help me! Whatever I've done, I'm sorry! Pea Soup, don't leave me! I'll die! Blast it, Pea Soup, *help me!*"

I begged and pleaded until Pea Soup was gone and my begging faded to weeping.

I was alone. Although a battle raged about me—men crying out, cutlasses singing, muskets firing, cannon blasting—I was alone.

I squeezed my eyes shut, panting, my heart jumping like a rabbit.

Jaws snapped beneath me.

Something splashed.

My arms began burning, quivering like harp strings. For a moment, a dreadful, awful moment, I thought of letting go, of giving up and letting the night—letting death, the sharks—just take me. All I'd have to do would be to release my hands.

Just let go.

But in that instant I thought of Mrs. Gallagher, of her kind face. Of her saying, *Do you promise,* absolutely promise, *to come home and see us again, my little English boy? I promise,* I'd replied. And now I knew I'd do anything in the world to see her and Mr. Gallagher again.

I thought of my miserable life under Master Crump. I thought of my vow to make something of myself. To be like Uncle. To never be hungry again. I thought of the thin-lipped satisfaction Master Crump would feel if he knew I'd been devoured by sharks.

A strength born of resolve flowed through me.

Climb, I ordered myself. *Climb, Philip Arthur Higgins!*

And where moments before I'd have doubted my ability and my strength, indeed I climbed the rope. Amid the battle, sharks snapping beneath me, I climbed the rope like a born sailor.

After, I tumbled onto the deck, collapsing in a heap. I wanted to put my face in my hands and cry, sob, weep, wail—do all sorts of unmanly things—but someone shook me by the shoulder. It was McGuire, the second mate. "Surgeon's been looking for you. There's wounded to attend to. Do your duty, he says to tell you."

"You—you must find Pea Soup and place him in confinement. Immediately. And—and please don't ask why."

So, for the rest of that night, I did my duty. Long after we left the American vessel far behind. Long after every naval soldier or officer had been beaten back and either slain or forced overboard.

And as I did my duty—sawing, sewing, bandaging, covered with bodily fluids so wretched I thought I'd surely never eat again and surrounded by shrieks, thunder, and lightning—three thoughts kept running through my head.

Pea Soup hates me.

Pea Soup wants me dead.

Pea Soup speaks English.

CHAPTER 10

*T*he air was hot as a kiln. A sultry breeze whispered over the deck, this way, that way, seeming undecided whether to move us forward or backward, forcing the crew to trim the yards again and again.

Finally the slaves were allowed to come on deck. As it was one of my few moments of rest and relaxation, I leaned against the bulwarks, watching as, two by two, the Africans crawled out of the hold. Day after day, while we'd finished loading our cargo and subsequently battled with the American cruiser (the British cruiser we never saw again), the slaves had been locked below, without fresh air other than what filtered through the grated hatch coverings. Now, six days after our escape out of the Bonny, they were a miserable lot, moaning and crying and gasping, some so bent they could hardly stand, all of them covered with filth, their stench unbearable. At the sight of them, my breast swelled with pity. I couldn't have endured it, except I knew that from now on the slaves would be able to take their air and exercise. *From now on,* I told myself, *all will be well.*

I'd been in the hold, twice. On the day we'd first received slaves into our hold, I'd followed Jonas as he visited them in his capacity as ship's surgeon. But no sooner had I stepped off the companionway into the suffocating darkness than, to my embarrassment, my chest had tightened and I couldn't breathe, as if someone were squeezing the life out of me. "Jonas," I managed to say. That was the last thing I remember as I fainted dead away, lantern glass shattering, candle wax spattering. I lasted five minutes before fainting again the next time. After that, Jonas went into the hold without me.

When Jonas found any indisposed, they were carried to the bow of the vessel, to a room under the fo'c'sle that was reserved as the slaves' infirmary, where I waited, damp with sweat, and where proper remedies could be applied. We administered calomel for digestive upsets, sulfur for skin disorders and chronic catarrhs, salves for festered sores acquired from lying upon a hard surface without relief, and more, until the infirmary became a blur of vials, spoons, and powders. During it all, Jonas kept a bottle of brandy near him, gulping it down whenever his hands shook, or if I talked too much, or if someone screeched in his ear.

Now the breeze ruffled my hair, hot as a fever. More slaves crawled from the hold, until over three hundred fifty milled about. With a signal from the first mate, Billy Dorsett climbed atop a spare boat, tuned a fiddle, then scraped the bow back and forth a few times before plunging into a merry jingle. I'd thought him too dull for such fine music-making.

"Dance!" cried Jack Numbly, the first mate, mimicking what he wanted the slaves to do. "Dance!"

Billy played louder. Surrounded by crew and with a few cracks of the whip, the slaves began to move. Chains clanked. Black skins glistened with sweat. Hot tar oozed from the deck seams, blackening their callused feet. Many slaves grimaced with pain. Others appeared sullen, as if they didn't want to dance. Most watched us warily, as if fearful of what we intended.

I watched until Uncle spied me and approached, looking pleased as a butter-fed fox, rubbing his hands together. "Fine-looking lot, eh?"

"Yes, Uncle," I agreed, knowing that, miserable though they appeared at present, a few days of exercise and air would do them wonders.

The second mate, McGuire, joined us by the bulwarks, whip coiled on his hip, pistol in his holster. Though a chap of handsome proportions, McGuire wasn't much for words. As usual, he said nothing, just leaned against the bulwarks and, like us, watched the slaves dance.

"Doctor's orders, isn't that right, Philip, my lad?" said Uncle. "Keeps them limber by exercising those stiffened joints and muscles. And if that isn't jolly well good enough, the fine fiddle music helps to civilize them, which eventually contributes to their overall happiness in life. What's the condition of the hold, McGuire?"

"It don't smell like Paradise Street in Liverpool, I'll tell you that much, Captain," McGuire replied.

Uncle lighted a cigar, blew out the match, and then said, "It's a comfort to me, McGuire, to know that our influence has a civilizing effect upon their savage natures. That without our influence, these brutes would live and die as mere animals, knowing not their Creator nor their purpose or proper station in life."

"Aye, sir. I'm sure you're right, sir."

"It's a mercy that we've fetched them aboard."

"Aye, sir."

"See to it that the men—black or white—do not mingle with the women. I'll not be responsible for a passel of spotted pups running round. It's indecent."

"Aye, sir."

McGuire left, and Uncle clapped me on the back. "Well, it's been a pleasure, but it's back to business, eh?"

As Uncle went aft, I glimpsed Pea Soup, his ankle shackled to that of another male slave. Within minutes of my near-death escape, Pea Soup had been confined in the hold along with the other slaves. Even after just a few days in such conditions, I was shocked by the change in him. His head was bowed to his chest; he scuffled his feet; filth matted his hair; he seemed thinner.

Seeing him, I broke out in a fresh sweat. Ever since he'd tried to kill me, Pea Soup's face had snarled in my dreams. Every time I closed my eyes, he spat at me. Sank his dreadful, pointed teeth into my neck. Said those horrid words, "Tonight you will die!" over and over, until I gasped awake every few minutes. Why did Pea Soup hate me so? What had I ever done to deserve death at his hands? But now . . . seeing him in such a deplorable state . . . *Perhaps he's learned his lesson,* I thought, feeling the familiar stir of pity. But even so, I couldn't bring myself to release him. Not yet.

Instead, I returned to the infirmary, only to find Jonas lying senseless on a pallet, empty bottle smashed on the floor, rats poking about the shards.

Over the next couple of days, while Jonas and I labored feverishly, the holds were scoured. Hot vinegar fumes wisped through every crack and cranny of the vessel, chasing away rotten odors and filling the infirmary with a suffocating heat.

"Never mind washing the crockery," Jonas ordered. "Leave it for later. Have we any clean spoons? No? And where the devil is my brandy? And stop making so much racket! A man can hardly think."

After piling the crockery and utensils for washing later and scooping the laundry into a pile high as the Tower of Babel, I set about sewing a gash on a slave's hip. According to Jonas, the man had gotten it in a scuffle. He was now unconscious, lying on his stomach. A crisscross of whip marks bloodied his back, which, Jonas said, was the price of scuffling. (I *did* wonder why the price of scuffling had to be so *bloody*.)

Jonas stood on the other side of the pallet, his brandy breath strong, his face like wax in the yellow candlelight. Taking a moment to steady myself, I poked the needle in, glancing at Jonas to see if I was doing it right. The patient twitched. Sweat trickled down the sides of my face, under the bandanna covering my nose and mouth. I caught the other side of the flesh with the needle and pulled the thread tight. After several more stitches, the wound began to close.

"That's it," breathed Jonas. "You've got it. One or two more stitches should do the trick."

I pulled the last stitch and knotted it. Jonas snipped the thread with scissors.

"Right, then." I pulled my bandanna down, yawning and stretching, for it was very late. I hoped Jonas would dismiss me. "Another patient finished."

Straightening up, Jonas steadied himself on his feet, casting a glance about at the dozen or so patients lying on their pallets. He closed his eyes. Opened them. Focused them unsteadily on me. He spoke, his voice oddly different. "It never changes, this—this madness. One after another after another, till all the faces swim together and you can't see nothing but flesh."

For a second I stared at him, not sure I'd understood such a speech coming from bug-eyed, donkey-bray Jonas. "But doesn't—doesn't it get better? Soon? Now that they're exercising and taking the air?"

He gestured toward the man's bloody back. "Does it look like it's getting better?"

"But Uncle says—"

"Your uncle says a lot of things."

A vague doubt niggled through my breast, wormlike, as if it'd always been there, waiting, gnawing. *Jonas is right—it's not getting better. It's getting worse.* But as quickly as the doubt surfaced, I pushed it away. *No, Jonas is just an old drunk. Uncle is right. Uncle is always right. . . . Isn't he?*

Jonas reached for his bottle, knocking it over. The golden liquid dripped from the table onto the floor. Cursing, he kicked the bottle across the room, where it shattered against a bulkhead. He winced and put a hand to his forehead. "I used to be a respected surgeon," he wheezed. "Now what am I? Huh? Tell me what I am."

But I'd no answer for him, finding his comments unsettling, and after I cleaned up the broken glass and washed a few spoons, he finally dismissed me for the night.

Twice a day the Africans received their meals: at eight in the morning and at four in the afternoon. They gathered about their various tubs, ten to a mess, using the wooden spoons fastened about their necks. For the most part, they were fed beans and rice mixed with palm oil and seasoned with pepper and salt. Their favorite, though, was peeled yams, cut up thin and boiled with pounded sailor's biscuit.

All male slaves were kept shackled in pairs as a precaution, while the women and children roamed freely so long as they stayed on the quarterdeck, away from the slave men. Some of the women were put on the forward deck to assist the cook. The first time these slaves set eyes upon the giant cooking cauldrons, they set up such a wail that I was certain we could be heard all the way to China. Some fainted. Some tried to leap overboard before they could be subdued. "They think we're gonna eat them," Billy had told me, his smug expression making me want to punch him, virtuoso or not.

"Oh, really?" I said dryly. "Perhaps with a bit of rum and sailor's biscuit?"

He shrugged. "Ask your uncle. He'll tell you I'm right."

Later, Uncle confirmed what Billy had said. "They're like children, really," he explained with a cockeyed grin. "Believing any silly tale, no matter how preposterous."

Thankfully, the Africans calmed once they saw us cooking rice and beans in the cauldrons.

Each morning after breakfast, all slaves were made to wash their hands and faces, clean their teeth with sticks, and rinse out their mouths with vinegar. For the ill, Jonas and I provided hearty soups, port wine mixed with sugar, and an additional meal at noon.

Then, in the evening, before the crew began stowing the slaves in the hold, several pipes of tobacco were lighted and allowed to be shared among the slave men. One of the slave men was Ikoro.

Billy had told me that all the fight had been branded out of Ikoro, the warrior who'd branded me—that you could poke him with a sharp stick and nothing would happen. But I'd not believed it till now. He was meek and obedient as a lamb: dancing when ordered, eating when ordered, moving from here to there when ordered, taking his turn at the pipe. Indeed, Ikoro appeared ready to accept his parcel in life. Perhaps this was, as Uncle said, evidence of our civilizing effect. In all my times of scurrying back and forth on various errands, Ikoro never once glanced at me, and I truly believed he'd forgotten the incident between us.

I sincerely hoped so, for it was an incident best forgotten.

CHAPTER
11

"You see, Philip," said my uncle one evening as we supped together in his cabin, his mouth full of roasted chicken, "what did I tell you? The slaves are well cared for, and if we can last the next seven weeks or so without disease, we'll have made a tidy sum for our efforts, even if we lose a few here and there."

The evening air, cool and breezy, swirled through the open stern windows. I sipped my wine, intoxicated by the smell of fermented grapes and our greasy dinner. "How much is a tidy sum, I wonder?"

Uncle shrugged. "Buy a slave for twenty dollars in Africa, or in goods worth that amount, then sell him for as much as fifteen hundred dollars—even twenty-five hundred—in New Orleans." He laughed when he saw my expression of amazement. "So don't fret, Philip, my lad, there'll be plenty for all of us."

"Then here's to us and the continued health of all concerned," I said, scarcely able to sit in my seat for joy. *Two thousand four hundred eighty dollars per slave!* If even I received the profits from just *one* slave, it'd be more money than I'd ever dreamed of in my life! We touched our wooden goblets together, sipped, and exchanged looks of satisfaction.

"Jonas says you're doing quite well; that you're learning, though you're still a bit squeamish."

"Really? Jonas thinks I'm doing well?"

"I believe you're rightly suited for the business. It's not everyone who is. You'd a difficult start, I'd say, but you've jolly well come about."

I thanked him, then asked a question I'd been pondering. "You told me once that you started in the business when you were just twelve. Is that why you ran away to sea, so you could be in the business?"

Uncle looked a bit surprised by my question. But he recovered himself quickly, wiped his mouth with his serviette, stood, and moved to the stern windows, gazing out absently. The breeze blew the hair back from his face. "What do you know of my father? What did my sister tell you?"

"You mean, my grandfather? Well, my mother didn't tell me much of anything. Only that he died long before I was born."

"He's dead, yes, thank the heavens." Uncle sighed heavily. "What she didn't tell you was that he was a wretched man. Made my life a misery with his drinking and his iron fist. After he died, I left home. Wanted to get away, see the world. I fell in with a slaver in Liverpool. Didn't know the first thing about the business, any more'n you did." Here Uncle smiled and returned to his chair. "But it was wages, food, a chance to be a man, and that was more'n I'd ever had from my father."

"And now you're rich."

"Indeed."

"Something else I've been meaning to ask you . . ." When he said nothing, instead tearing off a mouthful of bread and butter, I continued. "Jonas told me that the United States has made slaving punishable by death, by hanging. Is—is this true?"

Uncle laughed. "He's a sour sort of fellow, Jonas. Always ready to douse any fire worth burning."

"Is it true, though?"

"Aye. In May of last year it became law." He hastened to add, "Why do you look so glum? You're not American; you're English. Even so, the United States government hasn't yet acted upon the law, to my knowledge. Probably never will. Again, it's a ploy designed to make them look good in the eyes of the British—as if they mean to stop the slave trade when they really don't give a fig. It's all about foreign relations."

I remembered the face of the blond, mustached captain of the American warship, illuminated in the first startling flash of lightning. Despite Uncle's reassurances, I did not believe that this man didn't give a fig. Even in that split second, I saw the devil in his eyes. And he certainly put up a deuce of a fight.

"Your uncle says a lot of things. . . ."

Jonas' words—rising unbidden. And like the press of icy fingers against my spine, the thought *Perhaps Uncle doesn't know everything.* I took a gulp of wine, swallowing down the thought, not wanting to argue. Not with Uncle. He was helping me to better my position in life, and for that I owed him my gratitude.

Uncle was saying, "I hear that your servant—what's his name, Pea Soup, is it? I understand that he's still in confinement. Has been for ten days. Anything you want to tell me?"

I suddenly paid great attention to my roasted chicken, feeling my pulse jump in my throat. Even the mention of Pea Soup's name made my stomach seethe and roil like snakes in a basket. How could I forget his treachery? His hatred of me, his leaving me to die in a most frightful way, his desire to jeopardize the entire crew of the *Formidable* . . . and for what? Why? I'd decided that when I reached New Orleans, I'd sell him.

Though I'd not looked up, I could feel Uncle watching me, waiting for an explanation. "I—he—you see, he . . ." I pushed my chicken about on my plate, from port to starboard, fore and aft. Gravy slopped over the side in a trail of grease. "You see, he—there was—I've never been—he—"

"Philip," he said, not unkindly, "a slave knows when you're afraid of him."

I looked up, blinking with surprise. "Wh-what?" *Am I that transparent?*

Uncle filled his goblet, then leaned back in his chair. The chair squawked in protest. In the waning light, Uncle's eyes looked not blue, but black, and deep as the ocean. "You see, there's something you mustn't forget. No matter your size or age, no matter your social position, no matter whether this is your first slave or your five hundredth, *you* are the master. Do you understand?"

"Yes, Uncle."

"Masters do not shrink from their duties. Masters do not cower in fear from their slaves. You must show him who is master and who is slave, otherwise—and you must trust me in this—he is worthless to you, and will defy you at every opportunity."

My head suddenly swam with wine. Queasiness rocked through me. *What the devil's the matter with me?* I clenched my jaw and swallowed hard, thinking that I must tell the cook to use less grease.

"Remember, slavery's a necessary evil, and can't be helped."

"Yes, Uncle."

"If you can't handle one slave, how do you expect to handle a ship loaded to the gunwales with Africans, and you the captain?"

He made to pour me more wine, but I covered my goblet with my hand, realizing I was shaking. "No more, Uncle. Please, no more."

For the briefest moment, his eyes met mine. Then he burst into laughter and whacked me between the shoulder blades. "I'll make a man of you yet, Nephew. Ha!"

I wished I were six feet tall. I wished I were burly-chested, well muscled, with a deep voice and big hands.

Instead, I pushed my way through Africans taller than me, a slight lad who looked as if he should still be in grammar school, afterward having tea and biscuits. Dark eyes stared down at me, as if remembering that this was the lad who'd branded them.

"Excuse me, excuse me," I said, shoving people aside, thankful for McGuire, who trailed behind me as I'd asked, pistol and whip ready.

I heard him before I saw him. His voice, easily recognizable, for I'd heard it a thousand times in my nightmares. "Master," he implored. "Master Philip, please. Please."

Africans moved aside now, parting the way as if I were Moses parting the Red Sea. To my surprise, Pea Soup was on his knees, his hands clasped before him, looking wretched as a beggar. "Master, please."

Sores covered his body. His loincloth, once clean, was now

soiled and shabby. The stench from him was the same as from any of those about me—like animals that have been caged too long. Beneath the iron shackle, his ankle chafed and bled.

"Master Philip, please. I will be good." Tears streamed down his face while I gawked at him. *Is this the same Pea Soup who hates me? Who hissed through pointed teeth and left me to be eaten by sharks?*

Where there had been fear just a second before—a wobbling of knees, a dryness of mouth, a clamminess of hands—now there was only pity. Pea Soup's time of confinement had done wonders. "I'm your master," I said to him, delighted with the firmness in my voice and wishing Uncle were here to see me. "Do you understand?"

Pea Soup nodded vigorously.

"From now on, you'll do what I tell you. Do you understand?"

Still on his knees, he shuffled forward, then pressed his forehead to my feet. "I will be good. I promise."

"Release him," I said to McGuire, thinking, *Now that's how to handle it. Just like that, the situation has been righted.*

McGuire unshackled Pea Soup, whereupon the boy stood shakily on his feet, a good half a head taller than me. "I am grateful," he said.

"My cabin's a shambles, and my bedding needs airing. Please see to it, and then take your dinner and rest."

"Thank you, Master Philip, thank you." Pea Soup nodded and, with a quick glance at someone in the crowd, turned and left.

I stood, blinking daftly, as the Africans watched me.

"Let's go," said McGuire. He was tugging at the back of my shirt.

I looked to where Pea Soup had glanced. There stood Ikoro, head bowed, meek as a daisy. An unsettled feeling came over me like a spell, for when Pea Soup had glanced at Ikoro, I saw not the wretched expression and the tears he'd given me, but instead a look of triumph.

"Yes," I replied, "let's go," suddenly anxious to be out of there, feeling as if I'd just made a horrible, horrible mistake.

CHAPTER 12

*F*evers, boils, bad eyes, sores, and rashes . . . .

I wiped my face with my handkerchief and then straightened my stiffened back, feeling it pop. I filled my lungs, praying for fresh air, praying for my head to clear. But the infirmary air still stank of candle smoke and the most vile of body odors and excrements. Much as I'd tried to keep up with the washing and cleaning of the infirmary, it was getting the better of me—rats, dirty medical instruments, and every towel and rag filthy.

I'd told Jonas that we needed to do something about the deteriorating conditions in the infirmary, but Jonas, lately falling into long periods of drunkenness, was of little help.

And if I'd thought that Pea Soup would be of assistance, remarkably transformed from his imprisonment, I could think again. If possible, he worked slower than before, disappearing entirely for hours at a time. Yesterday, overwhelmed, I'd commanded Pea Soup to help me in the infirmary. Acting deaf and dumb, he did nothing but get in my way and trip over things, in the process spilling the surgical tray and breaking two crockery bowls. I next gave him laundry duty, but the articles came back damp, gray, wrinkled, and smelling like seaweed and rotten eggs. Today I'd not the strength nor time to deal with him, and so let him be—wherever he'd disappeared to. I didn't want to admit it, but I feared Pea Soup's promises and tears had only been a charade, masterfully performed to obtain his release.

A headache was beginning at my temples. In the five hours I'd worked, I'd seen how many people? Twenty? Thirty? A stream of ailments and complaints.

Jonas himself was groaning in our cabin, too ill to venture out today, he said.

Only the most desperately ill slaves stayed in the infirmary. On this day, just our twelfth day out from the river Bonny, every pallet was full, sometimes with two to a pallet, stacked up the sides of the hull like shelves. Already four slaves had been tossed overboard that day to the ever-present sharks who shadowed our wake. Each death became personal to me, as if I'd somehow failed, failed in my effort to bring the slaves to a better life.

"Hold still now, lass," I told the slave girl who lay before me on a raised pallet. She was eight years old or so, her two front teeth large as a rabbit's. "This won't hurt a bit, I promise."

One of her eyes was gummed shut. As she clutched my wrists, no doubt fearful of what I was about to do, I drizzled warm water over the lids, then gently pried them open and began to cleanse the eye. It was reddened, swollen, and the other eye showed indications of following in the same unhealthy direction.

Second case of it today. Must remember to tell Jonas.

I bathed both eyes in mucilage of sassafras, hushing the girl when she started to wail and grip my wrists, kicking her legs up and down, almost preventing me from performing my duties. My temples began to throb. The familiar nausea rose inside me, as if I stood on the top of the highest mast of a ship as it rolled heavily, creaking and groaning through the swells.

When I finished, the girl closed her eyes. Her body relaxed and she released her grip. Her breathing evened, and I knew she'd fallen asleep. After wiping my hands, I gently tucked a doll made of oakum under her arm. It was something I gave to each of the girls, a gift that took me but a few minutes to make and that seemed to calm them. Often I was rewarded with a smile through the tears. For the lads, I made a braided length of oakum with a cowrie shell at each end.

She's too thin, I thought.

Many of the slaves were too thin—bone-thin, some of them. I'd mentioned this to Uncle: that perhaps we needed to increase their portions, that sometimes the stronger at the mess ate more food, while the weaker received less than their share. But he said he'd been in the business for twenty years. That he knew what he was doing. That yams were particularly bulky storage items and we could only store so many. Feed them too much now, he said, and we wouldn't have enough to reach the Americas. Couldn't have them dying of starvation at the very time they went to market. Buyers wanted healthy negroes.

I sighed and turned to the next fellow. He'd been sitting propped against the bulkhead, but now he lay slumped over sideways, eyes open, not moving.

He's dead, I thought.

And indeed he was.

My nausea surfaced just as someone whipped open the door to the infirmary. Normally, fresh air would brush through a cabin upon the opening of a door, but there was only more humidity and heat.

It was Billy the Vermin, as I'd come to call him.

"Holy Mother of God, it stinks down here," he said.

I vomited into one of the many buckets, my head throbbing like a drum. Afterward I wiped my mouth with my handkerchief. "What do you want, Billy?"

He was strolling past the pallets, eyeballing everyone. When he saw the corpse, he bent over and poked it. "Why, I'll be jiggered. He's dead."

"Unless you've a complaint, you need to clear off."

Billy grinned.

"Really, Billy, I must turn in." I yawned, stretched, and rubbed my eyes.

"You can't," he said, scratching his scalp with a disgusting vigor. "The king commands your presence on deck."

I frowned. "You mean, the captain."

"No, the king." And as I was shirtless, he tugged me toward the door by the waist of my trousers.

"Billy, I've not time for your silly games. Carry this man outside. He's dead."

Still tugging at me, he stared at the corpse. "But that's Mackerel's job. Mack's and Roach's."

"Then go fetch Mack and Roach."

"But first you gotta come with me. The king commands. He says if you don't obey, he'll chop off your head." He grinned again. "He said if you don't come, you'll be very, very, *very* sorry. Please come, please. . . ." And all the while, he tugged at my trousers.

I glanced about the infirmary. Really, it *would* be nice to see the sky. And it was probably the only way I could get rid of Billy the Vermin. "All right, then. Stop tugging, pretend to be normal, and I'll come with you."

It was as if I'd told him we were going to play in the dirt and smash worms. He bounced up the companionway, telling me to hurry, hurry!

But the moment I stepped out of the fore hatchway onto the deck, blinking like a mole in the brightness, wondering why everyone—sailors, cook, carpenter, and all—was gathered about, grinning at me, I was grabbed on each side by the arms.

"What the devil—" I cried as two sailors, Mack and Roach, pinned me securely between them and propelled me forward.

"Now none of your fancy English sass," Mackerel was saying. His name was Mack, but everyone called him Mackerel, not because he looked like a fish but because he smelled like one. Besides being stinky, he was a frightful-looking fellow. He was tanned nearly dark as an African, his chest and arms covered with tattoos of anchors, ships, and buxom women. "You're coming with us. Got business to attend with you."

"Aye, *important* business," Roach emphasized, his weasel face looking dour as a witch's, his breath pleasant as a summer sewer.

I noticed that none of the male slaves were on deck, though there were blue skies overhead and it was as stifling as a pigpen in July. Tar oozed from the deck seams under the boiling sun, and I winced and hopped as I kicked and struggled. "Uncle! Help!"

Uncle leaned against the bulwarks next to the two mates, cigar in his mouth, grinning his half grin.

"No sense crying to your uncle, you little baby," said Mackerel. "He can't save you, because *we're* in charge today. Now you either behave or we'll be forced to spank you."

"Blood and thunder," added Roach, "you sure do stink."

Mackerel grinned. "We'll soon take care of that, won't we, men?"

The sailors jeered at me, banging spoons and pans, calling me names, laughing and aiming an occasional kick at my bum as they followed us forward. Against my efforts to prevent their sport, whatever it'd prove to be, we now stood at the bow. My chest heaved and my face felt hot as a kettle bottom. The sails rippled with the light breeze, rigging swayed and tightened, swayed and tightened, as the *Formidable* rolled first one way on an ocean swell, then the other.

At a signal from Mackerel, music of a sort began. Billy played his fiddle while the rest of the crew banged pots or drummed on buckets. Then, from under the bowsprit, from the very place where I'd clung for my life over the water, came a voice.

"*Shiip ahoy! Shiip ahoy!* Back your main topsails and let me aboard. I'm King Neptune, I am, come to greet the Sons o' Neptune. *Shiip ahoy!*"

By the deuce, it was Jonas' voice! What was he doing out of bed?

To my shock, Jonas climbed up and over the knightheads, dripping wet and breathing hard. Protuberant, yellowed eyes stared at the crowd from behind a canvas mask that only reached to the end of his nose. Whiskers of oakum covered his lower face. Layers of fishnet hair flowed from beneath his red crown. He wore a blanket for a robe, all of it draped with rope yarn painted green to look like seaweed, likely. He carried a three-pronged spear, which I knew was meant to look like a trident. "You scurvy dogs!" he barked. "Why in hell didn't you send me down a boat? There must be one among you who has not yet joined the Order of the Sons o' Neptune, or else such a blunder would never have happened. Now which of you is it? Don't keep me waiting all day!" He thumped his trident on the deck.

My captors forced me to my knees. "Here's the scurvy knave," said Mackerel.

"Philip's the only one who hasn't crossed the line, O Father Neptune," said Roach.

"Never crossed the line, have you?" asked Father Neptune.

While the *Formidable* had voyaged toward Africa, we'd managed to keep her above the equatorial line, but now we were forced to head into the southern hemisphere to catch the trade winds that would take us home. "No," I replied. "Never. I mean, this is the first time."

Father Neptune pointed his trident out to sea. "Well, look! There it is! The equator! A line round the waist o' the earth."

When I looked where he pointed, everyone burst out laughing. My face flushed as I realized he'd been joking. Of course there was no actual *line;* the equatorial line was only drawn on charts.

Father Neptune glared at me. "You stupid, pathetic waste of fish food! Who says you're worthy to join the Order? You look more like a scurvy rat than a Son o' Neptune!" Though Jonas' voice was nasty as bilgewater, I could see the laughter in his eyes. I saw I was in for it but knew no one would hurt me—at least I didn't *think* they'd hurt me. Not with Uncle watching. Not with Jonas in control of things. I decided to let them have their sport.

Cookie, the cook, stepped forward. "I think he's worthy! He stomachs my food, anyways, and that's got to count for something."

"No he don't," said Billy. "He was puking just a minute ago."

"Come, come!" cried Father Neptune. "Surely someone must believe this pathetic runt is worthy."

There followed a moment in which the men variously added their twopence on the subject:

"Well, I just don't know 'bout this feller. He's always got his nose in some book. No self-respecting Son o' Neptune would be caught with his nose in a book. All books're handy for is wiping those hard-to-reach places."

"Yeah, 'cept Shakespeare can be a bit scratchy."

"The little rat probably can't read a word of it, anyways."

"Yeah, it's all Greek to him."

"Speaking of Greek, he's always babbling in different languages. You ever notice that? Pretending to be smart."

"It's just babbling, far as I can tell. Who's to know the difference? You know Greek, Calvin?"

"No, I don't know Greek. You know Greek, Harold?"

"Can't say I do."

"Well, he *is* a doctor, of sorts. Worked on my hangnail for seven hours straight."

"No, he ain't no doctor. I told him I'd a headache, and he told me it was all in my head."

They roared with laughter, and I stifled a grin.

"Clap a stopper on it, you Sons o' Neptune!" screeched Father Neptune, waving his trident. "I'll conduct the inspection myself, since all of you are too limited in brain matter to do it yourselves." He strolled about me, poking me with his trident. "What have you to say for yourself? Are you clean and ready, a fellow worthy enough to join the ranks?"

I heaved a deep sigh, pretending to be frightfully sore, though I realized I was enjoying myself. "Aye, I'm worthy."

At this, Father Neptune's eyes bulged as he screeched, "Liar! Liar! Your scales have to come off! I've got to give you a hearty shave before you can join this illustrious order of sea scoundrels."

They pinned me again and blindfolded me. No sooner did I smell hot tar than my face and hair were slathered with it. I clenched my teeth, determined to endure the rite, determined not to cry, though the tar was hot enough to blister.

"Bring my shaving kit!" Father Neptune cried.

"It's here!"

"Is the razor sharp, keen-edged as a razor clam?"

"Aye. It'll cut the throat of anyone not worthy."

And so I was shaved, the first shave in my life, though I'd not a whisker to my name. They shaved my head as well, fine curly locks and all. Then flour was thrown in my face and piled atop my scalp to more roars of laughter. Afterward I was christened in a sail filled with salt water. The sun was low and it was time for the afternoon mess as I clambered out of the water-filled sail and removed my blindfold, spluttering and grinning like a fool while the men clapped me on the back and welcomed me as a Son of Neptune.

Maybe, I thought, *they're not such rotten fellows after all.*

Two days later we finally caught the southeast trades. The *Formidable* now sailed like a gull before the wind on a heading of west-northwest.

It was near midnight, and I couldn't sleep. I sat at the desk in the cabin Jonas and I shared, practicing my Spanish, sounding out words and writing sentences while Jonas snored like a gristmill. The candle in the lantern burned low, swaying on its peg above me as the ship dashed along. Tonight—amazingly, thankfully—the slaves were silent, and I could hear water gurgling against the hull.

Dipping my pen in the inkwell, I wrote, *"Buenas tardes, Señor Towne. Confío en que su familia esté bien." "Buenas tardes, Capitán Towne. ¿Estuvo bien el viaje? Están los esclavos con buena salud y contentos?"*

After filling the page, I sat back and sighed, rubbing my temples, wishing I could sleep. Lately, my nights had been troubled. It seemed I had barely closed my eyes when I'd awaken with a start, heart pounding. There were vague dreams of New Orleans, of chained slaves shuffling along. Dreams of Ikoro coming at me with an iron that glowed like the fires of hell. Of Mrs. Gallagher, making me, her little English boy, promise to come home. Of my uncle visiting me at the workhouse, saying, *Take care, Nephew, for I shall return someday.*

I'd awakened from this last dream only this morning, sitting up in my berth, catching my breath: *Why, Uncle, why didn't you return to the workhouse for me? Why'd you leave me alone with no word from you? Why?* Ashamed, feeling as if I'd just kicked my favorite dog, I'd doused my questions in salt water from the ewer, vowing to never think on them again. I was finished with the workhouse. Forever. And I was here now, on Uncle's ship, with a respectable position as surgeon's mate.

Jonas snorted, coughed, rolled over, and quickly resumed his snoring. Weary of Spanish, I opened the Book of Common Prayer. Prayers were quite handy for putting one to sleep.

> *O Eternal Lord God, who alone spreadest out the heavens, and rulest the raging of the sea; who hast compassed the waters with bounds, until day and night come to an end; Be pleased to receive into thy Almighty and most gracious protection, the persons of us thy servants, and the ship in which we serve. . . .*

A few minutes later, just as my eyelids began to droop, I snapped to awareness. Goose bumps crawled over my skin.

Someone's watching me.

CHAPTER 13

I gasped.

Whirled about.

At that moment the candle burned out, plunging me into darkness.

My heart lurched.

Oh God, oh God, it's dark!

As surely as if a shark had seized me by the leg and shook me in his jaws, terror gripped me. Immediately my chest tightened. I couldn't breathe, though I heard the sound of my panting.

"Who's there?" I hissed as the hair rose on the back of my neck.

Nothing.

A light. God help me, I need a light.

I fumbled in the desk drawer, the thud of my heart in my ears, half expecting someone to grab me from behind.

I should've been watching the candle. How could I have been so foolish?

It took only a moment for me to grasp that there were no candles in the drawer. Only hours ago I'd ordered Pea Soup to fetch some, knowing he could understand me perfectly well, wanting to assert my position as master once again. Off he'd shuffled, and I'd assumed it'd be done.

But there were none. Just papers, pens, a book, a few odd shapes.

Blast Pea Soup! He did this on purpose!

I sat for a while, motionless, wanting to burst into tears, listening to my shaky breathing, willing myself to stand and walk through the darkness to find a light—*please, God, somewhere, a light*—until it occurred to me that Jonas was no longer snoring and hadn't been for some time.

"Jonas?" I whispered. "Jonas, you awake?"

Even with all the sloshing and creaking of the *Formidable*, my voice sounded dreadfully loud. I reached out to shake him but pulled my hand back, suddenly terrified of what I might find.

I rose from my chair so quickly it clattered to the floor. I fetched the unlighted lantern from its peg and groped for the door latch.

Please, God; please, God!

Finally I stumbled into the darkened passageway, up the hatchway, and out onto the upper deck. The breeze ruffled my sweat-soaked hair. Stars sprinkled the night sky like sugar dust.

McGuire was standing next to the helmsman.

"Higgins!" he cried. That was what he fancied calling me. "Is there a problem?"

"My—my lantern's out," I said, trying not to sound panicked and out of breath. "Just need a candle or two to tide me over till morning."

McGuire grunted, disappeared for a while, then reappeared with two candles. "You owe me."

"Aye. And may I trouble you for a match?"

Lantern finally lighted and McGuire thanked, I went below.

It was as I'd suspected.

Jonas Drinkwater, surgeon for seven years aboard the *Formidable,* was dead.

Clouds dashed across a sky of powder blue.

The canvas-wrapped body lay on a grating that was balanced on the bulwarks, held in place by several men.

We clustered about Uncle. Dressed in his finest black suit, with a tall beaver hat, he cleared his throat. "If anyone has anything to say, now's the time."

At first no one spoke. A hen cackled from the chicken coop. Hemp groaned, stretched tight. Feet scuffed as men shifted their positions.

Then: "Drinkwater was a fair surgeon, he was."

"Leastways knew how to dull your senses before he—well, you know. . . ."

"He didn't leave behind no family."

"That's good. I guess."

"I suppose we were his family."

Someone slapped an insect on his cheek. Someone else coughed.

"He made a good Father Neptune. Best I ever saw."

"Drinkwater was always free with his tobacco."

"He liked his liquor, though. Wasn't so free with that."

"Always knew he'd die at sea."

"The sea keeps her own."

"Aye."

"The devil won't be hard on the poor fellow."

After the comments trickled away, like sand through fingers, Uncle cleared his throat again, opened his Book of Common Prayer, and began reading. The pages ruffled in the breeze. Uncle's gold teeth glinted in the sunlight. On and on he read, stumbling over a few passages here and there: ". . . We therefore commit his body to the deep, to be turned into corruption, looking for the resurrection of the body (when the sea shall give up her dead,) and the life of the world to come, through our Lord Jesus Christ; who at his coming shall change our vile body, that it may be like his glorious body, according to the mighty working whereby he is able to subdue all things unto himself. Amen."

The crew echoed, "Amen," at which time the grating was tilted. The body slid off the grating with a whoosh of fabric and a deep-throated splash into the sea. As one, the crew replaced their caps and began to disperse.

I peered over the side. Swirls of bubbles rose from the sinking form. Large, dark shapes darted toward the disturbance. Weighted with cannonballs, the body quickly sank out of sight.

"I hardly think I'm competent to fill a surgeon's berth," I told Uncle later, in his cabin.

"Stuff and nonsense!" said my uncle. "You're not called upon to be a court physician. Brimstone and molasses, calomel and jalap, and salt water in buckets were Drinkwater's whole materia medica, and I think you can take a hand at them as well as he." He thumped me on the back, offered me a goblet of palm wine, and that was that.

So it was that I, Philip Arthur Higgins—small for his age and without a whisker to his name—became surgeon aboard the *Formidable.*

Responsible for the well-being of more than four hundred souls.

I ordered the infirmary scoured from top to bottom. Hot vinegar vapors to cleanse the air. Towels and bandages boiled in salt water. Every black beetle and rat smoked out and killed.

Next the hold. Since Jonas' burial, owing to some nasty weather, the slaves had been confined below. I knelt beside the hatch and stuck my head down, holding my breath. One glance was all it took. Excrement, vomit, and the devil knows what else was everywhere—in the aisles, smeared on bodies—all of it crawling with vermin and fat rats. I was horrified to see the latrine buckets overflowing with waste. Though it was raining, I ordered all slaves brought on deck and every inch of the hold scoured as clean as a baby's bottom.

"After this," I told the bo'sun, trying not to quail before him like a workhouse orphan, "the latrine buckets must be kept emptied."

"Begging your pardon, *Surgeon* Higgins," said the bo'sun, thrusting his face into mine. Teags was a greasy sort of fellow with rotten teeth and an equally rotten temper. "But they fill 'em up faster than we can empty 'em."

I backed away, my eyelid suddenly twitching, finding the deck boards quite interesting. "Uh—very well. Do your best, then."

He snorted and walked away, murmuring, " 'Uh—very well. Do your best, then,' " in a mocking tone.

The bo'sun wasn't the only one unhappy with my new authority. Plenty of grumbling and angry looks were cast my way, some saying I was no Son o' Neptune; that Jonas Drinkwater, surgeon for seven years aboard the *Formidable*, had understood the way things were, and they didn't need any boy to tell them how to do their jobs. Uncle just stood back with his half grin and let me fulfill my duties. I fell into bed each night, too tired even to finish mumbling my prayers before I slipped into a troubled sleep, my door bolted and a ready supply of candles on hand.

Besides the miserable conditions and the various illnesses and ailments, there were the pregnant women. One day I mentioned to Uncle that one of the women was due to deliver and that I'd never delivered a baby, nor cared for a baby's needs. He waved his hand as if dismissing the matter as trivial and said simply, "Do your best, Mr. Surgeon. And when she's delivered, bring the baby to me."

"To you?"

"Aye."

"So you can care for it?"

Here Uncle flashed his gold teeth, as if I'd told a joke. "Aye, Nephew, I'll take care of it."

I returned to the infirmary, where I spent the rest of the day, relieved, at least, that the infant would be cared for. After treating my twelfth case of sore, reddened, swollen, gummy eyes in just two hours' time, I buried my face in my hands and sobbed like a wretch. I longed for the kindly arms of Mrs. Gallagher; wished my own mother had never died; wished I'd a friend, a *real* friend—all the while filled with guilt because I wished I were anywhere but where I was at that moment, and that I'd never met Uncle.

That night, I awoke, my pillow drenched. *I've been crying,* I realized, only then remembering my dream—the workhouse, a beating upon the backs of my knees, cold, pasty porridge, my arm wrenched from my socket, Uncle saying, *Take care, Nephew, for I shall return someday.*

I arose, took the lantern from its peg, unbolted my door, and entered my uncle's cabin.

He sat up in bed, blinking with sleep, his covers rustling. "Something the matter?"

"Did—did you ever send money to Master Crump, as you promised?"

He knitted his brow. "What the devil are you carrying on about? Do you know what hour it is?"

I almost withdrew, went back to my room, making some excuse, but instead asked again, in a quavery voice, "Did you ever send money to Master Crump, as you promised?"

Uncle groaned and lay back down, waving his hand in a sign of dismissal, saying, "It's difficult to stay on top of family affairs when one is traveling about the world, battling storms and the like. You know how it is, Philip."

"Then you sent no money for my welfare?"

"I suppose I sent something a time or two; it's difficult to remember. Now that I think about it, I'm sure I did."

For a while I said nothing, not knowing what to believe, what to say, how to feel. The *Formidable* groaned and heeled, and the floor beneath me tilted. A pen slid across the table and onto the floor.

"What, are you going to just stand there like a twit? Let a busy fellow get his rest."

"But—but why didn't you come for me?" My voice suddenly sounded like a child's. "You said you'd return. You *promised*."

Uncle sat up. His blanket fell to the floor. "Bloody hell! Stop dribbling rubbish! Get out of my cabin and leave me be! You're a man now, engaged in a respectable occupation, not some starving waif." The dismay must've shown in my face, for he sighed and rubbed his forehead. He looked at me again and softened his voice. "Come, Nephew. Don't think harshly of your old uncle. I've always wanted the best for you. Haven't I? Haven't I done right by you?"

He laughed then and rose from bed. Taking the light from me, he steered me back into my cabin, hanging my lantern and helping me back into bed as if I were a wee child. Tucking the edges of my blanket under my mattress, Uncle leaned over me. I could see his teeth glinting in the lantern light, the shadow of his whiskers; I could smell his stale tobacco breath. "Now get yourself some sleep. The world always looks different in the morning." And he playfully punched my shoulder and left. I waited a moment before getting up and bolting the door.

When I finally drifted back to sleep, I dreamed Master Crump was beating me across my shoulders while I cowered in a corner, arms over my head, begging him to stop, stop, oh please, stop! Only this time, instead of camphor, Master Crump smelled of cigars.

It was the following afternoon. I'd decided to take a quick break from my duties in the infirmary, so I'd fetched a book and now emerged onto a steaming deck, where the sun had finally broken through the clouds, and where the slaves danced to the merry strains of Billy's fiddle.

"Well, I'll be," remarked Mackerel. He nudged Roach and pointed at me. "It's our respectable new *surgeon.*"

I ignored Mackerel's and Roach's snickering, found an open space against the bulwarks, and opened my book.

"Well, would you look at that," whispered Roach loudly, "he's reading Shakespeare. *'Oh, Romeo, Romeo, ahoy there, Romeo.'*" They burst into peals of piggish laughter, slapping each other on the back. I continued to ignore them.

"Hey, Roach."

"Yes, Mackerel?"

"Better go empty those latrine buckets. Surgeon's orders."

"*Again?*"

"Yeah. Someone pissed in them."

Again the backslapping, snorting hilarity.

Twenty minutes later eight bells sounded, and it was time for the change of watch and the afternoon mess. To my relief, Mackerel and Roach left for their duties.

I was beginning Act II of *King Lear* when someone shook my shoulder. It was Teags, the bo'sun, his cat-o'-nine-tails in hand. "Got a problem."

"What is it?"

"Got a darkie that's refusing to eat."

I frowned. "Use the speculum orb, as you always do. It's simple enough, isn't it?"

Teags scratched his scalp, looking perplexed. "But, Mr. Higgins, you're the surgeon. We have to watch you do it so we know how to do it right. A demonstration, so to speak. Otherwise we might bend a hair on their poor woolly heads."

Again I heard snickers from all about. Mackerel and Roach stood nearby, grinning like pirates. Then there were Calvin, Harold, and Billy the Vermin. All looking at me. I searched for Uncle, but couldn't see him. Surely this was a joke, a mean prank they meant to play on me. Pea Soup leaned against the longboat, absently picking his fingernails, watching me with interest. Just the sight of him, and knowing his mouth contained horrible, wicked teeth that had been filed to points, made my heart race and my insides tremble. This persistent fear on my part annoyed me. After all, I was the *master*. Master and surgeon.

I closed my book and looked right at Teags' meaty, greasy face. "Right, then. Show me the fellow and I'll see to it."

From the corner of my eye, I saw Pea Soup smile.

I followed Teags into the mass of slaves, everyone crowded so closely together about their various food tubs that I had to plan each step. Teags hollered, "Out of the way!" snapping the cat-o'-nine-tails at those who weren't fast enough for his liking.

"Here he is," said Teags, pointing. "That one there. The skinny one with red eyes."

I stopped short. Chained next to the skinny one with red eyes was Ikoro. He was bent over the food tub, shoveling rice and beans into his mouth with zest. His arms looked as if they could break me in half, and I didn't relish getting within reach of him, no matter how well behaved he'd been lately.

Teags shoved me toward the two. "Show us how it's done, Mr. Higgins."

Something about the situation wasn't quite right. Something was out of place, but I couldn't figure out what. Just the white men milling about on the periphery, I supposed, joking among themselves, laughing, and watching me and waiting for their sport, whips coiled on their hips.

"I need the speculum orb," I said.

Teags handed it to me. "Always keep it handy."

It was a long metal instrument with a thumbscrew at one end. The screw operated two pointed arms that opened and closed like pincers. The idea was to insert the closed ends between the teeth of an unwilling jaw and then screw open the speculum, whereupon the jaw would have no choice but to open.

"Now everybody pay attention!" hollered Teags. "The surgeon's at work."

I stood next to the skinny slave. He stared at me with reddened, pus-filled, fear-filled eyes.

I'll take him to the infirmary, I thought. *After he eats.*

Swallowing hard, I opened his lips and tried to insert the metal end of the speculum through his teeth. Except there was no place to put it—no gaps, no missing teeth, no misaligned jaw.

I began to press the instrument against his teeth, trying to pry it between, wondering if this was how it was done or if there was a trick to it. He struggled.

"Eat!" I ordered him in the African language I'd been learning, praying he could understand. The speculum slid across his teeth, back and forth, as I poked here and there. And all the while, he struggled, shaking his head, his eyes clenched shut, moaning as if I were killing him.

This will never work, I thought. *He's stronger than me.* "Eat!" I cried, hearing the desperation in my voice.

The white men were near collapse in their fits of laughter when I finally figured out what was wrong.

Ikoro and the skinny man were not chained together.

The chains had somehow been released.

I knew it was a ploy—not of the whites, but a desperate ploy of the slaves themselves—when Ikoro snatched the speculum orb out of my hand and in one motion stabbed Teags in the stomach.

CHAPTER 14

*T*eags' eyes widened.

He bent his head and stared at the object protruding from his stomach. At the black hand that grasped it.

We all stared.

Where before there had been the hubbub of mealtime, now every African, every white man, stared at Teags.

Again Ikoro stabbed him. And again.

All this took only a second, or half a second, but it lasted forever.

Teags groaned and sank to his knees, the cat-o'-nine-tails slipping from his hand.

Ikoro removed the speculum orb and cried to the crowd in his language, "Fight, Igbo warriors! Fight! It is war!" Then he bounded toward Mackerel, the nearest white other than myself, holding the speculum orb over his head like a dagger. A scream ripped from Ikoro, an animal, warlike scream that set my scalp crawling.

The skinny slave with red eyes grabbed the cat-o'-nine-tails and ran after Ikoro. Other slaves followed. Roach was hollering, his eyes bugging out with terror, wrestling to unloose the whip at his hip. From the stern, I heard women shrieking and children crying.

Mackerel had disappeared under a mass of black bodies, his shocked face the last thing I saw before a hand wrapped about my neck from behind and yanked me down hard.

I slammed onto my back, the world suddenly topsy-turvy, black legs running all about, some still shackled, others loose.

They're going to kill us all! I'll be stabbed to death!

And then Pea Soup was leaning over me, eyes narrowed with hatred, his lips pulled back in a snarl exposing his hideous, pointed teeth.

"No!" I kicked, flailing wildly, trying to reach his eyes, to gouge them out. "No!" My teeth found the flesh of his hand and I bit hard. Tasted blood.

His forehead smashed my face. I heard bones crunch. My body seemed to melt, no longer obeying my commands to fight, to defend myself, to keep Pea Soup's cannibal teeth away from my neck. Blood from my broken nose streamed down my throat. I heard myself groan. Heard gunshots. The crack of whips.

I'm sorry, Mrs. Gallagher.

Then Pea Soup lay across my chest, pinning me down, and his voice was in my ear. "Do nothing. You will live."

And so I lay under Pea Soup's weight, his words spinning in my head like a distant light through a tunnel of darkness, dimly understanding that he was saving my life, protecting me from being massacred.

Within minutes, it was over. Pea Soup released me. I lay for a moment, staring at the clouds scudding across the sky, surprised that the sky would still be blue, that the breeze still stirred, that the heavens seemed unchanged.

"Make certain they're all shackled," Uncle was bellowing. I heard the crack of a whip. "If anyone so much as blinks an eye, kill him."

I sat up slowly, my head spinning, watching blankly as blood streamed from my nose like water pouring from a glass. Pea Soup was sitting beside me. He glanced at me. Turned away. Said nothing. His face registered nothing.

And while the flow of blood from my nose slowed to a trickle, then finally a drip-drip, having spattered my chest and soaked my trousers and the deck, the crew moved among the slaves, securing shackles, their curses and whips flying through the air. When a slave was found no longer breathing—shot through the head or the heart, perhaps—at a signal, two crew members picked up the body, one by the shoulders, one by the ankles, and heaved him overboard as if he were a sack of rubbish.

I watched it all, and knew. I knew as surely as I knew the sky was blue and the ocean deep. *Ikoro should've killed me. I was the closest white man to him, an arm's length away—but he didn't. Not only did Ikoro spare me, but Pea Soup protected me, saving my life from the mob. Why? Why?*

A violent shaking overwhelmed me.

Nineteen dead. Fifteen blacks and four whites, including First Mate Numbly.

Ikoro was still alive, though several wounds glistened on his flesh.

Uncle wrapped a bullwhip about Ikoro's neck and dragged him to the bulwarks. Ikoro tried to gain his footing, but failed.

"Philip!" Uncle screamed, the veins bulging in his neck. He scanned the deck. "Where in the bloody hell are you?"

Shaking, still dizzy, I stood. "Here, Uncle."

"Get the hell over here!"

I stumbled through the crowd. No one moved for me. My nose started bleeding again. Throbbing and bleeding. It was some time before I finally stood beside Uncle.

Mackerel lay nearby, his body in a twisted and unnatural position, the speculum orb buried in his back, above his kidney.

Ikoro knelt before Uncle, gasping for breath, the bullwhip tight about his neck, his eyes nearly popping from their sockets.

"Interpret what I say," said Uncle to me, and without waiting for a reply addressed the crowd. "You people have foolishly tried to rebel. You've taken up arms against us, the very ones who feed you, who see to your comfort and keep you safe from harm. But as you can see, you can't defeat us. Our weapons are strong, and you are weak. And as punishment for this rebellion, six of you will die today." Uncle turned to me, and I saw rage snapping in his eyes.

And for the first time, I was afraid of my uncle.

I stepped back, hesitated, then licked my lips free of blood and said, my voice a whisper, "You—you'd *kill* them?"

In a second Uncle whipped a pistol from his gun belt. He cocked the pistol and aimed it at Ikoro's head. "Interpret, Nephew," he ordered me through clenched teeth.

Heart skittering, knees shaking, I floundered through my interpretation, having no idea whether I was making any sense. When I finished, every African eye was trained on me. I looked away. Sails fluttered, snapping, the helm poorly manned.

"McGuire!" barked Uncle. "You're my first mate now. Select five more male slaves. Those with the most wounds, preferably. Set six nooses on the main yard, and hang them along with this savage." And so saying, Uncle pulled on the whip until Ikoro's eyes bulged again and his tongue protruded, purple.

Those same eyes had burned into me as the brand had seared my flesh. But seeing Ikoro now, struggling to find his footing, gasping for air, clawing at the whip about his neck—knowing he could've killed me, but didn't . . . "Please, you're hurting him. Uncle, please, don't do this."

Uncle stared at me as if he couldn't remember who I was. As if seeing me for the first time. His gaze took in the blood trickling from my nose, my blood-spattered appearance. He blinked.

Then, suddenly, there was a movement among the slaves. Pea Soup began running toward us. Screaming, screaming.

Uncle cursed, raised his firearm, and aimed.

"No!" I pushed his arm away, and the pistol fired harmlessly into the air.

Pea Soup reached us and, to my astonishment, flung himself beside Ikoro, tugging at the whip about Ikoro's neck. *"Nnà!"* he shrieked.

"Father" . . .

The hair rose on the back of my neck and I knew. I *knew*.

Ikoro was Pea Soup's father.

"Nnà!"

As I watched the display between father and son, tears poured out of me. Then Pea Soup turned and grasped me about the ankles, his tears moistening my bare feet, crying, crying over and over, *"Bikó! Mèelu ānyi èbelè!"*—"Please! I beg you! Have mercy on us!"

I stood, weeping, my nose throbbing and dribbling, and in that moment all my fear of Pea Soup vanished, like a nightmare vanishes upon awakening. He was a boy, like me, desperate, begging to save the life of his father. "Spare him," I managed to say. "Please don't kill Ikoro. He's—he's Pea Soup's father. Don't you see? He's Pea Soup's father. Have mercy. Have mercy on all of them."

Uncle had been observing the scene with clenched jaw, his lips compressed into a thin line. Now he looked at me with the eyes of a stranger. "We all have fathers. Mine shot himself in the head when I was eleven. Yours was lost at sea." To McGuire he said, "Carry out my orders. And string up the warrior brute first."

"McGuire, don't do this," I pleaded, but McGuire looked over my head, as if I weren't there. "McGuire, you know it's wrong. Uncle, *please*. I'm begging you!"

I begged some more, feeling no longer the grand, intelligent surgeon of the *Formidable,* but instead the sickly, pale little lad cowering under the ferocious scowl of Master Crump, vainly begging for any mercy. I clung to Uncle's shirt, mucus and tears and blood all running together. But Uncle ignored me. Finally pushed me away as if I were an insect, and then I lay flat on my back again, sails and sky blurring into one awful scheme of white and blue, blue and white.

And so, on the twenty-second day of our homeward voyage across the Atlantic, six male slaves, including Ikoro, were executed, hanged from the main yard and then shot. They were then hacked into pieces and tossed overboard. The last part was a deliberate act on the part of my uncle, for it was well known that Africans believed that if a body was dismembered, the spirit couldn't return to the African soil of its ancestors.

I heard all this and more from Billy the Vermin, for I'd refused to watch. Like a fly that wouldn't shoo, Billy followed me about the infirmary as I cared for the wounded slaves, telling me all about the executions, though I hollered at him to clear off, that I didn't want to hear it. To clear off, clear off, *clear off*! He finally left, but only after I threw a scalpel at him that stuck, quivering, in the bulkhead.

It was midnight. Cries and moans and songs of grief bled throughout the ship. My nose throbbed. I kept the candle burning in the lantern.

I slept fitfully, gasping awake every few minutes, over and over again seeing Teags' look of surprise. The speculum orb sticking out of his stomach. I saw Pea Soup running toward us. Tugging at the whip wrapped about his father's neck. Weeping, sobbing, asking of me *"Mèelụ ānyị èbelè!"*—"Have mercy on us!" I saw my uncle, glaring at me with the eyes of a stranger. Six male slaves, including Ikoro, standing silently by my berth, watching me, wanting something. . . . The familiar nausea pitched in my stomach. I groaned.

Finally, hating my bed, hating my cabin, hating the stench of nighttime, I arose and took the lantern from its peg. I'd decided I'd go on deck and clear my head.

But outside my cabin door, confronted with the closed door of my uncle's cabin, which stood beside mine, a compulsion overtook me. Hesitating just a moment, I entered his cabin, again without knocking, lantern in hand.

I don't know what I'd expected to find. Him sitting at his chart table, perhaps, plotting the next day's course. Him pacing, stewing over the day's events. Him reading his Book of Common Prayer, praying for strength to endure the remainder of the voyage.

But what I'd not expected was to see him sleeping like a babe.

He lay crossways on his bed, shirt unbuttoned to his waist. His mouth was open. Gold teeth caught the shimmering light of the lantern. He was snoring softly. I saw beneath his curls that he didn't remove his earrings at night. His boots lay haphazardly on the floor next to the bed.

He looks as if he hasn't a care in the world, I thought.

And as I gazed at my uncle, the scales fell from my eyes and

I knew. For the first time since I'd met my uncle at the Magford workhouse four years previous, I saw him clearly, saw him for what he was. Surrounded by cries and wailing so piteous it'd melt the heart of the devil himself, my uncle slept peacefully.

You care for no one but yourself, Uncle. No one. Not even for me, your only flesh and blood.

You never sent money for my welfare. You left me to rot at the work-house.

You killed six slaves today as heartlessly as you'd swat a fly.

A horrible, seething wretchedness crawled through me, and in that moment, born of every beating I'd ever endured, born of the cries of suffering that shrieked in my ears, I despised my uncle.

CHAPTER
15

*W*ithin two days, life aboard the *For-midable* returned to its usual appearance.

The four dead crew members—including Teags, Mackerel, and Numbly—followed in Jonas' wake, sewn into their hammocks, weighted with cannonballs. Dry-eyed, I said nothing when their bodies plunged one by one into the briny deep.

And when Uncle asked me to continue with our daily lessons in navigation (which had been temporarily suspended, owing to my duties as surgeon), I silently complied. "Once you master navigation, you'll be worth double to me," he said jovially, seeming to have construed my begging for Ikoro's life as a childish moment, easily forgotten. "Besides, with Numbly gone now, I'm relying on you should anything happen to me."

The sextant, charts, parallel rulers, compass, and all things navigational were hateful objects to me now. I wished only for the *Formidable* to speed on her way under a full press of sail and for the voyage to end. I resolved that upon arriving in New Orleans, I would go my own way and never see Uncle again.

I'd have thought my uncle would've noticed my reticence and suspect that my feelings toward him had changed considerably. But he noticed nothing. This was another confirmation of my uncle's selfishness, of his inability to see beyond his own nose, beyond his own needs and wants.

My face had swelled from its injury. My nose felt tight; it was reddened, sore, and clogged. My eyes had blackened, as if I'd been punched with the old one-two. Uncle just laughed when he saw me, telling me how many times he'd broken his own nose and that it bloody well hurt, didn't it?

Because of the rebellion, the slaves were kept under guard in the hold. Not even the women and children were allowed on deck. And so it would remain until Uncle changed his mind. Of course it was all the talk among the crew just *how* the slaves had managed the revolt. They'd been found with all sorts of weapons hidden on their persons—iron bolts, scalpels, mallets, and such. The crew speculated as to how the slaves had obtained such materials, some mentioning Pea Soup as the only possible explanation. After all, he'd been confined in the hold following the battle with the American warship and had found his father, Ikoro. Doubtless, from that moment on father and son had conspired to rebel. Once free to roam the ship again, Pea Soup had taken the opportunity to bring weapons to the slaves.

"Someone should string that boy up, use the same noose as for his father," said Calvin one day at our noon mess. His mouth was full of biscuit and salt beef, and he spat crumbs as he talked. "Chop him into bits afterwards. It's all because of him Mackerel's dead."

Upon hearing his words, and with a ferocity that surprised me, I hurled my wooden plate across the deck, lunged across the space between us, and pointed my knife at Calvin's throat. Everyone stared at me as if I were a lunatic. A mashed chunk of salt beef plopped from Calvin's mouth. My voice sounded cold and dead, even to me. "If anyone so much as touches Pea Soup, the next time you beg for medicine I'll administer arsenic instead of quinine. Don't think I won't. My uncle's agreed that it's *my* responsibility to punish my own slave, and trusts me to do as I see fit. He's *my* slave, and you'll leave him be."

No one spoke as I stamped off. I was trembling with rage, hating the ease with which Calvin had talked of chopping Pea Soup to bits. As I stepped down the companionway, someone moved at the bottom step. Down and away, as if he'd just slipped down the steps ahead of me. "Pea Soup, is that you?"

Pea Soup turned and looked up, his face showing no more expression than if he'd been watching grass grow. I wondered if he'd heard the conversation.

For a moment, we said nothing. I realized then that I was wrong about his expression. Grief lined his face. Shadows circled his eyes. I'd been blind not to see it. Blind like Uncle. "I—I'm sorry about your father. Truly I am. My father died too. Before I was born."

He turned away then, disappearing into the shadows so quickly that had I not just seen and spoken to him face to face, I'd have doubted anyone else had been there.

It appeared that my little demonstration at the mess had been effective, for after this day no one, not even Uncle, mentioned Pea Soup. He was, however, constantly in my thoughts.

Even days after the rebellion, I was baffled as to why Pea Soup had spared my life. Had not only spared my life, but seemed intent upon preserving it. Why? Even Ikoro had not harmed me when he'd had the chance. After stabbing Teags, he could have dispatched me in a second, yet he'd left me behind, alive and well—a white boy, and an enemy. Again, why? It was possible that he considered me to be no threat, but that still didn't explain Pea Soup's change of heart.

Aside from our encounter in the companionway, I'd seen little of Pea Soup since the revolt. Truth was, between my time in the infirmary, navigation, and language studies, my every hour was occupied. Though there was evidence that Pea Soup was keeping up with his chores, I felt unsettled, haunted, as if something were wrong—something unsaid, undone—but I didn't know what.

One day there was a timid knock upon the infirmary door.

"Who is it?" I barked, praying it wasn't Billy the Vermin.

When no one answered and yet there came another knock, I strode to the door and yanked it open, ready to vent my spleen.

It was Pea Soup.

He stood straight as a spear, taller than me by five or so inches. One eye was gummed shut, the other pink and swollen. His pink eye gazed at me, unabashed.

I stared, mouth open like a dimwit, before recovering myself, remembering that I was the surgeon and that someone here was in need of medical attention. I said, "Come in," and stepped aside.

Pea Soup entered, his pink eye taking in the claustrophobic infirmary. The smoky darkness. The berths lining the hull, each filled with a sleeping shape. The basket of oakum dolls and braided rope. The medicine chest. The piles of dirty linen. The variety of medical instruments lying about. The pitcher of water and bucket of waste. My own filthy apron, covered with bodily fluids of every description.

"Lie down." I motioned to the examination table, wondering if I was making a mistake. Could I really trust Pea Soup? Perhaps he'd come to kill me. To finish what he'd started and then neglected. After all, it was he who'd broken my nose.

As with all the patients who'd suffered from the eye disease, I rinsed his eyes and treated them with mucilage of sassafras. Pea Soup never budged. Never stopped watching me with his pink eye. It was rather unnerving.

When I finished, he sat up, wiped his face with the towel I gave him, and then left without another glance back.

Well, I thought, sitting down and allowing myself a smile, *I suppose that's better than being thrown to the sharks.*

The baby was delivered in the dead of night, shortly after eight bells.

Billy awakened me to tell me one of the women was thought to be in labor and was in the infirmary. By the time I'd shaken the sleep from me, nervously skimmed the birthing section in one of Jonas' medical books, and arranged the necessary towels and medical instruments, the baby had been delivered into my hands with a hearty screech from the mother and hardly a word or action from me.

I cradled the squalling, slippery infant. It was pathetically skinny, seeming to lack the energy to cry. "It's a girl," I told the mother in her language. Tears welling in her eyes, the mother reached out her arms and took the child to her breast.

Within the hour, I'd taken care of the mother, washed the baby, and cleaned up the mess. And all the while a disturbing thought kept surfacing: *Even the babe's first breath is drawn in bondage.* I tried to convince myself that it was for her own good, that we were doing the baby a favor by taking her to civilization, but instead a melancholy stole over me, as if I'd awakened and found myself forty years older.

I'd dozed off, sitting upright in the chair, when someone burst into the infirmary.

It was Uncle, obviously having just roused himself from bed, his hair looking as if he'd caught it in a moss picker. "Where is it?"

I blinked with sleep. "Where's what?"

"The baby. Billy told me—" And before he could finish his sentence, he saw the baby, curled in the crook of the mother's arm. He strode over and, without a by-your-leave, snatched the infant up. The mother's eyes flew open. She shrieked and reached out for her baby. The baby squalled. Kicked.

I rose from my chair, mouth dry, heart pounding, with a sudden feeling of dread. "Wait, please—"

"I told you to bring me the baby, did I not?" Uncle scowled at me, looking displeased. Looking like the day he'd ordered Ikoro executed along with five other slaves.

"Yes, but I thought it could wait till—"

"Bloody hell! Shut her up, would you?" Uncle motioned to the mother. "She's going to burst my eardrums with her racket!" And without another word to me, he left the infirmary, taking the baby with him.

I rushed after him, pulse pounding in my ears.

My God, what's he planning to do?

He moved quickly, up the companionway and onto the upper deck before I'd even reached the first step. "Wait! Please, wait!" Up I clambered, my breath ragged as if I'd just run a mile.

The full moon cast a silver path along the waters. The sails hummed in the brisk wind. Uncle was striding to the rail. And while I watched, while my heart lodged in my throat, hesitating between beats, he reached the rail and flung the infant over-board.

"*No!*" I screeched, running to him, almost pitching over the gunwale. "My God, what've you done?"

Uncle caught my arm.

"What've you done?" I repeated. I could see nothing. Just the path of moonlight shimmering on the water. "We must save it! We must do something!" I was crying, the words bursting from my mouth like pus from a wound. I think I would've jumped overboard had Uncle's grip not tightened. He yanked my arm so hard that my head whipped back.

"Stop it! Stop this rubbish, this—this blood-gushing non-sense, before I beat it out of you!" he bellowed.

His hand, like an iron trap. Me, like an animal, struggling to get away. His eyes, now midnight black, narrowed.

Stop this blood-gushing nonsense, before I beat it out of you!

No, Master Crump! No!

I fought against him.

He cursed. Raised his hand to strike me.

No! Please, have mercy!

My bones turned to mush. I sank against the bulwarks. Rough wood scraped my cheek. Hard, damp. I slid down until I lay in a crumpled heap on the deck, curled into a ball.

Don't hit me. Don't hit me.

The man said, "What did you think, Nephew? That I'd turn the ship into a nursery? Grow up." He grunted with disgust and strode away.

I sat in the infirmary. It stank of bowels. Of birth. Of blood.

I stared at the hull. Its timbers stacked one on top the other. There was a knothole in one of them. A black beetle crawled along the edge of the knothole.

Except for the occasional groan, except for the never-ending gurgle of the deep on the other side of the hull, the infirmary was silent. The mother had stopped crying hours ago. She'd bled to death. I'd held her in my arms, begged God to save her. But her life oozed away until her eyes rolled back in her head.

My gaze fell to my hands. Dark, caked with blood. Rivers of black trailing between my fingers to my elbows. Blood crusted under the nails. I moved my fingers. They were stiff, sticky.

We're doing them a favor . . . saving their lives, in a way. . . . They'll be better off and thank us. . . . It's a necessary evil, and can't be helped. . . .

No, Uncle. It's not a necessary evil.

It's purely evil.

You've filled my ears with lies.

You've covered my hands with blood.

And I can bear it no longer.

CHAPTER
16

*U*ncle thumped me on the back when
I emerged into the early sun and thrust a
plate of food into my hands, saying, "Missed
your morning mess, my lad."

I could hardly stand the sight of him,
knowing him for a murderer, knowing
everything he'd told me was a lie. But I
took my meal, leaning over the rail, saying
nothing.

Uncle tilted his head back and breathed
deeply, lips curled in a smile, as if life didn't
get any better than this. "Grand day, eh
what? Wind's strong, ship's sound—ah,
couldn't be finer! What do you look so glum
for? Cheer up, lad, we're soon to be rich! Ha!
Did I ever tell you about my first voyage?
No? Made two thousand British pounds,
even as a cabin boy . . ."

And Uncle regaled me with his adventures while I picked at my food, sickened, wishing I were deaf, for his voice now set my teeth on edge. I looked away, out over the empty waters, half wishing I could follow the baby overboard.

Previous to the executions and the murder of the infant, I'd already witnessed much suffering—the paltry food rations, the horrifying conditions in the hold, the whipping of slaves—but all of it, *all* of it, I'd believed was a necessary means toward an end that was ultimately good. And much can be endured if one believes that all will, one day, be well. But now I knew differently. To kill helpless slaves, helpless babies, wasn't a means to an end that was ultimately good, a favor that we bestowed upon them out of a desire to better their state in life. No, it was murder. And for what? To make my uncle, and people like my uncle, rich.

Slavery was *not* a better life than the one the slaves had left behind in Africa. And even if it was, who was I, who was Uncle, or anyone, to decide for them? They were human beings, with intelligence and God-given choice.

Yes, the slave trade was evil. Anyone who spoke contrary to such a fact was lying. This I knew, just as surely as I knew I'd two arms, two legs, and one head. The thought of becoming a wealthy man based upon such a lie filled me with abhorrence. I'd no more be a party to such abuse than I'd become a workhouse master and make money off the sweat of poor, starving orphans.

Uncle put an arm about my shoulder, but I shrugged out of his grasp.

"Ah, you'll get used to it. It's as I told you. You must harden yourself to it. You're too sensitive. Must thicken that skin of yours! Ha!" And here he turned, shouted an order to the helmsman, and strode aft, leaving me with my mouth full, chewing a piece of salt beef over and over again, unable to swallow. I leaned over and spat it into the sea.

Six men stood in my cabin, watching me. Black eyes, black faces. They held spears. Said nothing, just watched me sleep. *They want something . . . but what? What?* I tried to awaken, but couldn't.

Someone knocked on the door.

I pried a babe from its mother's arms. She was screaming, but I took it anyhow. I ran to the upper deck and tossed it overboard, weeping at the same time, trying to claw over the gunwale to rescue it, but Master Crump held me back, beating me across my shoulders and head.

"Foolish boy. Mind your catechism and grow up."

Again someone knocked on the door.

I ran through the streets, naked. Uncle saw me through the tavern doorway, took his cigar from his mouth, and laughed. And laughed. His roars of laughter filled my ears. He pounded the table with his fist, tears streaming from his eyes, pointing at me as if I were a twopenny show.

A voice penetrated the heavy curtain of sleep. "Philip!"

I opened my eyes. I was in my cabin aboard the *Formidable*. The candle was burning. Waves of sleep clung to me. Two days had passed since the death of the infant and her mother, but it seemed a hundred years ago, a lifetime.

"Philip!"

It was Billy the Vermin.

"Bugger and blast, don't you ever go away?"

"Captain wants to see you."

"What hour is it?"

"Six bells. He wants to see you now. I think you're in trouble."

Once I'd sloshed cold water on my face and dressed, I found

Uncle pacing the quarterdeck. He saw me coming and flicked his cigar over the bulwarks into the sea.

"Finished with your beauty sleep?" Uncle's voice held no trace of humor, and I saw a storm brewing on his brow.

"Told you," whispered Billy. He'd followed me, no doubt anxious to see me in trouble.

"Sorry, but I was up late again last night with several complaints."

"And what was the nature of those complaints?"

"Sore eyes."

"Really?" His voice was sharp as a knife edge. "And how many cases of sore eyes have you treated since the voyage began?"

I shrugged as fear stole over me. My heart began to race. Much as I despised my uncle, he frightened me too.

Behind me, Billy giggled.

"How many?" Uncle repeated.

"A hundred or so. I don't really know. I—I've not counted. Over eighty in the past five days, I should think."

Uncle inhaled deeply, as if trying to control himself. "I see. Please tell me why I've not heard of this until now."

"I—I told Jonas when I saw the first case. He told me to wash the affected eyes with warm water and mucilage of sassafras. That's what I've been doing."

"And he said nothing else?"

"He—he was drunk. Three sheets to the wind."

"Well, he's *dead* now."

I said nothing.

"And because he's *dead,* you report to me. Didn't you understand this?"

"But you said I could handle the job. And I have, Uncle, I have. I've done everything Jonas told me to."

At this, Uncle grabbed me roughly by the arm. He stuck his face into mine. "You want to see how you've handled it? Do you?"

I blinked. Smelled his tobacco breath. My mouth went dry. I wondered, desperately wondered, what catastrophe had occurred to make Uncle so livid with anger. "What is it? What've I done?"

Billy snorted with barely contained laughter.

Uncle released me. "Come with me."

I followed him as he strode to the main hatch. Roach was waiting there with a musket in one hand, a lantern in the other. Without a word, Uncle took the lantern from Roach and disappeared into the darkness of the hold.

"What're you waiting for?" said Billy the Vermin. "Go." And he poked me in the spine with a rigid finger.

"Clear off, Vermin." I hesitated at the lip of the hatch, smelling the darkness beneath. My knees shook. I blinked the sweat from my eyes.

Billy hissed in my ear, "You're scared. You ain't nothing but a cow-hearted *dog.*"

That did it. I summoned every ounce of courage and descended the companionway, leaving Billy behind. Uncle waited for me, lantern in hand. His face was cast in shadow. At the bottom, I clung to the ladder. *It's so dark!* Immediately my chest tightened. A vise about my lungs, squeezing, squeezing. I wanted to shriek and climb out of there.

"Uncle, Uncle, I can't breathe."

Again Uncle grabbed my arm. His fingers pressed hard into my flesh, down to my bone, and I knew I'd have bruises to show for it. I gasped.

He growled, "You'll come with me now or I'll lock you down here for the remainder of the voyage. Which will it be?"

"No, please, don't lock me up, please!" I screeched, my voice shrill as a fishwife's. "I—I'll follow."

The smell of so many bodies crammed together—the stench of waste, of every bodily fluid, spilled on the tiers, in the narrow aisles—was overpowering. I choked back vomit.

I can't breathe!

As we passed through the aisles, my uncle first, then me, arms reached out from every direction—from the tiers high above, from the middle section, from the ground. Chains clanked; hands grabbed my trousers, my shirt, my hair. I tore away from them, stifling my urge to scream, brushing them away as if they were insects.

I can't breathe!

A chorus of wails attended us, growing louder as we approached each area of the hold, then fading as we left. Throughout, Uncle stopped and held up his lantern, grabbing me by the scruff of my neck and forcing me to look. . . .

Look . . .

Blind eyes stared at nothing. Filmy white membranes covered the brown irises like fog. Hundreds of them. Hundreds.

All blind.

CHAPTER
17

*T*he *Formidable* plunged on through the Atlantic waters, unaware of the frightful illness she carried in her holds.

Ophthalmia.

That's what my uncle told me it was, once he'd returned to his cabin and scrubbed his scalp and face with cold water.

Highly contagious.

"If you'd told me when it'd first occurred," he said, now looking tired and drained, "I could've thrown the affected ones overboard." He sat and poured each of us a goblet of palm wine. "Then we could've avoided this mess."

I thought of the little girl with the rabbit teeth. I thought of her being tossed overboard, still alive, simply because her eyelids were gummed together. I stood there, ignoring the goblet of wine Uncle proffered me, hating this vessel, this voyage. Hating this relative of mine, who'd the compassion of a toad and the remorse of an onion.

Uncle drank deeply.

"What happens now?" I asked.

"You're the bloody surgeon, you tell me."

I made no response, knowing that he knew the answer, while I knew nothing.

"We ride it out, that's what we do," he finally said. "There're too many affected. It's all over the ship. Our only hope is that the blindness isn't always permanent. Given enough time, in fact, it often reverses itself." He drained his goblet and poured himself another. "Let us pray God will be merciful. I *cannot* lose this cargo."

"I didn't know you prayed."

He mustn't have heard the sarcasm in my voice, for he said simply, "Aye, I pray. What God-fearing man doesn't? And though I'm forced to work in a thankless occupation, God has blessed me." He suddenly looked at me. "I'm thankful for you, Philip. And I'm sorry for losing my temper. I'd never have locked you down there. You know that."

Again I said nothing, my heart tight, wishing things had been different between us.

Uncle frowned, then sighed. Set down his empty goblet and stood. "Well, then, best get started. We must see to the organization of the slaves into two groups, those who are afflicted and those who aren't. It'll take the rest of the day, I judge." And out he went.

I followed, saying nothing, not telling Uncle that the whites of his eyes had turned to pink.

It was everywhere.

The ophthalmia.

Almost every slave was afflicted with it, to one degree or another. Pea Soup too was now as blind as if he'd been carved from obsidian rather than flesh. I saw him upon occasion, sitting and staring at nothing or pathetically feeling his way along, going goodness knows where.

Uncle flogged several of the crew for not telling him about the ophthalmia.

Roach said he thought Harold had told him. Harold said he thought Calvin had told him. Calvin said it was the surgeon's responsibility, so why should they get in trouble for something that was my fault?

Uncle flogged them all.

It was a day of flogging, of vinegar vapors, of grumbling, crying, moaning, whining, and vicious looks cast my way. More than once, someone bumped into me, hard, or put an elbow in my face, or stamped on my toe, saying, "Oh, excuse me, Mr. Surgeon, I didn't see you there. You being so small and all."

Food and water rations, which had already been stingy, were halved.

As for myself, I felt hideously inadequate, furious that Jonas had left me with this disaster. I'd already done everything I knew to heal the slaves' eyes, and yet they'd gone blind. What more could I do? Bleed them? Blister them? Cup them? I spent much of my day poring over Jonas' ancient medical books, as musty and yellowed as their former owner, but could find nothing helpful.

One said to apply the pulp of rotted apples over the inflamed eyes, but we'd no apples. Another said to apply a lukewarm decoction of poppy heads, but we'd no poppy heads. Another said to apply leeches, but our supply of leeches had died a fortnight ago. Another said to "stir the whites of two eggs briskly with a lump of alum till they coagulate," and then to apply the mixture to closed lids at night. But Uncle had finished eating all of the chickens and their eggs a few days past. Regardless, all of these remedies were for *inflamed* eyes, not for curing blindness.

The sun hung over the watery horizon on this evening in mid-May, the conclusion of the thirty-first day of our homeward-bound journey. I closed the last of the medical books. Nothing. I stood at the rail, wishing all this were a dream, until Billy fetched me, saying I needed to report to Uncle's cabin.

"I say, Billy, do you ever wonder why you do this?" I asked on impulse.

An expression came over Billy's face that I can only describe as daft. "Do what?"

"*This.* Trade in human flesh."

He shrugged. "No. Not really."

I sighed. "No, I don't suppose you would."

Uncle was lying on his bed, a wet rag over his eyes. When I entered his cabin, he lifted it up and peered at me. "I have it, don't I?"

To my shock, he was weeping.

"I have it, don't I? The disease."

"Yes, Uncle. I'm sorry."

One by one, the crew contracted the disease. They wandered about with pink, pus-filled eyes until they too became blind. First the gunner, then nine of the sailors, then the carpenter, then Uncle . . .

Soon there were only six of us who could see to set the sails. We plied on every scrap of canvas, reeling toward the Caribbean. According to the charts we were more than halfway to Havana, but owing to our condition we'd resolved to make for the nearest port, cutting a fortnight off our journey. I was solely responsible for navigation of the ship now. Uncle stood beside me each day at the rail, clutching my arm like a child who can't let his parent out of his sight for fear of being lost. "Are you quite certain it's high noon?" "What's the compass heading?" "Are you sure your figures are correct?" "Have you—"

"Yes, don't worry. We're on course."

"How long till our destination?"

"Hopefully no more'n ten days."

"Have you forgotten that you're my Don Felipe, should we be boarded by the Yanks?"

"No, Don Pedro, I've not forgotten."

"I can't do this without you, Philip."

"I know, Uncle."

"You're my eyes. I'm trusting you."

"Yes, I know."

"Why've you not gone blind too? You're the surgeon. You of all people should've been affected; the ill are constantly about you."

"I've stopped trying to figure it out. Luck, probably."

"Certainly not your manly constitution."

"I suppose not."

"Have you seen to it that rations have been cut again?"

"Yes, but everyone is thirsty. We can't cut the water rations again."

"How many died today?"

"Seven."

"Pray tell me, what did they die of?"

"Breathing toxic vapors."

"We can't keep them down there for the remainder of the voyage. It's unhealthy. Negroes must have their exercise. They're like dogs in that regard."

"Exercise would do them well."

"But how do we bring up hundreds of blind negroes when we ourselves are blind?"

"I don't know."

"It'd be madness." He slammed the rail with his fist. Tears dripped from his blind eyes. "Oh God, Philip, I pray every moment to see again. I pray God take this blindness from me!"

"Yes, Uncle. I pray that as well."

I took my first trick at the helm. An enormous burden of work fell upon those of us who still had our sight, allowing us only a couple of hours of sleep per day. Not only that, but we were already shorthanded, as our crew now numbered only thirty-four, twelve of us having been lost to disease, battle, and rebellion. Of course the ship's wheel was too massive and stubborn for me to control alone, so I was flanked by two sightless sailors who followed my instructions. "Left, left! No, no, too much!" I would cry. "Right, right!" "Hold her steady!" "She's luffing. Quickly, which way should I go again?"

It was a fine, windy day, the blue skies marred only by distant clouds. The *Formidable* plunged through the waves, tossing spray over her bow. It would've been magnificent had our situation been different. Had we carried coal or rice or fabrics instead of slaves. Had we been healthy, well fed, and with all the drinking water we desired. Today three of the six men who still had vision now bore signs of the disease. It was a race to reach port before it claimed us all.

When I wasn't giving orders, I clung to the wheel, the bracing wind tossing my hair and making my eyes burn and water.

Eight more days at most.

I prayed for strength and sight to guide the ship safely to harbor. For though I despised my uncle as well as the crew, I wished no one ill, and wouldn't rest till both crew and slaves had proper medical attention and plenty of food and clean water. This was the task appointed me and this was the task I'd fulfill, as nephew, surgeon, and one who knows what it is to suffer.

After my trick, it was near noon. Every muscle ached, and I was so stiff and sore I couldn't move properly. Twenty slaves took their exercise on deck. Blind, tripping over one another, they danced to Billy's fiddle music. Chains rattled and the deck thumped as they stamped about. While we couldn't exercise hundreds at a time, we brought them up on deck in small numbers, where they could be handled easily for a couple of hours before being exchanged for the next lot.

I watched for a moment before disappearing down the aft companionway. It was time to sight the noonday sun. After that, I was to help Cookie with the evening mess, for he was as blind as the rest of them and fumbled about his pots and pans and food stores like a lost sheep, all the while mumbling like a madman. I paused outside my cabin door, longing to slip inside and study my languages, read Shakespeare, sleep, perhaps, but instead I took a deep breath and prepared to rap on Uncle's cabin door to fetch the nautical instruments.

It was then I heard voices from within. Heard my name.

Uncle was speaking. "Philip has proved to be quite useful to me. He says we're at most eight days' sail from the nearest port. Barbuda, I believe, if our course remains true."

"It'll be a mercy if we make it safely." I recognized the second voice. It belonged to the new first mate, McGuire. He'd been promoted from his position as second mate upon the death of Numbly during the rebellion. Now, like Uncle, McGuire was afflicted with blindness.

Uncle lowered his voice, and I strained to hear. "When we're within a day's sail, I want you to jettison all cargo that hasn't yet recovered their sight."

There was a silence.

My heart skipped a beat.

Jettison the cargo? I'd heard those words before. Somewhere. And what exactly did they mean? I dreaded I was soon to find out.

"Sir?" asked the first mate.

Uncle laughed. "Think about it, McGuire. Who would buy a bunch of blind slaves anyhow? Whereas every slave that's lost must be made good by the underwriters. Did you think my cargo would be uninsured?"

"But—but, Captain . . ."

"Besides, my good man, would you have me turn my ship into a hospital for the support of blind negroes?"

"No, of course not."

"Unless they regain their sight, they're useless to me. A dead slave is worth more to me than a blind slave."

"Of course, Captain. I understand."

I heard the knife edge return to Uncle's voice. "That's all, McGuire. Now get out of here."

Quick as a blink, I slipped into my cabin and shut the door. My ears roared with the frantic beat of my heart as McGuire trod the passage.

Finally the sounds of his passing faded. All that remained was the scrape of the fiddle, the rattle of chains, and the *thump-thump, thump-thump* of feet on the deck.

Three hundred thirty-six remaining slaves. All of them blind now. And if Uncle had his way, they'd be *jettisoned,* thrown into the sea. Why? So Uncle could collect his insurance money for their deaths and still make good on the voyage. A dead slave was worth more to Uncle than a blind slave.

It was the wee hours of the morning and I sat at my desk in my cabin, candle burning in the lantern as usual, unable to sleep.

My eyes kept watering, aching with weariness. What was I to do? I was the surgeon of the *Formidable,* responsible for the well-being of every person aboard, black and white. How could I sit idly by and let 336 of them be murdered? Tossed into the sea, still alive, still shackled, to drown—or worse, to be devoured by sharks? There were girls and boys, men and women—some of the women pregnant.

That my uncle would consider such an act no longer surprised me. I was only mortified that it'd taken me so long to understand his true character.

In approximately one week we'd arrive at port; in only six days Uncle planned to jettison the cargo. I agonized over what to do. How could I stop it from happening? I considered begging for their lives, but remembered my piteous begging for the life of Ikoro and my uncle's callousness in executing him anyhow. No, begging would be quite useless. What, then, could I do? Me, Philip Arthur Higgins, of no particular importance in the world? Me, Philip Arthur Higgins, who was the sport of the crew, whom no one took seriously?

And as I sat there in my cabin, a great helplessness seized me, and I laid my head upon my desk and sobbed.

It's not fair that I should be in this position! It's not fair!

An ache heavy as a millstone weighed upon my heart, and I longed to be home. *Home.* My real home, where the Gallaghers waited for me, loved me. For the first time, I knew with a simple clarity that they were, and had been, my family—my foster mother and father. *Oh, forgive me for not realizing it before! I promise I'll make it up to you, if only I can be home again! I promise! I promise I'll be a true son, as you deserve!*

I sobbed myself to sleep, my forehead pressed onto my quill pen. When I awakened—an hour, two hours later—to a sharp rap on the door, my room was black as coal dust.

"Philip, take your trick at the wheel. Must we wake you for everything?"

The candle's gone out! Dear God, the candle!

Wanting to scream, chest already tightening like a vise, I whisked open my drawer for a fresh candle.

"Philip! Wake up, for God's sake!"

My hands wrapped about a candle.

In a moment I'll have light. Hurry, Philip, hurry!

I stood and reached for the latch on the lantern door, then stopped, my hands on the metal casing.

But—but how can that be? The lantern. It's hot.

And in that instant the awful truth dawned.

The candle still burns, only I can't see.

I did scream then. A wail erupted from deep down, bubbling out of me in a terror greater than I've ever known. As if I'd awakened one morning to find that the sun had disappeared from the sky and all was cold and night forever.

CHAPTER 18

*F*or the first day of my blindness, I thrashed and screamed and blubbered like a madman.

Uncle ordered me locked in my cabin until I stopped this childish nonsense. "Bloody hell!" he hollered. "You're a man, aren't you? Act like one!"

I pounded on the door and screamed until I was hoarse, screeching over and over, "I can't breathe! I can't breathe!" Finally, hours later, I crumpled to the floor, weeping, begging to be let out, to be taken on deck, to feel the sun on my face at least, at the very least, oh please, please. I promised to stop screaming then.

When I lay prostrate on the floor, tears spent, five years old again and shut in the darkness of Master Crump's cupboard, the door opened. I didn't hear it, but I felt it. A gentle breeze.

"Who's there?" I raised myself up, half expecting a cane to descend upon me.

The door closed again. Someone was beside me.

"Who—who is it?"

"You are thirsty?"

It was Pea Soup.

"You are thirsty?" he asked again.

I hesitated only a moment before I croaked, "Yes, yes, please help me."

A hand touched my face, my nose, my mouth, and then a goblet was held to my lips. I drank deeply, gasping for breath between gulps, until every last drop was gone.

"Thank you," I said, wiping my mouth, only then realizing that I'd drunk twice the normal ration, that Pea Soup must've given me his own. I was reminded of steerage, of being aboard the *Hope*, and of the poor Irish family who fed me, though they had scarcely a crumb to their name. Such kindness moved me deeply.

I lay down again and began to weep.

Pea Soup sat beside me.

"I'm blind," I told him, as if he didn't already know. "I—I can't see. Everything is dark. I hate the dark. It frightens me. They used to lock me in the dark."

For a long time I cried. Pea Soup said nothing.

By and by I stopped weeping and lay still, utterly spent, only then falling into a deep, dreamless sleep. Once I briefly awoke to find myself in my bunk, with Pea Soup snoring in the berth above me.

By the next day, every last one of us was blind—slave and crew.

Uncle having unlocked my cabin door at last, I emerged on deck to learn this news.

"But what will we do?" I asked Uncle.

"I don't know." I heard the tightness in his voice, the despair, and my heart swelled in sympathy despite myself.

"But how will we return home?"

"We've no course now but to pray. It's in God's hands."

So we wandered the seas, aimless, God as our steersman.

We kept the sails up, praying we'd make land somehow, knowing that even if we did, it'd likely be to founder upon a reef, or an atoll, or rocks. Everything—rigging, blocks, yards—creaked, slapped, or knocked about, for we could do nothing. It was impossible to trim the sails. We couldn't figure out which rope went where.

It was the deepest sort of blindness, without even a glimmer of light. Even on the darkest nights at sea, a seeing person can discern the glitter of the waters and the white crest of the wave, and half perceive, half guess, the form of surrounding objects. And even in the midst of the darkest night, a seeing person knows that soon the sun will rise, bringing new light to the world.

A bleak part of me wondered if jettisoning the "cargo" now might be the most merciful thing we could do, for the slaves' cries and moans were so piteous, and yet we were powerless to help them. No longer were they allowed to come on deck, for it was rotten enough that we, the crew, stumbled about, arms in front of us, feeling our way from mast to hatch to bow, only to discover we were headed in the wrong direction, without having three hundred some-odd slaves to worry about as well.

Uncle tried to keep order. He maintained the watches,

having us estimate four-hour stretches. He kept a "lookout" at all times—ordering someone with keen ears to listen for the sound of the surf, of breakers crashing against a reef or rocks. And when several men pillaged the spirit-casks and lay in a drunken stupor, Uncle whipped them to their senses with his rattan cane and set a guard with crossed swords over the storeroom. Uncle commanded the crew to enter the hold, as usual, to feed and water the slaves. To find those who were dead and heave them overboard before the stench of their decay overwhelmed us. The sound of bodies plunging into the deep was becoming increasingly familiar.

Uncle kept saying, "Surely *one* of us will regain sight and direct us. Surely God doesn't mean for us *all* to die." Thrice daily my uncle summoned us for recitations from the Book of Common Prayer. He knew only three passages by heart, and it was these he repeated morning, noon, and night. The morning prayer was "Lord be merciful to us sinners, and save us for thy mercy's sake. Thou art the great God, who hast made and rulest all things: O deliver us for thy Name's sake. Thou art the great God to be feared above all: O save us, that we may praise thee. Amen."

"Amen," we echoed.

While I indeed wanted to be delivered—prayed to be delivered, in fact—I wondered why the Divinity would save us only to let us then turn and murder hundreds of innocent souls. What right did we have to be saved at all?

Pea Soup, who'd seemed to have gotten his bearings, now shared my cabin. Oddly enough, it gave me comfort to have him there—the one I'd feared for so long. To be alone in the dark would've been unbearable. Sometimes I'd awaken in a fright, disoriented, my chest tightening in that familiar panic. I'd cry out, "Pea Soup! Are you there?" He'd answer, "Here, Philip. I am here." (Except that when he said my name, it sounded more like *Hileep*.)

One day again I cried out, "Pea Soup! For mercy's sake, where are you?"

His voice came from the berth above me, startling me with its firmness. "No, Philip. No more Pea Soup. I am not Pea Soup. I am Oji."

"Wh-what?"

"You asked my name. Long time ago. My African name. I am Oji, first son of Ikoro."

I lay back, the tightness in my chest easing, my breathing returning to normal.

Oji, first son of Ikoro.

I rolled his name on my tongue, as if it were a sweet— "Oji . . . Oji"—finally pronouncing, "Why, it's a grand name. Much better than—than Pea Soup. To tell you the truth, I hate pea soup. I prefer potato."

It was a dumb joke, but I laughed anyhow. It was the only laughter I'd heard in days, and it felt and sounded good. After my laughter died away, I lay there. Then: "Why are you so kind to me, Oji?"

I admit, part of me wanted Oji to say that all was forgiven between us, that he was wrong to have ever hated me. Instead, I was disappointed and somewhat hurt when he replied, "My father said to be."

"I—I don't understand. Why would Ikoro want you to be kind to me? Truth was, I wasn't so kind once to your father. I'm ashamed of what I did."

But Oji wouldn't answer me, saying only that one day I would know. One day. But not yet.

That night, while I slept, Ikoro and the five executed slaves watched me. And I dreamed that the scar on my chest glowed a burning red.

I tried to invent remedies to reverse the effects of my blindness: Seawater mixed with mashed yams, heated to a slow boil and afterward some smeared on the eyelids. Saliva mixed with tobacco juice, then drizzled into the eyes. Setting over Uncle's cigar while he smoked, my eyes watering, and him saying, "Well, Mr. Surgeon, I'd say that if this were the remedy, I'd see clear as crystal by now."

The worst attempted remedy, though, was the lime juice. I thought that if lime juice could prevent scurvy, perhaps it'd cleanse the eyes and heal blindness. So I lay upon my bunk, braced myself, and ordered Oji to squirt it in my eyes.

"It will hurt," he said.

"I know."

And it did. A knife stabbed in the eyeball couldn't have hurt any worse. I screeched and thrashed as Oji pried open my eyelids and rinsed my eyes with seawater. An hour later all I'd accomplished was to drench my corn-husk mattress.

"You are brave," pronounced Oji.

"Or daft."

"You are like the man in my village who goes to hunt the lion."

I removed the wet towel from my eyes, staring through the darkness as if I could see Oji sitting beside me on my mattress. "You've hunted lions?"

"I was eight years old when I was taken from my village. Boys do not hunt lions. Only men."

"I hardly think squirting lime juice in my eyes compares with hunting lions."

"You are still brave."

"So you were only a boy when your village was attacked?"

"My village was not attacked."

"But—but you were captured as a prisoner of war. Weren't you?"

"A boy setting traps to catch animals is not war. I was kidnapped."

"Kidnapped? But Uncle told me—" And before I'd even finished my sentence, again I knew Uncle had told me another lie. I tossed the towel against the hull and cursed.

Oji leaned across me, fumbled about, and then placed the towel back over my eyes. "Cursing does not go well with you. Leave the curses to your uncle."

Later that day, Oji and I stood at the bow, where the spray misted over the ship, tormented by the never-ending cries issuing from the hold.

"I was happy that day," Oji told me, speaking in his own language, for the dialect I'd been learning was his native tongue, and he was now my teacher. "Come moonrise, my village planned to have a feast and dance. All day the drums beat. I was almost finished checking and setting my traps when arms grabbed me and a bag fell over my head and the sun disappeared from the sky."

"What happened?"

"I kicked and screamed and cursed, but no one from my village heard me."

"Because of the drums?"

"Yes. I was chained with many others and made to walk for three full moons until I reached the river's shore. I never saw my village or my family again."

"Until you found Ikoro."

"Yes."

I wondered what it would've been like to have been stolen from one's family, from everything familiar. Even worse, I imagined, than having one's parents die at an early age and going to live in the workhouse under the guardianship of Master Crump.

Oji's voice tightened. "Every day I think about my village. I remember my father's vast yam fields, and how the smoke from the cooking fires smelled, and how sometimes it rained so hard you could not tell sky from ground. I remember the stories my mother used to tell—about the tiger and the monkey, about how the tortoise got his shell and how the pigeon learned to fly." Oji sighed. "Even today my mother watches the horizon, waiting for my return. She will watch every day until she is buried and cannot see through the dirt."

A thought came to me. "Then you were chained in the hold as well . . . as they are."

"For many days and nights. I thought they were going to eat us." He paused. "Today, when I hear my African brothers and sisters cry in the belly of the ship and I can do nothing to help them, my heart is full of holes."

I picked at a bump on the rail, picked and picked, as a heavy shame settled on me, each desperate cry from below searing my heart as with a brand. I could never know what it must be like. To have one's very self stolen away and then to be treated worse than an animal. *Yes, a heart full of holes.* "I'm sorry, Oji."

"Why?"

"I—I'm sorry for taking you again on this voyage. I'm sorry for locking you up again. I'm sorry for everything."

"You are wrong. You think it was your decision. But it was my personal god, my *chi*, who made it happen. For I was able to see my father again. One last time. And to hear that my grandparents, my mother, my brothers and sisters, are all well. Someday I will return to them."

I imagined Oji returning to his village, and the thought eased my shame. I said in English, "I've a family too. Well, they're not my *blood* family, but they love me like a son. They're waiting for me to come home. Like you, I'll return to them someday."

"Then I wish you success in your journey."

I paused, not certain how to say next what I'd been thinking except just to come out and say it. It was something that I'd been pondering for some time. "Oji, you're not my slave any longer. I release you. You're free now."

To my surprise, Oji laughed, but it was a laugh without humor. "Even you, Philip, cannot release what was never yours to begin with."

And he left me then, silently. He left me alone by the rail, left me groping in the spaces about me, calling "Oji? Oji?" and finding nothing except the thick of darkness.

We estimated that we'd been sailing blind for three weeks now.

God only knew where we'd drifted, or what the filthy state of our vessel was. Our water had turned nasty, tasting like bog water.

On one particular day (I knew it to be daytime, for the sun was hot on my face, hurting my sensitive eyes), I was lying near the bow. Oji was beside me, and our conversation had faded to nothing. Waves slapped heavily against the hull. My tongue was thick, my mouth pasty, for we were allowed only a quarter cup of water per day. As I lay there, I imagined drinking a cold glass of water straight from the workhouse well. Glass after glorious glass. Droplets of water glistening on the outside of the glass, sliding down.

Then from over the sea came an odd sound. At first I didn't notice it. But as the sound grew closer, I stopped dreaming and listened. The creak of wood, the snap of canvas, the slap of water against the bow . . . coming closer, closer.

I sat up, my pulse quickening. "Do you hear that, Oji?"

"Yes. They are coming."

CHAPTER
19

$\mathcal{I}$ jumped up and screeched, my voice cracking. "Sail ho! A ship's approaching! Off—off the port bow!"

In just moments a mass of sweating, stinking bodies jostled and pushed into position beside me.

And then we were silent, listening.

There it was.

The unmistakable sound of another ship at sea.

Closer, much closer.

Joy burst from my heart as a simultaneous cry erupted from every throat. And in that instant our cry was answered from across the water.

They've seen us!

A part of me wondered whether perhaps this was a warship come to capture us, but I was beyond caring.

We dissolved into a frenzy of sobbing. Someone grabbed and hugged me. Then someone else. I was jumping up and down.

"Praise God!"

"They see us!"

"We're saved!"

Then Uncle was hollering through his speaking trumpet. "Ship ahoy! Ahoy! What ship?"

"The *San León* of Spain. I am its captain."

We're saved, I thought. *And praise be to the saints, it's not a warship.*

"Where from?" asked Uncle.

"From Old Calabar, in the Bight of Biafra."

"Then you're slavers?"

"Aye. We have a full cargo."

"As do we!" replied Uncle. "Please, then, I implore you, as one slaver to another—"

But before Uncle could say more, the captain of the *San León* cried, "Help us, for God's sake! Before it is too late! Before we sail past one another and all is lost!"

There was a slight hesitation in Uncle's voice. "We want help ourselves. We—"

"Please, please help us! We are dying of hunger and thirst. Send us some provisions and a few hands to work the ship, and name your own terms."

"We can give you food," said Uncle, "but we're in want of hands. Come aboard our ship and we'll exchange provisions for men."

"Gold! Gold!" replied the captain of the *San León*. "We will pay you in gold, a thousand times what the food and hands are worth, but we cannot send any men. We have slaves on board; they have infected us with ophthalmia, and we are all stone-blind."

At this announcement, a silence fell among us. A silence pure and deep as death. It was broken by a fit of laughter, and then all of us were laughing, an awful hysteria like that of a man marching to the gallows, knowing he no longer had to settle his debts. My sides hurt from laughing. Tears streamed down my face. I could scarcely catch my breath, but when I did, when our horrible laughter subsided, we could hear, by the sound of the curses that the Spaniards shouted at us, that the *San León* had drifted away.

That night, a storm blew in.

The wind howled. The *Formidable* shrieked as if it were alive. Every timber groaned. Masts creaked. I cowered in my bunk, hearing things rip apart, the sails bursting their bonds with a sound like musketry, imagining the unmanned wheel spinning wildly from side to side, the waves dashing across the decks, sweeping away everything not tied down.

"The gods are angry," said Oji. "We will die in this great lake of water."

I feared the ship would burst apart and water would rush into my cabin, and that I'd sink into the deep and die in the darkness, not even knowing where I was or what day it was. I thought of Mr. and Mrs. Gallagher. Of their waiting year after year, finally realizing that their little English boy was never coming home, then being laid in their graves, never knowing how much their foster son truly loved them.

Home, I thought, and for the thousandth time wished I were there.

Again and again the bow of the *Formidable* rose as the vessel climbed a monstrous wave; I tumbled in a heap at the foot of my bunk. When the *Formidable* reached the crest of the wave, there was a moment of hanging, indecision, almost—and then down she plummeted into the trough between this wave and the next one as I slid to the other end of my bunk, banging my head and crunching my neck. Screams of terror echoed throughout the ship.

And mixed with those screams, I heard a cry.

A baby's cry.

A newborn.

Just one cry, then nothing.

And as I crashed from one end of my bunk to the other, waves hammering the bows like thunder, I hoped I'd imagined it. I knew what happened to babies born aboard the *Formidable.*

Moments later, to my anguish, I heard the cry again. It was cut off quickly, as if a hand had been placed over its mouth. It would've been easier for me to cover my ears, to pretend that the cry had been lost in the storm's rage. But I couldn't. "Oji, did you hear that?"

"Yes."

"We must find it before my uncle does."

"Yes, and we must hide it. Quickly."

The women's hold reeked of vomit.

We were surrounded by shrieks of terror, sobbing, children crying for their fathers and mothers in their African tongues.

And because they weren't chained like the men, many women and children were lying in the aisles. Tossed from side to side, I lurched down the passage, stumbling over and between them, my gorge rising. Oji followed, his hand gripping my upper arm with a strength of which Ikoro would have been proud.

Then Oji asked in a loud voice where the baby and its mother were. As he spoke, it seemed to me that the shrieking abated. No doubt the women were surprised to hear the voice of a male, and not just a male, but a native African. He told them to trust him, not to worry. That we were there to help them.

Someone called out to Oji—a woman's voice, speaking in a dialect I didn't completely understand, though I recognized a few of the words.

"This way," Oji said to me, and he pulled me in the opposite direction, until I was completely disoriented. All the while, Oji conversed with the woman and her voice grew closer.

And then a baby was in my arms. A scrawny, bony baby.

"The mother wants to know where you are taking them."

"Them?" Until that moment, it'd not occurred to me that I'd need to take the mother too.

But Oji voiced what I should've known: "A baby belongs with its mother. It will die without milk."

The baby moved. Let out a mewling sound. I shielded it as the *Formidable* pitched, tossing me into the tiers and bruising my shoulder. Fresh screams pounded my ears.

"The mother says one of the girls has broken her leg. And a little boy his wrist."

"The infirmary," I replied, surprised at the steadiness in my voice. "No one goes in there anymore. Can you carry the girl with the broken leg, and can the boy and the mother follow?"

Again Oji spoke to the women, then said to me, "Yes. Let us go."

It was a long way to the infirmary. Three times the baby cried and I had to clamp a hand over its mouth. Twice we lost our way. Once we bumped into a fellow whose voice I recognized as Roach's, but he merely carried on about how we were all going to die miserably, that he didn't know how to swim and that his father and his brother had both died at sea. After that burst of wretchedness, Roach pushed past us, leaving us alone in the corridor.

In the infirmary I settled the mother and baby as best I could considering that we were being tossed about like rag dolls. The boy refused to lie down, instead clutching the waist of my trousers with his good hand. The girl whimpered as I probed her broken leg. I spoke to her in the only African language I knew, telling her it'd be all right, that I'd take care of her. That I was a surgeon. That it'd hurt only for a moment and then all would be well. Oji interpreted for me when I faltered.

I pulled hard on her leg, feeling the bones move back into alignment, feeling her squirm. Hearing her pant as she stifled her cries.

Dear Lord, how it must hurt!

Next to me, the boy began to cry softly, his arm now about my waist, his hand clutching my shirt. And in the midst of the storm, like a dam trembling under the pressure of the water until it finally rips asunder, my heart tore open and I was flooded with compassion, not just for the girl, but for all of them. For the mother, the newborn, the boy with the broken wrist. For Oji, and for every African aboard—all of whom had names, families, villages, where loved ones watched the horizon, awaiting their return.

During the three days the storm lasted, Oji and I brought all the injured to the infirmary—men, women, and children. It was easy to do, in a manner of speaking, for there were no guards at the holds and, as surgeon, I'd a skeleton key that unlocked any shackle. Together Oji and I set and splinted broken limbs, clumsily stitched gashes, and bound wounds.

Although I *was* the surgeon and it was rightfully in my capacity to act as such, I'd decided not to tell anyone that I was filling the infirmary with injured Africans. I'd a dread of what would happen to slaves who broke their limbs—rather like horses, I supposed, they'd be quickly dispatched. For the slaves' part, like the little girl, they stifled their screams, Oji having warned them to be silent.

Oji and I raided the food stores and the spirit-casks as well, all unguarded during the storm. Once, while I was loaded with an armful of yams, a wave dashed me off my feet. Horrified, I smashed into the bulwarks in a cascade of seawater and yams. Surely another wave would've washed me overboard, but Oji's strong hand grasped my ankle. I clung to him, choking, fighting the waves, until we made it safely back into the storage locker. There, both of us sopping wet, Oji filled my arms with more yams.

"Oji, listen." I spoke above the storm's clamor. "There's something I've been meaning to ask you. Why, during the rebellion, did you spare my life? Why did you protect me from harm instead of killing me? I know you broke my nose, and that hurt like the dickens, but you could've killed me and you didn't."

Oji continued to pile yams into my arms. Finally he said, "My father ordered me not to kill you."

"Ikoro ordered you not to kill me?" I remembered Ikoro turning his back on his opportunity to kill me, instead killing Mackerel. "But why—"

"He believed you had a powerful god, a powerful *chi*, and that you would do great things in your life because of your *chi*."

"Then—then you only spared my life because your father said so?"

"On that day, I wanted you to die. I thirsted for your blood. And in my homeland we keep the heads of our enemies as trophies. I wanted your blood *and* your head."

162

I was shocked into silence.

He continued. "But my father insisted. We were to kill all the white men except you."

A lump grew in my throat, and my eyes burned. "Then why are you standing here talking to me if you hate me so much, Oji?" My voice sounded as hurt as I felt. "Why do you share my quarters, and why did you give me water when I was thirsty? And why did you just now save me from being washed overboard? You should've just let me go."

Water swirled about my ankles, cold and biting. My teeth began to chatter. The door to the storage locker slammed shut, then opened, then slammed shut again with the rocking of the ship.

"Are you really so blind?" said Oji, his voice as calm as if he were talking of yam soup. "Does a man beg for the life of another if he has hatred in his heart? When you begged for my father's life, I knew then that you were not like the others."

"That's not saying much. They're murderers, the lot of them. And if they're not murderers, it's only because they've not had the chance yet." The door flew open again, and the wind roared through the shelter. I braced my legs against one of the shelves, still hurt that Oji had admitted to hating me for so long.

"It was only after they killed my father that I understood. My *chi*, my personal god, must have sent you to me as an exchange for my father. The more I have noticed your actions toward others, the more I have understood that my father was right. You have a powerful *chi*."

I staggered under the weight of so many yams. "Well, my *chi* is getting tired and hungry, and I can't carry another yam. Please, let's go." But as I turned, Oji caught my arm.

"Do not be angry. I no longer hate you."

"Well, that's some comfort," I said, and though I'd meant it sarcastically, I realized that this was indeed a comfort. That what Oji thought of me was actually quite important.

The six executed slaves gathered round my berth and watched me, looking inside my dream. And in my dream, as in all my dreams, I could see.

The *Formidable,* her sails as tattered as a battle flag, her hull thickened with barnacles, had arrived on the coast and dropped anchor. The air smelled of jungle—rich, damp, alive. Thousands stood along the shore, waiting. Boatloads of slaves from the *Formidable* were rowing ashore. As each boat scraped the sand, the occupants sprang out and into the crowd, leaving their chains behind.

They flung themselves into the arms of those who'd been waiting. There were exclamations of joy, tears, laughter. Fathers were reunited with sons. Daughters with mothers. Brothers with sisters.

Oji cradling the baby.

And me, standing at the helm alongside the Gallaghers, smiling.

Then, like a strike of lightning on a sunny day, cruel and unexpected, my uncle cried, "Fire!" and the cannon blasted. The crowd disintegrated like matchsticks.

I screamed—a real scream, shrill and loud. I sat up in my berth, my blood roaring with the pounding of my heart.

"Philip?" It was Oji.

He killed them! He killed them all!

Then Oji was beside me. "Philip? Are you ill?"

I was trembling, panting, my mind's eye still seeing the bodies—of men, women, children. Everyone dead.

Oji pressed his hand against my forehead. "Philip, if you die, we all die."

My corn-husk mattress crunched as I sank back. Water slapped gently against the hull. Timbers creaked. And in the women's hold, someone was singing:

"My apple tree grow, Nda-a,
"Grow, grow, grow, Nda-a,
"Grow for the fatherless, Nda-a,
"Grow for the motherless, Nda-a . . ."

I said, "The storm has stopped."

"Yes. We have life."

And as I lay there listening to the woman sing, my breathing still ragged, I remembered what Oji had said. "What did you mean when you said that if I die, everyone dies?"

For the longest time, he didn't answer. He didn't move, nor could I hear him breathe. If I'd not known he was there, I'd have thought I was alone. Finally he whispered, "When you asked me why my father and I spared your life, I did not tell you everything."

I said nothing, waiting for Oji to continue.

"He had a vision that you would be the one to lead us back to Africa. He said that because of your knowledge of how the great hut sails on the water, you would use this knowledge to help us."

I was stunned.

Lead them back to Africa? Me?

If he'd told me this even a short time ago, I'd have laughed. But now I thought of the six slaves who always visited my sleep; of my increasing shame; of my dream of families reuniting while the scent of jungle lingered in the night. . . . "Oji, this vision of your father's . . . I'm just a boy, and a blind boy at that."

"The gods do not lie."

"But—but I don't *believe* in your gods."

"But you believe in yours."

I said nothing.

"And your *chi*, your god, is powerful."

The song from the women's hold faded into a silence filled only with the sounds of the ship. "She was singing a song of my childhood," whispered Oji. "Philip, I *will* return to Africa again. I *will* be free. We will all be free. It is our right."

In the dark I groped for his hand and clasped it. It was warm and dry. "Yes, it *is* your right. Your right as human beings." My voice tightened. "And I pray that someday you will all return to your homeland."

I was surprised by the ferocity with which Oji now clutched my hand. "Take us there, Philip."

"But—but I don't know how."

"The gods will show the way. Your *chi* will lead you. Take us there. *Please,* I beg you. *Bikō.* In the name of every African aboard."

I swallowed, my throat dry as parched earth, my heart hammering as if I stood at a great precipice and had been asked to leap off. But something larger than me was at work. As if my whole life had led me to this moment, to hold the hand of Oji, to prompt me to say, with all sincerity, "If I weren't blind, and if it were in my power, I'd take you there. All of you."

Then an odd thing happened. As soon as I had uttered them, my words went beyond me, no longer belonging to me alone. They echoed through my cabin, piercing timbers, whispering through the deepest shadows and holds of the *Formidable,* penetrating my being, written upon my heart with the finger of every black man, woman, and child aboard.

And in that moment it was as if Oji and I were no longer alone—as if six male slaves stood in the cabin with us, filling the space with their presence.

Goose bumps danced up my arms like wind rippling across the water's surface. I bowed my head, thinking, *Is it really possible? Can such a thing be done?*

I don't know how much time elapsed before I awoke again—two hours? three?—but I sat up straight, the ship still gripped in the silence that followed the storm.

Something was different.

I crawled out of my bunk and felt for Oji's to determine if he was still there.

He wasn't.

That's when I noticed something that caused my heart to skip like a rock tossed across the surface of a pond.

In the direction of the porthole, I saw a hazy light. I blinked. Thinking it'd disappear. That it was another dream. A cruel dream. But no, it was there. A light. Grayish, like the pre-light of dawn.

My heart began to thump wildly, a bird trapped in my chest. As if Uncle had just screamed "Fire!"

I hauled on my trousers and hastened into the passageway, up the dim outline of the companionway, and out onto the deck. I gasped. About me I saw rigging hanging like vines in a jungle, sails torn and shredded, yards askew, everything damp and puddled.

And there, in the east, hues of purple light brushed the predawn sky.

CHAPTER 20

I basked in the sights all morning and afternoon.

The sun. The freckles on the backs of my hands. The infant suckling at the breast of his young mother. The towering masts. Oji. A beetle crawling across the deck. All of it amazed me, as if I were seeing everything for the first time.

Yet when in the late afternoon I joined the crew as we gathered about Uncle on the quarterdeck, I was equally appalled by the desperation and ugliness that now surrounded me.

Uncle's left eyeball was rotting out of his head.

His clothes hung slack on his frame. His cheeks were sunken, his whiskers unkempt; his usual healthy complexion had been replaced by a gray pallor. "We collected several casks of rainwater before the storm became too violent," he was saying. "If we ration them carefully, our supply will last another few weeks. After that, well . . ." His voice trailed away.

The sky was clear, the air stiflingly hot. Steam curled up from the deck. The crew was a filthy and haggard lot, their clothing sweat-stained and damp. Their eyeballs covered with a cloudy film, they stared blindly at nothing. Billy the Vermin plucked something from inside his nose and ate it.

Uncle continued. "Men, we've been dealt a harsh blow, I judge. But God wouldn't have preserved us had he not intended for us to accomplish the task entrusted to us from the beginning. We've been divinely commissioned." His voice rose, as if he were delivering a fiery sermon. "And just as Paul the Apostle obeyed the laws of the Lord by returning the runaway slave Onesimus to his master, we too must obey. And for our deliverance and continued safety, I give praise to the Almighty, who governs the heavens and the seas. Could I see to read a prayer of thanksgiving, I'd do so."

"Amen," murmured several of the men.

I looked away, sickened. My uncle's capacity to twist words— to procure the blessing of everyone, even God Almighty, for his purely evil purposes—amazed me.

How wrong you are, Uncle.

"But what can we do?" asked the gunner. "Our sails have been torn to shreds and we're sailing as blind as we ever were."

"Again we must trust to Providence to deliver us," replied Uncle. "You're born sailors. Nimble as cats in trees, you are. And while the wind is mild and the weather friendly, we'll bend new sails to the yards."

"*Blind?*" someone asked incredulously. "You expect us to climb up there *blind*? Even cats can see!"

"Trust God to preserve you. Mr. McGuire will oversee."

Now was my time. My moment of performance, a performance that Oji and I had planned carefully. "Uncle!" I cried.

He peered sightlessly in my direction. "Philip? Is that you?"

"Aye, Uncle. I believe that—" I gasped, and paused for effect. "Yes, yes indeed, it's true! I believe I'm recovering my sight!"

Everyone gasped.

Surprise splashed across my uncle's face, as if he'd been dashed with a bucket of water.

I continued my charade. "Just now I saw a glimmer of light, and even as I speak it grows stronger. Yes, I'm certain of it now. The light grows stronger and clearer!"

"Is it—is it true?" Uncle pushed through the crowd, arms groping, until I reached out and took hold of his sleeve, pulling him in front of me.

"See, Uncle? I saw you coming toward me. I can see. *I can see!* You're wearing a white shirt with gray trousers, and you've forgotten your hat."

Uncle's face crumpled. He sobbed and embraced me. I endured the damp smelliness of his embrace, surprised to realize that a part of me still loved my uncle. Finally he pulled away, holding me by the shoulders as if to inspect me with his sightless, rotting eyes. "You'll guide us," he pronounced, his voice clogged with emotion. "Praise God that I took care of you for all those years so you could succor me in my hour of greatest need. Praise God that I'd the foresight to teach you navigation. You'll guide us home. You'll sing out the compass readings. I'll tell you how we must trim the sails, and you'll guide us through the rigging. You'll restore the well-being of the ship and of the stock."

"Aye," I replied. "You can trust me to do what's right and good."

"That's my Philip," said Uncle.

And then the crew surrounded me, as if they'd never said a disrespectful word or played a mean trick on me—little Philip Arthur Higgins, surgeon aboard the *Formidable*. They clapped me on the back, congratulated me, and called me a true Son o' Neptune while tears streamed from their sightless eyes.

Yes, go ahead and cry, I thought. *For Oji and me and every African soul aboard—we're headed to Africa, and you're taking us there.*

"So? Where are we?" It was the next day, and Uncle drummed his fingers on the rail, waiting for me to finish my navigational reading. Uncle didn't know it, but I'd already taken a reading the day before. This day was overcast, making a reading impossible, but Uncle, with his rotting eye, didn't guess the truth, for it simply didn't occur to him that I would deliberately deceive him.

"Halfway between Freetown and Barbuda, I'd say" was my false response.

Actually, we were dangerously close to the coast of South America, off the eastern tip of Brazil. My spirits plummeted the first time I took a reading, knowing that in another day or so, had we kept upon our same course of directionless meandering, we'd have washed ashore.

I couldn't let that happen.

Not now.

Trying to stay calm, though my palms sweated and my stomach was clenched, I hastened the bending of new sails to the yards with my crew of blind men, ordering the new course as soon as the mainsail was set. "Bearing west-nor'west," I told them, ordering the wheel turned and the yard adjusted so that the compass actually read east-northeast.

I planned to head for the nearest portion of the African coast instead of the river Bonny. If all went well, we'd make landfall in a bit over a month's time. To head for Brazil or the Caribbean was certain death for the slaves aboard, as Uncle would jettison them to collect his insurance money. To head for Africa was life, freedom—God willing.

Truth was, our chance of returning to Africa was slim as a reed, as was the chance of my ever seeing the Gallaghers again. But I now knew I could never look them in the face, call them Mother and Father, love them as dearly as they deserved, were I not to make every effort to bring the Africans home to their own villages and families first. Oddly enough, upon our decision to return to Africa, I felt closer to the Gallaghers than ever before, as if somehow my words, my vow, had traveled across the waters and entered the chemist's shop on the Rue du Dauphine in the French Quarter, where they heard it and approved.

"Are you certain your bearing is correct?" Uncle asked me.

"Trust me. The nor'east trades will compensate for our northerly heading."

He smiled then, gold teeth flashing, and I briefly glimpsed the hale and hearty chap he used to be. "Like I've always told you, Philip, my lad, you're fashioned from the same mold. A chip of the same block."

"Aye, sir."

Uncle believed we were headed west-northwest, and that soon the northeast trades would blow from our starboard. In actuality, we were headed east-northeast, and the southeast trade winds would soon blow from our starboard. A blind man wouldn't know the difference. Only the rising sun on Uncle's face would tell him of my deception. I prayed to God hourly, every second, to keep the sky clouded, my uncle deluded, my shipmates blinded, and to speed us on our way. If any of the crew gained their sight before my plans could be carried to fruition, all would be lost.

Oji and I had discussed the merits of an outright rebellion—how easy it'd be for the now 193 remaining male slaves to overcome and imprison 33 blind sailors. But we needed the sailors, blind as they were. We needed them to operate the sails and rigging, for though I was their eyes and could direct them, I knew little about seamanship and would've been helpless without their knowledge and without Uncle beside me, telling me what to do next.

"But once we arrive home, I will have your uncle's head," said Oji, his voice hard and angry. "It is my right."

I could only imagine the hatred smoldering in Oji's heart for my uncle, the killer of his father. "Oji, please . . ."

"I will have *all* their heads." And he stumbled away, his back straight, looking more like Ikoro every day.

Because of the return of my sight, it was no longer necessary for me to conduct my duties as surgeon in secret. Everyone knew that I had patients in the infirmary, but as I was the only one with sight, they couldn't know that over a dozen slaves were recovering from broken limbs, nor could they know that one of my patients was an infant.

Oji became my assistant. He stirred the medicines, dosed the patients, bathed them—all under my supervision. He spent much time soothing the infant, taking it gently from its mother when she slept and holding it as if he were the proud father. "His name is Onwuha. It means 'Death, may you let this child live.' "

It was a mercy that baby Onwuha rarely cried, only making quiet, mewling sounds upon occasion. As a precaution, we'd loosened some of the boards beneath the mother's bunk and lined the empty space with soft cloth. It was here we'd hide him should it become necessary.

But I'd much more on my mind than the well-being of a single baby. The well-being of every person aboard the *Formidable* was still my responsibility.

Of grave concern was the declining state of our food stores.

Already we'd been at sea for approximately eleven weeks, yet we'd anticipated a homeward voyage of no more than nine weeks (although we'd taken extra provisions, as well-seasoned sailors do). Again I feared, judging from Uncle's previous conversation with McGuire, that Uncle would jettison the cargo, believing food was wasted upon blind, and therefore useless, slaves. I decided, then, to use Uncle's greed to our advantage.

"Uncle!" I said brightly one evening, rushing inside his cabin as if I'd wonderful, exciting news.

Uncle sat up in bed, rumpled and dazed, as if he couldn't remember where he was.

"I was down in the hold just now, and I've made the most jolly discovery!"

"What? What?" cried Uncle.

"Most of the slaves have recovered their sight!" In actuality, the number was only three.

Uncle rose from his bed. He stumbled to his desk and laid hold of his Book of Common Prayer. He crossed himself. His shoulders heaved. "Praise be to the Almighty," he whispered. "This cargo may yet be saved."

Uncle's relief was a mixed blessing. Though he wouldn't likely jettison any of the slaves now, believing that in just a couple of weeks he'd be a wealthy man, his "godly" mission accomplished, we were still desperately short on food. A half a yam a day and a meager handful of rice and beans were all that was allowed each slave; less was allotted for children. I fired up the galley once a day for Cookie, helping him until the rice and beans were cooked through, the yams roasted.

The provisions for the crew were equally reduced, and they complained bitterly of hunger. Indeed, it looked impossible that their emaciated forms could climb the shrouds, and I feared that there would come a day when they'd lack the strength or the will to do so.

I ate no more than anyone else. My stomach shriveled with pain. My limbs wobbled with weakness, and if I moved too smartly my sight dimmed and my knees buckled. Memories of the workhouse and cold, watery gruel flooded back, and I realized I'd forsaken my vow to never be hungry again. I hated hunger.

God, when will this be over? I prayed constantly. *I'm tired and hungry. And what happens when we reach the coast of Africa? What then? Release the captives into the jungles to shift for themselves?* I'd no answers, only prayers.

I was plagued too by the terrible fear that one of the crew would recover his sight, as I had.

One glance at the compass would reveal the truth of my deception.

One glance at the slaves in the hold would reveal the truth of their condition.

It was a fear that seeped into my dreams like poison, startling me awake, making my heart pound. Sweating, I beseeched God to help me again and again, in prayers that seemed to go no farther than the walls of my cabin.

CHAPTER 21

$\mathcal{O}$ne and a half weeks into our voyage toward the African continent, we sprang a leak.

Cookie had been sent down to the lower hold with Billy to fetch yams. What Cookie told us when he returned shocked us all. "There's seawater in the hold. Lots of it. Up to my waist. Ruined much of the food, it has."

You'd have thought Cookie had just thrown a shovelful of dirt upon each of our caskets. Roach wailed, saying he didn't want to drown; he'd a fear of drowning. Billy told him how your life flashes before your eyes and how when you sink for the third time, you're a goner. Uncle said nothing, just stared off with his one clouded eye, as if he could see beyond the horizon. McGuire ordered the men to the pumps.

In the lower hold I drew a chalk line at the water level. After a day of pumping, I returned to see if the chalk line was above or below the water level. If above, we might live. If below, unless the leak was mended and despite all our pumping, the *Formidable* would slowly fill with water until she became too heavy, and would sink.

I crawled out of the companionway onto the deck, my body trembling with fatigue and my chest heaving with even this simple exertion. The crew was waiting to hear what I'd found. Whether or not I was to give them a death sentence.

"The line is above the water level," I said.

They sighed as if with one body and went back to the pumps, day and night. Some of the healthier male slaves were brought out of the upper hold to aid with the pumping.

Because of the spoilage caused by the leak, food rations were cut yet again.

Working the pumps on our meager diet sapped a man's energy, as if he'd run a mile at full tilt. I took my turn but could scarcely work the pumps. I panted like a cart horse on a July day, my muscles no stronger than string. Roach pushed me aside and took my place, saying that little Philip the surgeon shouldn't man the pumps. That I was too important, and very busy.

"Thanks," I said, gasping.

"Ah, think nothing of it. Just save your strength for getting us home again. Got three kids, you know. And another one on the way. Got to get home."

"Oh, uh—well, congratulations are probably in order, then." And I ambled off, glad Roach was blind to my guilty countenance.

Owing to the diet and the relentless exercise at the pumps,

twelve of the crew collapsed, stricken with fevers and flux. I confined them to their hammocks. Their illness increased the workload for those who remained.

And although my uncle believed we were each day sailing farther north from the equator, we were, in fact, soon to approach it again from the south. Because the skies were overcast, I didn't know our precise position; only that if I kept true to our heading, we'd indeed run into Africa, for the continent was impossible to miss. Where exactly we'd land I couldn't know.

"To a fine windy day!" my uncle said one evening, raising his wine goblet, his hand shaking like an old man's.

"To a fine windy day," I echoed, touching my goblet to his.

We both drank, him gulping half the contents, me a sip only. We sat at the captain's table. Before us lay our wooden platters; upon each were two hard biscuits and a lemon-sized lump of stewed salt pork, tough as shoe leather.

"Probably made near two hundred nautical miles in the past day or so," Uncle said cheerily. "At this rate, we should arrive in Barbuda in, oh, say, a few days, I should think." He devoured his biscuit. Among the crumbs, a weevil dropped from my uncle's mouth to his beard. Its white body wiggled blindly for a few seconds before disappearing into the hair.

"Aye. In just a few days, God willing." The truth of the matter was, we were still two weeks from land, according to my best approximations. I gnawed off a hunk of pork and exercised my jaw. I planned to tell Uncle that I'd made a slight error in my calculations, and that we'd sailed unknowingly past Barbuda and would therefore head for the next-closest island. This would buy me another few days, at most.

I talked around my pork, not wanting to speak of navigation. "First thing I'm going to do when I arrive in port is take a bath. It's the simple things in life one misses most when one's at sea, at least that's my experience. As if—as if I've had much experience! Ha!" I laughed, hoping I sounded natural, afterward panting for breath. "Mrs. Gallagher used to sprinkle rosemary and thyme in my bathwater. Mind you, I smelled like a herb-roasted chicken, but she believed it a remedy for whatever ailed the skin."

I jabbered on, sounding more and more like a fool in my own ears. A fool and a liar.

"I wonder what shall happen to me," Uncle murmured of a sudden.

I stopped mid-sentence. "Uncle?"

"Think on it. I've known nothing but the sea. I can hardly remember a time when I didn't feel the ship rock beneath me, or breathe the salt air. What will happen to me now—now that I'm blind?"

"But surely your sight will return, as did mine. In your right eye anyhow."

Uncle shook his head. "No. It's permanent. I know it just as I know the feel of wind upon my face."

I said nothing, devouring my two biscuits as quickly as Uncle had his, trying not to think of the weevils that now crawled about in my stomach.

Uncle looked at me then. Or at least his right eyeball turned in my direction. The other one dangled out of its socket, attached by a few shriveled and blackened cords. "You'll tend an old, useless uncle, won't you, Philip, lad? By the deuce, you're all I have. My only relation. I've money enough to keep us both quite well."

"Of course," I lied, feeling as guilty as if I'd stabbed him. What would happen to him I didn't know. If Oji had his way, he'd eat Uncle's brains and use his skull for a drinking vessel. "Uncle, now that we're just a few days from land, perhaps we could allow the slaves some exercise—"

His face hardened. "No."

"But—"

"We've discussed this before. You're the only one with sight. Are you going to single-handedly prevent a rebellion if these devils have a mind to act against us? It's especially made dangerous when they can see and we can't."

"Then at least allow the women and children to take the air and move round."

He groped about the table. "Where's that bottle?"

"Here, let me pour you some more." I handed him his goblet and prompted him: "Well?"

He drank deeply, belching and wiping his mouth on his sleeve. "All right. But they're to be chained while on deck." He straightened up in his chair, as if this moment of magnanimity had restored him to his former person. "You'll remove my left eye. It's become quite bothersome; I've snagged it a couple of times. And I must look decently presentable upon our arrival in port. You'll do it tonight. And you'll sew me an eye patch."

A few moments later, when I opened the cabin door intending to fetch my medical instruments, I saw Billy the Vermin feeling his way down the corridor, moving away from me. And just as Uncle knew he'd never recover his sight, I knew Billy had been on the other side of the cabin door, listening. What that meant I didn't know, other than that Billy was a snoop and not to be trusted any more than one trusts a maggot with meat.

The women and children were a sorry-looking lot. Eyes blind, and with every bone jutting from their skin, they felt their way to the stern of the vessel, where I oversaw the shackling. It seemed ridiculous to require an eight-year-old child or a twig-thin middle-aged woman to wear a shackle, but my uncle would brook no argument.

Billy struck up a tune on his fiddle. The poor blacks shuffled about, clutching one another for support. Heart aching to see them so afflicted, I shouted in their language that when the moon reached its next fullness, they'd arrive at the shores of their homeland again. That on that day, God willing, they'd be free.

At this announcement, one of the women began to sing. Others joined her, their voices weak at first, then growing stronger until the song filled the ship. From below, the enslaved men's voices began to sing too. It was a melancholy song, rhythmic, yet I sensed within it strains of hope. And as their voices swelled, Billy's fiddle fell silent.

"What the devil did you tell them?" Uncle asked me, frowning, his arms crossed.

"That their circumstances would soon change."

He sighed. "God willing. I'm heartily sick of this."

"Aye. Me too."

Four days later, when I told Uncle that I'd made an error in my calculations and we'd missed the island of Barbuda, he laid his head upon the table in his cabin and wept.

Everything and everyone demanded my attention. The ship's heading. The management of the sails and rigging. Firing up the galley. Appeasing my uncle. Continuing the deception. Seeing to the rotting and diminishing supply of food and water. Caring for the ill—the slaves in the infirmary, and the crew wherever else they lay, in their hammocks or strewn about on the upper deck.

Try as I might, even with Oji's constant help, the situation decayed. To my dismay, five of the crew and sixteen slaves died overnight of the bloody flux. Seven more of the crew contracted the ailment, including McGuire, bringing the total ill to fourteen, leaving only fifteen of the crew to work the pumps and man the ship. That number diminished yet again when Cookie fell in a faint as he stood over his cauldrons, whacking his head on his way to the deck. He died the next day. The sailor Uncle chose to replace him burned the rice and beans. Uncle cane-whipped him. The odor of scorched food wormed through the ship's timbers. I smelled it night and day.

And as at the cotton mill when I was but a wee lad, exhaustion plagued me and I was tormented by a high fever that left me sweating and gasping. In one of my rare moments of rest, I leaned against the bulwarks next to one of the long guns. My body trembled with chills. My tongue was thick, my lips cracked and bleeding.

What've I done? I thought miserably. *We were but one day from land, and I turned about and headed back across the ocean.*

And then, mercifully, Mrs. Gallagher was there, dabbing my forehead with a cool, damp cloth, afterward giving me a spoonful of medicine and squeezing my hand while I choked the liquid down.

"There, there," she said, her voice sweet as an angel's. "My little English boy. You did what you had to do."

CHAPTER 22

The child stared sightlessly at me before his eyelids fluttered closed. His breathing slowed and his body relaxed.

"The medicine's taken effect," I said, releasing the boy's hand. "Agim will sleep well now, I should think. And his wrist is healing cleanly."

"The gods be praised," said Oji. He sponged the frail black body with seawater, attempting to cool the fire raging in the child. "Fight, little Agim. You are a warrior."

Each day, following the morning mess, I visited the infirmary. I treated the patients and left instructions for Oji. The incidence of fevers and flux was increasing, and two or three patients lay in each pallet, strewn across the floor in various stages of misery, eyes clouded and shrunken in their sockets, skin stretched across their skulls as if they were skeletons already.

I was tempted, sorely tempted, to burst into a wretchedness of weeping, to say I was only Philip Arthur Higgins, not God Almighty, and how could I be expected to stem the flow of disease and death? But I clamped my fevered lips shut, ordered my stomach to stop its dreadful demands, rolled up my sleeves, and went to work. If I didn't do it, who would?

I tried every remedy I knew. Blisters, plasters, pills, baths, ointments, and more. I mixed concoctions of pine pitch, yellow wax, mutton tallow, Peruvian bark, and Spanish fly; of bittersweet, winter evergreen, and jalap.

Try as I might, my patients were dying. They slipped away, one by one or by the handful. On this day, after leaving Agim in Oji's care, I moved on to the next patient, a tall man, thin as a hat rack, his bony protrusions festering with the familiar sores that resulted from lying upon a hard surface without relief. Would I ever get used to the sight of suffering? I hoped not. Never would I harden my heart as had Master Crump—and Uncle, who viewed human suffering as one might view a mosquito stuck in honey, with little interest and no sympathy, concerned only that the honey was ruined.

"May you receive health," I said to him in his language.

The man struggled to speak. His mouth bubbled with a bloody froth. "They say—they say you are taking us home. That you have blinded these men so they cannot see their straight path."

Rubbing his sores with a strong decoction of wormwood, I stammered, "Don't talk. Only rest."

"They say you have been sent to us by the gods." And as if he could see, he touched the brand on my chest with a shaky finger. "This is the sign they gave you."

I stopped my treatment, blinking at him.

Whereupon he reached out and took both my hands in his. His hands trembled, hot and moist. He stared at me with milky eyes. His breath smelled like rotted meat. "I am Ikeotuonye. It means 'the strength of one person.'" He cried out a word I didn't know, then said, "I—I give my name to you." After two more raspy breaths, he quivered once and then relaxed, his arms falling, exhaling for the last time.

The infirmary had grown quiet. I closed his eyelids, aware of the rhythmic sloshing of the water on the other side of the hull, the gentle roll of the *Formidable,* my own labored breathing.

I've failed again.

"Ikeotuonye," one of the other men whispered. And it was whispered in such a way that it sounded as if he were sitting in the vastness of Saint Louis Cathedral in New Orleans instead of in a crowded, stench-filled infirmary in the gut of a slave ship.

"Ikeotuonye," others whispered.

Someone lying on the floor touched my ankle. Another my foot.

"Ikeotuonye."

And they surrounded me, those that could. Touching me, chanting my African name.

"Ikeotuonye . . ."

"Ikeotuonye . . ."

I was digging in my medicine chest, searching for antimony, when Uncle threw open the door to the infirmary.

One look at his reddened face, milky eye glaring, was enough to know that something was frightfully amiss. Behind him stood Billy the Vermin, a smug expression playing upon his normally dull features.

Uncle said, "Billy heard the sound of a baby coming from inside this infirmary."

I glanced quickly at Oji, who was sitting cross-legged, holding the infant. Oji looked as if he'd been caught committing murder. His blinded eyes widened. He stiffened. The baby squirmed and opened its mouth to protest. Oji clamped his hand over the child's mouth and whispered in its ear.

"Where is it?" demanded Uncle.

"There's no infant here," I said. My words sounded calm, yet my stomach turned topsy-turvy and my pulse pounded up my neck and into my head. I approached Uncle, praying Oji would quickly place the infant in its hiding spot, praying the infant would settle.

Uncle brushed me aside and began to search the infirmary.

None of the patients made a sound, no doubt frightened by this intrusion. But I wished they'd cry, moan, groan, and weep, to cover any noises little Onwuha might make.

I saw Oji stumble toward the mother's bunk, feeling his way. Meanwhile, Uncle began touching everything that came within his grasp. A pallet with three children, all ill with the flux. A woman dying of a lung disorder. The girl with the broken leg. Uncle seemed not to notice her splint as he stumbled over prostrate bodies, searching, searching for a baby.

"Uncle, please, this isn't necessary." I followed him, urging the people in their native tongue to make noise, my head pounding with the beat of my heart even when the infirmary filled with a symphony of misery.

"But I done heard it, Captain Towne," said Billy, standing inside the door. "Ain't no doubt. My mama had ten babies, and I know what they sound like."

By the time Uncle reached the mother's bunk, Onwuha was safely stowed in his hiding place beneath the planks. Uncle felt the bunk, then the mother, and moved on.

I breathed a sigh of relief, but it wasn't until Uncle finished his search of the entire infirmary that the throbbing in my head began to lessen.

"There's no baby here," Uncle said to Billy. "You heard wrong."

"But, Captain Towne, I heard—"

"Philip wouldn't disobey my instructions." Uncle looked in my direction. His voice hardened. "He knows the consequences. He knows I do not like to be made a fool, don't you, Philip?"

"Yes, Uncle."

"Quite right. You see, Billy? There's no baby here." And with that pronouncement, Uncle left.

Billy stood there, staring into the infirmary as if he could will himself to see the truth.

"Clear off, you worm," I told him. "And don't you ever listen outside my door again or I'll set Pea Soup on you. He *loves* white meat."

Billy cast me a look of hatred.

I blinked and stepped back, alarmed.

The hatred didn't bother me. Indeed no. What did I care if Billy the Vermin hated me? What made me gasp were his eyes.

Billy the Vermin's eyes were looking horribly, horribly healthy. It'd be only a matter of time before he could see.

The wind died.

Where before our beautiful white sails had been filled to bursting with a fine, fresh wind, now they hung slack. Rippling with an occasional breath. Hanging this way, then that, depending upon which way the *Formidable* was listing. The slackened ropes dangled, useless.

All was still.

"I don't like it," said Uncle. "Never happened to me before in this part of the world. Are you certain you're on the correct heading?"

"Quite certain."

"You've made mistakes before."

"Yes, I know. But never again."

The leak continued to require pumping. So many crew became ill with the bloody flux that it was necessary to force them to work despite their illness, despite the pain that gripped their bowels so fiercely. They hunched over the pumps in agony.

"Pump!" Uncle ordered. "Your lives depend on it."

"God save us!" cried Roach. He stood in a wooden tub meant to catch his bodily wastes, for the flux was relentless in its release of liquids. "I need water."

"You can survive thirst, you filthy, stinking mongrel!" shouted Uncle, the veins bulging in his neck. "But you can't survive drowning! Or must I dunk you over the side to prove my point?"

Roach looked alarmed. "But—but, Captain, there are sharks."

"At least it would end," said McGuire, his voice as shrunken and disheveled as his once-handsome person.

Billy spoke. "We could take the boats and leave this tub."

At this suggestion, there was a silence. Only the *scree, scree, scree* of the pumps.

I couldn't breathe. My fever suddenly pounded in my head. *Leave the ship?* "Uncle—"

"Philip, how many slaves have recovered their sight?"

"Last—last I counted, which was several hours ago this morning, it was—let me think—"

"How many?" he screeched, his face turning an unhealthy red.

"One hundred thirty or so," I lied, hoping the number didn't sound too falsely inflated.

"Too many for the boats," he said. Beneath his eye patch, he frowned.

"Please, sir," gasped Roach. "Let's just leave. I'm—I'm dying. Truly, I am."

Several others murmured their agreement.

"Nephew, how many days till we reach land?"

Again my head filled with a fevered pounding. I wanted to lie down and sleep. Die. Do anything except stand on my feet and answer a question of life and death. If I said too many days were left, Uncle would abandon ship this minute. If I said too few and we didn't arrive as promised . . .

Ikeotuonye, I said to myself.

"Philip?"

The strength of one person . . .

"I—I don't know. Without the wind . . ."

"If the wind were to return?"

"Three, four days at most."

Uncle smiled grimly. "Hear that, men? You can survive the pumps for another four days. After that, if we've no wind we'll take what slaves we can and leave the ship where she lies."

Billy the Vermin looked at me then and smiled, his irises clear and unclouded.

I swore that he could see me.

But then he looked past me, his eyes unfocused, and I released the breath I'd been holding.

Two days later I lay on the deck after a morning mess of one weevily biscuit and a quarter cup of scummy water. It was time to visit the infirmary, but I couldn't find the strength to rise. Oji lay beside me, his eyes closed, his face drawn with pain, his pointed teeth chattering with the chills.

The sails still hung slack.

Uncle had the boats down and the carpenter was running his hands over them, checking them for leaks.

The pumps still operated.

Scree, scree, scree.

I heard someone calling my name, begging for help, saying he was dying. The voice stopped; there was a cough, then silence.

Scree, scree, scree.

Across from me, the gunner lay on his back on top of the arms locker, his head hanging over one end of it, his long hair sweeping back and forth, the strands clotted with deck filth.

Scree, scree, scree.

I stared at the gunner's body, at his mouth hanging open, at the flies buzzing in and out.

There was something wrong. I blinked. Then knew.

I looked up. The sun was blazing overhead, its round orb staring at me like an eye.

My cloud cover.

It's gone.

Latitude 4°01' N and longitude 8° W.

I took the reading again, wiping the grime from my hands onto my trousers.

Yes.

A frightful trembling seized me that had nothing to do with fever or hunger. Once again I felt like a diminutive child shivering under the glare and cane of Master Crump.

We're but forty miles south of Africa. If the wind picks up (dear God, let the wind pick up!), we could arrive tomorrow.

I peered north, willing my eyes to see land. A ribbon of brown, stretching across the horizon. But there was nothing. Nothing but the endless ocean.

CHAPTER
23

"We'll shackle them together," I whispered, "after we've taken control of the ship."

"We will kill them," said Oji.

We sat together on the floor of our cabin, candle burning in the lantern above. It was well past midnight.

The *Formidable* was still dead in the water, still forty miles from Africa—her sails slack as a dead man's mouth, her bow pointing this way, then that, rising and falling on the ocean swells.

Tomorrow Uncle planned to abandon ship. It was necessary that Oji and I develop a plan to save the captives, who would otherwise die, trapped inside a sinking vessel. Their only hope was a lone white boy who didn't know how to operate the sails and who lacked the strength to man the helm or the pumps.

Oji clenched his fists and pounded the side of my bunk. He threw his head back and exposed his pointed teeth in a silent cry of rage. "They have taken my father and my sight," he finally said. "They have taken everything from me."

"For now we must concentrate on getting all our people into the boats," I told Oji.

Oji had buried his head in his hands. "There must be strong men in each of the boats."

"Yes, and before we cast off, I'll release the crew from their shackles."

"Leave them shackled. They can sink and die."

"With no surgeon aboard and with everyone blind, they'll probably sink and die anyhow."

"Then it will be in the hands of the gods."

"Once we leave the *Formidable* behind, we'll have other concerns."

Oji raised his head, gazing sightlessly at me. "Yes. What happens when we reach land? What then?"

"I—I've not thought that far ahead."

"Whatever we do, we will all succeed or we will all fail."

Through the night, we discussed every detail. The placement of the arms. The moment at which to unlock the captives. The vast numbers to squeeze into just three boats. The possibility of building several rafts to tow behind. Where to stow the provisions of food and water. Praying for calm seas and strength enough to row. Even as we discussed the plan, it seemed impossible. Ridiculous, even. As if I were a child moving toy soldiers about. As if it'd no relation to real life and real people.

And through it all, I couldn't help but feel sorrow for the crew, especially my uncle, left behind on a rotting tub, all blind, all betrayed by someone they trusted. Me, Philip Arthur Higgins, surgeon aboard the *Formidable,* nephew of Captain Towne.

I didn't want to do this. I was too ill; my bowels were beginning to loosen with the gripes. Fever clouded my thoughts so that I could scarcely remember what we'd discussed even a few minutes before. I had to concentrate—*had* to concentrate!

Blast it, I'm so ill!

"We'll take the medicines," I was saying.

"I will let the infant bellow like a horn as we row away across the great lake," Oji said.

Through my feverish thoughts, I pricked up my ears. I'd heard something. "Did you hear that, Oji?"

"Is the devil listening outside our door again?"

"No, no. *Listen.*"

And there it was. A creaking, a moaning; a shifting of the vessel, ever so slowly.

"It's—it's *wind,*" I whispered.

Under the moonlit predawn sky, the breeze was fine and bracing. The hair was blown from my fevered forehead. Chills raced down my scalp.

"We're saved!" breathed Calvin.

"Saints be praised!" said Roach.

Harold said, "I hope I live long enough to feel grass beneath my feet again. In just a day or two we'll be on land, right, Mr. Surgeon? Right?"

I ordered the new heading, and with Uncle beside me, instructing me sail by sail, line by line, I became the eyes of the crew as they climbed about with a newfound strength that defied their illness.

"No, not that line, the line next to it, I believe. Yes, that's right. Pull now. Give it all you've got. There. The yard's turning to port. That's what we want, isn't it, Uncle? The yard to turn to port? To catch the wind coming from our starboard quarter? By the deuce, Uncle, if I keep this up, I'll become a sailor through and through. Ha!"

I continued my charade until finally the course was set and every sail trimmed. I estimated our speed at eight knots. At this rate, we'd arrive in five hours or so.

Oji and I returned to our cabin. There was much to discuss.

We'd still need to disembark all of the captives while keeping the crew at bay, but now we'd five hours to accomplish it rather than twenty-four as before.

"I'll carry the arms into the hold a few at a time so as not to attract attention," I told Oji, groaning and clenching my teeth.

My bowels! Bugger and blast, my bowels!

The cabin swirled about me in a haze of dizziness. I groped for the chamber pot. It was ten minutes before I could talk again. "When it's time, the crew mustn't be able to find a single weapon."

"They will resist anyway."

"I know."

"How will we get them to submit?"

A wave of helplessness washed over me. I'd asked myself this question again and again and had no answers. Beg them, I supposed. Ask them nicely. This much I knew: I didn't wish to use violence. I was heartily sick of it. I put my head in my hands. "I don't know, Oji. We'll think of something. Lure them somewhere one by one, maybe. Use their blindness against them."

For a long time, we said nothing. Uncle was calling for me from the deck. "We will leave the food and water here," Oji said.

"Leave it? But—"

"We will take half the Africans and come back for the rest. Come back for the food as well."

"Oh, right, right, of course. We'll be close enough to shore where we can do that. We needn't overload the boats unnecessarily. Oji . . ."

"Yes?"

"Help me off the pot." And as Oji helped me, and as Uncle kept calling my name, demanding my presence on deck, I thought, *This will never work. We're doomed to failure.*

I've brought them this far only to fail.

A pathetic boy and a pathetic plan.

I emerged on deck, shaking with weakness, blinking away the brightness of the morning sun, anxious to satisfy Uncle's demands so that I could begin emptying the arms locker.

Scree, scree, scree.

Hands clasped behind his back, Uncle stood aft beside Harold, who stood at the helm. One look at Uncle's blood-suffused face, his narrowed eye and his clamped jaw, and I knew, once again, that he was angry. I was, by this time, quite used to his temper tantrums. Still, I didn't fancy the idea of facing him when he was in one of his moods. To make matters worse, Billy the Vermin sat on the deck not far from Uncle. He'd a hand under his shirt and was vigorously scratching his armpit.

I took a deep breath, straightened my aching backbone, and approached. "Here I am. Just had a bit of a spell on the chamber pot."

Upon hearing me, a strange light entered Uncle's eye. His voice, not as I expected. Quite civil, to be sure, yet the hair on my arms and the back of my neck stood on end. "Philip, my nephew, my single surviving flesh and blood, dear and only son of my sister, do be so kind as to tell us our heading."

A sudden panicky urge to flee came over me, but I suppressed it with a will. I looked at Billy, but his face was bland as pudding and I was uncertain as to whether he could see me or not. I cleared my throat. "Excuse me? What, then? Our—our heading?"

Uncle gestured toward the binnacle that encased the ship's compass. "Yes, our heading. *If* I can trouble you to be so kind."

Scree, scree, scree.

I looked at the compass, already knowing what it indicated.

North-northeast.

My lips stuck together, as if my mouth were glued shut. I forced them open, dreading to utter a word.

"West-nor'west."

"Ah. West-nor'west. How very intriguing. Come now, don't you think that's intriguing?"

"I—I don't know," I stammered.

"And why wouldn't you know?"

I shook my head, a dreadful fear filling my chest. The fear of my nightmares, every one of them, crammed into this single moment.

He knows.

Again I wanted to flee. But I forced myself to sound perplexed, as if I'd no idea what the problem was. "I—I don't understand. Please, tell me. What's this about?"

Uncle propped a hand under his chin and furrowed his brow, as if contemplating something highly intellectual. "Hmm. 'What's this about?' he asks. Did you hear that, Billy, my cabin boy? He asks, 'What's this about?' "

"Yeah," said Billy, looking right at me. "I heard it."

"Did you hear that, Harold?"

"Aye, I heard it."

Uncle turned back to me. "Then I'll tell you, Philip, my nephew. I'll tell you what this is about." He closed his eye and breathed deeply.

A silence followed in which my every nerve was afire. Should I run? Should I sound the alarm? Should I call for Oji?

Scree, scree, scree.

"I can feel it on my skin," Uncle said finally. "The morning sun. Rising from the north. How very intriguing. The earth has changed its rotational axis in relation to the sun. Either that or you're lying. Which is it?"

I began to back away, but suddenly, like a snake that strikes, Uncle snarled and grabbed me by the scruff of the neck, lifting me entirely off the ground. "The compass must've broken!" I screamed, kicking and flailing at the empty air.

Billy laughed as if this were the funniest thing.

By the deuce! He can *see me!*

Uncle shoved his face into mine. His breath smelled of decay. His voice was calm as the dead. "Where are we, Philip, my lad?"

"Barbuda!" I said. "I can see it from here!" I pointed at the thin ribbon of land in the distance. "There it is! It's a miracle! We've arrived! See? See?"

"Of course I can't see!" screamed Uncle. Now the veins stood out on his neck and temples. "And you're a bloody liar!"

And so saying, he shook me like a rat. The sky bobbed. The ship bobbed. Blackness pulsed at the edges of my vision. Africa, Billy, my uncle, the *Formidable*—all disappeared into a whipping back-and-forth blindness.

I heard Billy laughing, laughing. I heard others of the crew shouting, telling Uncle just to kill me, that I'd been a pest and a liar from the beginning.

And then I was on the deck again. Lying on the deck, chest heaving, vision returning, world swirling, neck aching, my uncle still screaming. He grabbed me by my shirt front and squeezed. "Tell me," he snarled, flecks of spit landing on my face, "where we are. Tell me what you've done with my ship. Tell me what you've done with my cargo."

"Barbuda," I gasped. "We're in Barbuda. Uncle, please, please, I—I c-a-n-'t b-r-e-a-t-h-e."

Uncle let go of me then; I didn't know why. I only knew that one moment I was choking for breath and the next there was nothing. Just me, lying on the filthy planks, the minutes passing while I gasped and vomited, thinking, *After all this, I've failed.*

That's when I heard the baby cry.

"*G*ive it to me," demanded Uncle.

Spitting out the last of my vomit, head pounding, I watched Billy place the infant in Uncle's arms, Billy saying, "See? Told you so. They was hiding it."

Without a word, Uncle stumbled to the bulwarks, and after a moment of fumbling, grasped the infant by the ankle and dangled him over the water. Onwuha wiggled, then squalled, while I stumbled to my feet, screeching, "Stop! Stop!"

"If you want him to live, you'll tell me our precise location," my uncle commanded, his voice calm once again.

"Africa!" I screamed. "Africa! Africa! Africa! We're off the coast of Cape Palmas! I can see it from here! It's the truth!"

Uncle paled and staggered, falling against

one of the long guns. Onwuha squalled and kicked. "Then—then it's true. You mean to say, all—all this time, you've deceived me? Your own flesh and blood?"

"Please, give the baby to me. I've told you what you wanted. *Please.* I beg of you."

"You've deceived me? After all I've done for you? After all I've *wanted* for you?" And to my surprise, tears sprang to my uncle's eye, as if I'd truly wounded him.

"Just hand the baby to me. Then we can talk. I'll tell you everything."

But Uncle continued to look bewildered, holding Onwuha over the water. By now Onwuha was crying lustily, his face scrunched. I became aware of the rest of the crew closing about us, like the dead risen from their graves. "But why, Philip? *Why?*"

"Because they're people with homes and families, people who deserve to live their lives in freedom, just as you do. Please, hand me the baby now." While I spoke, I crept toward Onwuha, to wrest him to safety before Uncle could stop me. But someone grabbed me from behind. It was Billy. I struggled in his grasp. "Let go!"

"He's been lying to us the whole time!" cried Billy. "About everything! Only eight slaves can see. The rest of them's blind as the rest of you!"

"That's a lie!" I screamed. It was then, as I kicked Billy in the shins and yanked his hair—hating him, oh God, hating him so much—that I saw Oji streak through the blind crowd and past me. Directed no doubt by Onwuha's wailing and with a savage cry, he dove into Uncle and sank his pointed teeth into Uncle's neck. And as Uncle instinctively released Onwuha to grasp at his throat, Oji snatched the baby and fled, crying, "Run, Ikeotuonye!"

Shocked, I stared as Uncle slid down the bulwarks, grabbing at the long gun, and collapsed upon the deck. Blood seeped from his gaping wound. His one milky eye was wide and dazed. "Good heavens," he said. "That black devil of yours has killed me, I should think."

Roach said, "Uh—Captain Towne? Are—are you all right?"

Uncle gasped, "Find—find that black devil and string him up. And toss my nephew overboard. I—I'll be bloody well damned if he's commander of this vessel."

I sank my teeth into Billy's hand. He shrieked, did a dance of pain. I heard one of his bones crack, and then I was off and running.

"He's over there!" cried Billy. "Beside you, McGuire!"

McGuire lunged for me, but I dodged his blind grasp. "Oji!" I screamed. "Help me!" Past the mainmast and down the hatch I went, like a rabbit down a hole. I don't remember using the steps, only knowing that suddenly I was in the hold, in the darkness, the only light coming from the open hatchway. I ran down the aisle, between the tiers filled with men, into the utter darkness, my eyes still blinded from the morning sun. Slime squished under my bare feet. Bones crunched. The stench was like a musket ball to my brain. *"Nyèlụ m̄ aka!"* I cried—"Help me!"

Hands reached out and pulled me down. I fell heavily on one of the men, our heads bumping. Chains rattled. Everyone was shouting in various languages. And then I was under the bodies, under the filth, under the stench. "Ikeotuonye," someone said to me. "Stay still. Do not move."

I lay beneath the bodies in the darkness, shivering with fever, bowels cramping, lungs screaming for air.

Oh God, oh God, help me! Help us all!

They came down the aisle. If I opened one eye a crack, I could see them from between the bodies. Billy the Vermin, cradling his wounded hand, blood seeping down his arm. McGuire with a lantern held high. Three sailors with muskets.

Billy looked from the right to the left, from the upper tier to the lower tier, poking, prodding. "Keep going," he said. "He's here somewhere."

Sweat dripped down every crease in my body. I could feel the pounding heart of the African who lay atop me.

"I think I'm going to be sick," one of the sailors said.

"Son of a gun," said Billy, wiping his forehead and leaving a dirty smear. "That one's deader'n a turd. Rats chewed off his toes."

On they came. Closer.

When they neared me, I bolted. The Africans all screamed at once, throwing the hold into an uproar. I tumbled over bodies. A musket exploded. Another. More screams. "Get him! He's heading toward the hatch!" Panic tore at my chest, and I thought I might faint out of sheer fright.

I flew up the companionway. A blast from a musket splintered the wood beneath my feet. A shard pierced my foot. Out I sprang, onto the main deck. Oji was there, blind eyes wide, a knife in his hands, swiping at the empty air, calling my name: "Ikeotuonye!"

From somewhere came a distant boom. But I didn't have time to ponder what it was, for I sped for the shrouds, ducking out of the grasps of the men who grabbed for me. I kicked one of them who'd gotten hold of my shirt; he fell back, tearing part of my shirt away. Then I ran. "Oji!" Scrambling atop a long gun, grabbing the shrouds, I shouted in his language, "Fetch the key and unlock all the men below! They'll be tossed overboard anyhow. They can at least die fighting! Unlock them all! Quickly!"

And up the shrouds I scrambled, never in my life having climbed anything so high. The mast swayed, rocking in giant arcs through the sky. My stomach lurched. I forced my legs to climb. A swirl of dizziness took my breath away. My vision dimmed. I clung to the rigging, panting.

They were after me. Ten men at least, their skill as sailors evident despite their blindness, climbing up the shrouds beneath me—and across from me, on the starboard side as well.

"Get the turncoat!"

"We'll toss him overboard, all right! After we smash his arms and legs!"

"Don't worry, Captain Towne, he's mine!"

"Come here, little Mr. Surgeon, we won't hurt you!"

Up I climbed, hearing my own panting, my ears roaring with the thunder of my heart, suddenly thinking once again of Mr. and Mrs. Gallagher, thinking how disappointed they'd be to learn that their little English boy would never return, that he'd fallen to his death off the coast of Africa.

Someone grabbed my ankle. I screeched, kicking. My toes hit teeth. Pain shot up my foot, as if I'd stubbed it on a door.

Someone let go. Cursed.

I reached the main yard and paused, having only a second to make up my mind. Above me was the maintop with its lubber's hole. I could crawl through that and continue up. But even as I contemplated this, the men climbing the starboard shrouds caught up with me as our shrouds converged on the mainmast. Milky eyes stared. Hands clawed the empty air.

A cry escaped me and I climbed away from them, out onto the main yard, the only course left to me.

Below me, Oji dodged the crew and disappeared down the main hatch.

My legs trembling, my feet on the footropes, as quickly as I could I slid across the main yard, as I'd seen the sailors do countless times. Below, Billy shrieked, "He's on the main yard! Get him!"

Again I heard a boom. Closer this time. Then a shout, sounding as if it came from across the water.

Then, to my embarrassment, my bowels released themselves. High as I was in the air, the contents splattered directly onto Billy below, who screeched like a hog at the slaughter. I must admit to no small satisfaction, despite the fact that I was soon to die.

In moments I reached the end of the yard. Beneath me was no longer the deck, but the rolling swells of the Atlantic, dark shapes swarming just beneath the surface. A wave of dizziness shot through me, as if I'd twirled round and round. I clutched the end of the yard.

Below, Billy was still screeching. Black men were flooding out of the hold. Uncle was still lying slumped against the bulwarks.

Scores of blind crew members had followed me onto the main yard. Gaunt, whiskered, shriveled, yellowed. Clouded eyes stared at nothing. All of the men were clawing the empty air, trying to find me. One of them reached out, grasped a handful of my shirt, and yanked.

I screamed.

My feet slipped off the footrope.

For one precarious second, I clung to the yardarm.

Then my weakened fingers gave way and I plummeted.

My heart in my throat.

Thinking, *Farewell.*

Screaming, screaming.

Arms and legs windmilling through the air.

Down, down, down, into the ocean.

CHAPTER
25

I hit the water.

Its coolness closed over me. Except for the gurgling of bubbles and the sound of my heart throbbing in my head, all noise ceased. Salt water entered my nose, my ears, my mouth.

Immediately I began to drown. To thrash and drown, wondering if it hurt more to drown or to be eaten by sharks. My lungs screamed for air.

I bobbed to the surface, choked, and then sank again.

Something brushed up against me.

Hurry. Make it quick.

And then it had me by the scruff of the neck and was pulling me up, up, out of the water and onto something hard and dry.

A wave of shock pulsed through my body, as if I'd just had a tooth yanked out.

I spluttered and choked, my eyes stinging, blinking back salt water.

There, still holding me by the scruff of the neck while I dripped like a sewer rat, was a familiar figure. Blond, mustached, hat upon his head, it was the young officer from the American vessel from what seemed so long ago. His mouth was hard, lips drawn tight, eyes ablaze.

And without saying a word, he shoved me away; he stood at the bow of his longboat, where I lay in a heap, and drew his cutlass, pointing it at the *Formidable*. "Attack!"

Men in the longboat, and there were many—forty, maybe—scrambled over me and swarmed up the ship's sides, grasping anything they could find to help them aboard. I heard shouts and cries from above. Several men remained behind. One of them deposited himself next to me, cocked a pistol, and aimed it at my head. "You so much as twitch," he growled, "and it'll go worse for you than it has already."

I closed my eyes and lay back, only too happy not to twitch. *You've done it, Philip Arthur Higgins. A blind and weakened crew will be no match for trained marines.*

I think I slept for a while—I'm not sure—but I was startled, dreams floating away like feathers, when the American sailor pulled me to my feet. "Up you go," he said. "Let's get you aboard with the rest of them."

After all this, I couldn't climb. My muscles failed me, and I groaned. Again I tried, and again, until finally the sailor heaved me over his back, complaining about my wretched smell, and climbed up and over the side of the *Formidable*. He deposited me like a sack of potatoes on the sun-soaked deck, then shackled me to Harold, who, like the rest of the *Formidable*'s crew, sat chained about the mainmast.

It took a long time.

The liberation.

The crew of the American naval vessel tied handkerchiefs about their noses and mouths. Occasionally someone vomited. Some cried openly as more and more slaves crawled out of the holds. Some slaves had to be carried. Some were shackled to dead bodies. Those that were shackled were released. Blinking in the bright sunshine, most of the men, women, and children couldn't stand. Skeletons with skin. Covered with sores, bruises, vomit, and feces.

Finally the holds and the infirmary were empty.

I'd looked and looked for Oji, but couldn't see him anywhere. I called his name, but my voice was no more than a whisper.

Oji, where have you gone? Fevered tears slid from between my eyelids. *Are you dead?*

Meanwhile, American sailors moved among the blacks, giving them food and water. The naval surgeon administered what relief he could—ointments, balm, pills. I longed to join him, but I'd released my bowels again, my fever was raging, and I believed I was about to die.

The rest of the *Formidable*'s crew wasn't in much better condition. Uncle wasn't far from me, a crimson-soaked bandage wrapped about his neck. He declared in Spanish that they had no right to seize his vessel, that he was a Spanish gentleman of legal commerce. McGuire had his head in his hands. Roach sobbed, proclaiming his innocence over and over. Billy clutched his injured hand, looking dreadfully unhappy. Next to me, Harold was groaning, stinking, dying of fever too.

"You're the captain?" asked the naval captain of my uncle, coming to stand before him.

For the past half hour, Uncle had spoken nothing but Spanish, declaring his indignation with an ever-increasing weakness. He'd been ignored until this moment.

"*Sí.*"

"Name?"

"Don Pedro." Uncle then spoke in heavily accented English. "You have no right to take this vessel. I am a Spaniard, the ship is owned by Spaniards, and the American navy has no jurisdiction over us."

The American captain didn't blink. "I'm Captain Marshall of the U.S.S. *Stinger.* Unless you can prove that you are the Spaniard you declare yourself to be and that this is a Spanish ship, I hereby take command of your vessel. Do you have any papers?"

"*Sí.* In the captain's desk in my cabin, aft."

Captain Marshall gave a signal and one of his men disappeared below, returning a few moments later with the papers in hand. I could see the captain's shoulders sink as he read them.

"Please, sir," I said, my voice raspy as dust.

No one heard me. I said it again. "Please, sir, please. Do listen. It's quite important."

The captain looked about, perplexed. "Who's saying that?"

"It's the boy, sir," said one of the American sailors. "The boy we fished from the water."

"That boy is a liar," said my uncle. "Believe nothing he says." And from his lips issued a stream of Spanish curses designed to send me to hell.

Captain Marshall ignored Uncle and strode to where I lay shackled next to Harold. The captain pierced me with his pale blue eyes. "You can see, can't you?"

"Yes."

"Name?"

"He is a liar!" cried my uncle.

"Philip Arthur Higgins, surgeon aboard the *Formidable*."

Captain Marshall raised an eyebrow. "You're the surgeon?"

"Aye."

"How old are you?"

"Fifteen, I think."

"I—see." He glanced at one of his men next to him, then said, "You have something to say?"

"Yes. Those—those are fake papers."

"He's a liar! I *am* a Spaniard! I am Don Pedro of Castile! My papers are authentic! Touch one hair on the heads of my slaves and I will take you to Spanish court and crucify you!"

"Do you know the location of the real papers?" the American captain asked me.

"Stuffed in his mattress."

Captain Marshall touched his hat to me. "Thank you, Surgeon. Much obliged. Men, you heard him."

EPILOGUE

A prize crew was put aboard the *Formidable:* a dozen stout men, including the surgeon.

Though some had their doubts as to whether the *Formidable* could make it as far as Sierra Leone before she sank, make it she did, arriving at Freetown with 199 slaves on August 19, 1821, four months after she'd set sail from the river Bonny with 368 slaves aboard.

During the voyage, given fresh food and water, the Africans recovered under awnings constructed on the deck, while the crew of the *Formidable* was chained in the hold, where they remained until it came time for their trial.

I'd have liked to have helped the *Stinger's*

surgeon—to learn some of his techniques, perhaps—but I'd fallen deathly ill and became a patient myself. Oji told me later that I'd died at one point, that my lungs had ceased to draw air and that my spirit had left my little body, but that upon his cry of grief I'd revived. Yes, Oji was with me then, through that short voyage to Sierra Leone. On the day the *Formidable* was taken, he'd fought to release as many Africans as he could, but had suffered a blow to the head when he emerged from the hold. He was knocked senseless, thought to be dead; his last memory was of hearing me scream as I plummeted from the main yard into the ocean.

Oji had told the captain of my "heroics," as he called them. Everyone treated me as a hero—Captain Marshall and his crew; the *Stinger*'s surgeon; the Africans, who still called me Ikeotuonye. But I didn't think of myself as one. My guilt and shame wouldn't allow me to. I merely thought of myself as a formerly luckless lad who'd once been blind, but whose eyes had miraculously been opened.

Upon arrival in Sierra Leone, the sixteen men of the *Formidable*'s crew who'd survived, including my uncle, were tried at a mixed tribunal, found guilty of participating in the illegal slave trade, and sentenced to fifteen years in prison. I testified at the trial, deeply moved when I saw my uncle in chains, a shrunken vestige of his former, jaunty self.

I visited him during his confinement. Just once.

Uncle sat on a cot in his cell, his beard unkempt, mumbling to himself. My feet scuffed the floor and he jerked his head up, listening, gazing about with his one milky eye, the left socket still shrouded with an eye patch. "Who's there?"

"It's me, Uncle." I grasped the bars, the press of steel cold and hard. The cell stank of mildew and urine.

He turned his eye away. Busied himself with unraveling the threads of his blanket. First one thread, then another, then another.

"If you keep that up, you won't have a blanket left." I shifted uncomfortably after he said nothing. "I—I could send you things to keep up your spirits. Blankets, candies, cigars and matches, fresh clothes . . ." I almost said "books," but stopped myself in time.

He arranged the threads in a row. Scratched his beard. Hunched over his threads and began counting them, the breath whistling in and out of his nostrils.

"I'm—I'm leaving for New Orleans on a vessel come Tuesday. If you want, I can bring a message to someone, should you have a need. I can tell them where you are, if there's anyone."

Uncle divided the threads into three piles and began to braid them. The braid was sloppy and kept falling apart. I looked away as sorrow overwhelmed me. My throat squeezed painfully. *So it's come to this.*

I released the bars. "I'm leaving now. Goodbye. I—I wish things could've been different between us. I never meant you harm." From outside the barred window came the sound of a goat bleating. "Take good care, Uncle." And I trod the prison corridor, leaving him behind with his threads and his milky eye, knowing I'd never see him again.

I did as promised and for fifteen years sent him articles for his comfort. Four of the crew eventually regained their vision, but my uncle never did, just as he'd predicted. Lately I've heard that he lives with a mistress on the island of Cuba, in a small dwelling by a river surrounded by lemon trees and fat goats. In an odd way, I don't begrudge him his happiness, nor any peace he might find.

On my last day in Africa, I saw Oji again. Like the other captives of the *Formidable,* he'd been given his freedom. And though some of the Africans had recovered their sight, Oji hadn't. He'd settled in Sierra Leone, having been granted his own plot of land, as had the others.

It was a fine plot, the vigorous weeds promising good soil beneath.

"You can grow yams," I said. The day smelled of soil, of goat droppings, of sun.

Oji felt one of the weeds with his hands, then yanked it up by the roots and tossed it away. "Yams are good," he said. "A man with many yams is a man with much wealth." He straightened up and gazed into the late-afternoon sun as if he could see it. "I will work very hard and provide much for my family."

From inside his grass hut came the nonsense sounds of Onwuha, burbling like the healthy baby he was. I heard Onwuha's mother, Nneka, as well, humming as she tended her household. After a while she came to the doorway and looked out at us, her eyes healed and whole. Next to her stood the girl who'd broken her leg in the great storm, Anyanwu, a name meaning "sunshine; dazzling beauty." Anyanwu had her arm about Agim, the boy who'd broken his wrist.

"Someday I will return to my home village," said Oji, resuming his attack on the weeds. "Someday I will see my mother and my brothers and sisters again."

I knelt beside him and pulled a few weeds. "Then I wish you success in your journey. Wherever it takes you. And may your new family be blessed."

Oji nodded. "You are not crying again, are you?"

I laughed. "Yes, I'm afraid I am. Can't help it, I suppose."

For a while we pulled weeds, sometimes in silence, sometimes chatting about this and that, until finally our shadows lengthened with the setting sun. I stood stiffly. "Well, I—I must go now, Oji. My ship leaves in the morning."

He tossed away another weed and straightened up, gazing down at me, his clouded eyes shimmering. Groping for my hands, he found them, rubbing them with African soil; then he clasped them warmly. "Farewell, Ikeotuonye. Farewell, friend of my heart. The distance shall not separate us."

To this day I can still feel the soil upon my hands, and smell it in the evening sun.

Bells jangled. A rush of air greeted me, hinting of yellow jessamine and camphor. I entered the shop, my brogans clicking on the hard-planked floor, and took my place in the queue behind a customer, a tall gentleman in a gray frock coat and silk hat.

"Give her two in the morning and two in the evening with plenty of milk," the chemist was saying. His spectacles had slid to the end of his nose, and he pushed them up with a finger as he handed the package over the counter. "That'll be twenty cents, please."

The man stuffed the packet into his coat, dug in his coin purse, then dropped the money into the chemist's outstretched hand.

"Let me know how she is come tomorrow evening, Mr. Dyer," said the chemist as he rang up the sale. "She should be back to her usual activities in no time at all."

"I'll do that, Mr. Gallagher, that I will. Merry Christmas now!"

"Aye! A jolly Christmas to you and yours as well!"

And out the customer went, humming a carol, bells ringing.

Mr. Gallagher wiped his hands on a towel, smiled at me, and then said, "Well, then. What can I do for you, young man?"

All the months of waiting, all the dreams of home, the forever ache in my heart—all were distilled into this moment. I removed my cap. Kneaded it between my hands. I opened my mouth to speak, but couldn't.

Mr. Gallagher's smile faded. His eyes widened. The towel slipped from his hands. "My God, my dear God—Philip? Is that you, lad?" His eyes glistened with sudden tears and his lips trembled.

I nodded.

And out he came from behind the counter, hollering, "Mary! Mary! Come quickly! He's *home*! My God! Our Philip is home again!"

With a cry of joy, he swooped me into his arms, pressing me against him. He smelled of balm and blackberry. I hugged him back, laughing. And then Mrs. Gallagher was there. "My little English boy, you're home! Dear me, you're home!" She wrapped her arms about us and I kissed her cheek, and soon all three of us were laughing and jumping up and down as if we'd just won the biggest, grandest prize in all the world. Which, I suppose, we had.

After a while we drew apart, gasping for breath, still gripping one another's hands, me grinning till I thought my cheeks might split. I gazed from one to the other, drinking in the sight of them—their crowns of silver hair; their kind, gentle smiles; their eyes filled with love for me.

I squeezed their hands and said simply, "Mother, Father, I've come home at last."

If you happen to wander into a bookshop in these northern United States, you might chance across a bestselling book, Reflections Upon the Slave Trade, *written by one Philip Arthur Higgins, Physician,*

Poet, and Abolitionist. It is said he endured much upon a slave ship, the Formidable, once upon a time, even losing his sight, and then steered the craft back to Africa, where all the slaves were redeemed. But no one, not even the northerners, really believed every single word of it.

But stretched truth or not, no one denied the power of his convictions, and many a person succumbed to his preachings, dissolving into flurries of tears and paroxysms of guilt over the peculiar institution of slavery. Dr. Higgins, graduate of the renowned Yale College Medical Institution, was a pale man of slight build, somewhat weak in the eyes. Nevertheless, he had moved entire crowds to tears by the end of his impassioned speeches. But some called him a liar. Others threw rotted tomatoes at him. Once, he had bared his chest, revealing a most hideous scar. Twice, he'd had to flee for his life, rushing out the back door to where a gray-haired couple waited with their carriage to hurry him safely home to his wife and newborn son.

But if you were to ask Dr. Higgins himself of what accomplishment he was most proud, likely he would not say it was his poems, or his speeches, or his advancements in medicine, or even his bestselling book, exaggerated as it might be. No, likely he would remove his spectacles, polish them for a bit, and then tell you of the time he returned to Africa. Of the time he pushed up the Niger River with a small expedition, accompanied by one African companion named Oji and Oji's adopted family. Dr. Higgins would likely relate how they had found a village, a small village of no repute, where a woman had daily watched the horizon for the return of her son, gone these twenty years. And how there Dr. Higgins had at last laid his guilt to rest, finding a sense of fulfillment that has never left him to this day.

AUTHOR'S NOTE

Originally, the hero for *Voyage of Midnight* was to be a midshipman in Nelson's navy, stationed off the coast of West Africa during the era of the illegal slave trade (1807–1869). I imagined him cruising the coast of Africa, chasing down slaving ships and generally acting heroically. Or so I thought. I was neck deep in research when I stumbled upon a reference regarding some letters written in 1819 by a young passenger aboard a slaving ship. After some searching, I found the letters reprinted in their entirety within the book *Slave Ships and Slaving*, by George Francis Dow, published in 1927. What I read shocked me.

Twelve-year-old J. B. Romaigne was the son of a plantation owner from the French West Indies island of Guadeloupe. Having completed his education in France, Romaigne took passage aboard a slaving vessel, *La Rodeur*, bound for Guadeloupe via Africa. Headed over the Atlantic with a cargo of slaves, the entire crew of *La Rodeur* and all of the slaves were struck blind with ophthalmia. Romaigne wrote letters to his mother even as his own sight dimmed. Finally, some of the crew, including Romaigne, regained their sight, and *La Rodeur* staggered into Guadeloupe, but not before the blind slaves were jettisoned, for, as the captain explained, ". . . would you have me turn my ship into a hospital for the support of blind negroes?"

Lost in the dusty volumes of history, this was a story begging to be told. So I set my midshipman hero adrift and started over. Besides the obvious, many of the incidents and impressions in *Voyage of Midnight* were taken directly from Romaigne's experiences, such as "The Captain is very fond of me and is very good-tempered; . . . he is a fine, handsome man and I am sure I shall like him very much." And when the slaves were first brought aboard, Romaigne wrote somewhat irritably: "I wish the ignorant creatures would come quietly and have it over."

One of the most telling incidents regarding the captain's character occurred on a night when Romaigne could not sleep because of the sounds issuing from the hold: ". . . the sound froze my very blood; . . . jumping up in horror, I ran to the Captain's state-room. The lamp shone upon his face; it was as calm as marble, he slept profoundly, and I did not like to disturb him." And when the captain executed six slaves as a lesson to the other slaves—shooting three and hanging three—the distraught Romaigne thought he saw the six slaves "passing to and fro through the cabin. . . ."

Conditions aboard *La Rodeur* deteriorated, as did the captain's good temper. "All the crew are now blind but one man. The rest work under his orders like unconscious machines; the Captain standing by with a thick rope, which he sometimes applies, when led to any recreant by the man who can see. My own eyes begin to be affected; in a little while, I shall see nothing but death." Soon after, all blind, they suffered a storm in which "no hand was upon the helm, not a reef upon the sails." That they survived the storm was remarkable. But perhaps even more remarkable was the incident of the two ships passing. Much of the dialogue between the two captains, as written by Romaigne, is reproduced in *Voyage of Midnight*. The *Saint Leon* of Spain was never heard from again. Eventually, the captain of *La Rodeur* lost an eye, and most of the crew remained irretrievably blind. Romaigne recovered his sight completely.

But a problem still remained for me. Who would be my hero? Rather than end the story with the jettisoning of the slaves, I wanted to develop a character who had the moral fiber to attempt a rescue. I felt I could not fashion my character after Romaigne, for although it was obvious that some of the events of his voyage bothered him deeply, he was nonetheless the son of a planter and did not have the perspective to question what for him was a "fact of life," a long-standing cultural institution that put the bread on his family's table. Instead, I needed a character who could question the institution of slavery from an authentic viewpoint, a viewpoint that emerged from his own life experiences.

Enter Richard Drake, who supposedly dictated an autobiography called *Revelations of a Slave Smuggler*, published in 1860.[i] Drake was orphaned and sent to a workhouse, and worked at a cotton mill for upwards of eighteen hours a day until, as a self-described "feeble" and "sickly child," he collapsed and nearly died of a fever. During his confinement, he was visited by a long-lost seafaring uncle, who promised to send money for his keep . . . You know the story, for I patterned my Philip character after Richard Drake. And just like my Philip, the young Drake searched for his uncle in New Orleans, worked for a pharmacist, ran across his long-lost uncle in a tavern while making a delivery, and eventually signed aboard his uncle's ship as a surgeon's mate. Here the similarities end, for Drake goes on to detail decades as a slave trader, whereas my young Philip cannot forget his abuses in the workhouse and is grounded with a moral integrity that shines through once he realizes the true character of his uncle and witnesses the horrors of the slave trade.

Another event in my novel was based on facts. Sir Henry Huntley, in his book *Seven Years' Service on the Slave Coast of Western Africa*, describes two warships chasing two slavers up the Bonny River and into a forked tributary, where the warships split up, separated by a foliage-covered sand spit. During the chase, the slavers frantically loaded the slaves into canoes and took them ashore, and, when the warships came too close, began tossing the slaves overboard, still shackled in pairs. The slaving ships were eventually captured, but not before one-third of the five hundred slaves had drowned or been devoured by sharks and crocodiles.[ii]

Herman Melville, author of *Moby-Dick*, said, "Sharks . . . are the invariable outriders of all slave ships crossing the Atlantic, systematically trotting alongside, to be handy in case a parcel needs to be carried anywhere, or a dead slave to be decently buried. . . ."[iii] And, as in the river chase described above, eyewitness accounts of shark attacks in freshwater abound. Sharks literally *waited* alongside slaving ships.

While at the time it was not noted (at least not to this author's knowledge) what species of shark was responsible, in all likelihood it was the bull shark *(Carcharhinus leucas)*. Bull sharks have been found in freshwater as far as 2,500 miles inland, and can also live in saltwater.[iv] They can grow up to 11 feet in length and weigh 500 pounds.[v] Bull sharks have a wide distribution around the world's waterways, including the Bonny River. Shark experts believe that the majority of shark attacks worldwide today are by bull sharks. Not only are they extremely aggressive, but they lurk in shallow freshwater, where people least expect them.

Because of the willingness of callous slavers to fling slaves overboard just to avoid prosecution, in 1841 the law in the United States was changed so that slavers could be prosecuted solely upon evidence of slaving *activity,* such as the presence of shackles or handcuffs, huge cooking kettles or boilers, spare planks used to build tiers in the hold, an overabundance of food and water stores, and so on.[vi] Convictions of slave traders greatly increased with the enactment of this new law, and the practice of tossing slaves overboard ended.

Public sentiment in the United States in the early part of the nineteenth century was, generally speaking, supportive of slavery, although anti-slavery feelings were gaining momentum. Simply put, slavery was big business, profited many people, and was foundational to the American economy.[vii] When Britain passed a law prohibiting the slave trade in 1807, the U.S. government was far more interested in protecting its own economic interests and the interests of its well-to-do citizens. Due to pressure from Britain, however, the United States reluctantly passed a similar law in 1808. Yet the United States did little to enforce the new law, at times providing no more than a token force to patrol the coast of Africa, at other times having no force at all. The War of 1812 further distanced American interests from those of Britain, the United States seeking autonomy at sea regardless of whether or not a vessel was suspected of engaging in illegal ventures. The additional U.S. law passed in 1820 equating slave trading with piracy and making it punishable by hanging was, once again, an empty gesture. The death penalty was enacted only once, in 1862, when anti-slavery sentiment was at a fever pitch and civil war was imminent.[viii] Along with the Cuban slave trade, that of the United States was brisk up until the Civil

War, which ended slavery once and for all in the United States in 1865. The Cuban slave market was not closed until 1869.[ix]

In contrast to the U.S. government, the commanders of the American squadron, whose task it was to patrol the African coast, were zealous in their pursuit of slavers and in their desire to see justice served and the slaves liberated.[x] And unlike their respective governments, the American and British squadrons often cooperated cordially in their efforts at capturing slavers.[xi] Besides having to catch the slavers "red-handed" with slaves aboard, the difficulties of successful capture were compounded when slaving ships began carrying multiple sets of papers. One American captain reported in frustration, "We have made ten captures, [and] although they are evidently owned by Americans, they are so completely covered by Spanish papers that it is impossible to condemn them. . . . There are probably no less than 300 vessels on the coast engaged in the traffic, each having two or three sets of papers."[xii]

There are literally hundreds of autobiographies and eyewitness accounts written by individuals—captains, cabin boys, surgeons, passengers—who were involved in the slave trade. Understandably, descriptions of the conditions aboard these vessels varied according to era, nationality, the vessel itself, the character and philosophy of the captain and its owners, and countless other factors. There were extremes at both ends—ships in which there was unspeakable brutality and suffering, and ships in which the slaves were allowed to roam freely and were given as many comforts as could be provided. The vast majority of narratives, however, reveal inhumane conditions as the norm. Conditions deteriorated even further once slaving became an act of smuggling. Government regulations that had previously protected slaves against overcrowding and underprovisioning were gone. Captains crammed the holds with as many slaves as they could, to make up for the losses caused by the inevitable seizures.[xiii]

The human cost of the slave trade in terms of death and displacement is staggering. Records regarding how many slaves were exported from Africa between the years 1450 and 1850 are inaccurate, but estimates range from 10 million to 28 million persons, sold worldwide from the Americas to Asia.[xiv] This figure swells grotesquely when one realizes that these are the numbers of slaves who arrived at their destination *alive*. It is estimated that half of all slaves captured died during the march to the African coast and from their time spent in the baracoons. (One slave recounts that it took *seven months* to march to the coast.[xv]) An additional quarter died during the Middle Passage.[xvi] Despite the lack of exact numbers, it is clear that this was one of the most horrific holocausts ever perpetrated against a race of people.

Often, criticism has been aimed at the African tribes for their participation in the slave trade. While greed and power no doubt played a role for many of the indigenous participants at that time, it is important to remember that for most the choice was stark: take or be taken. In other words, they could participate in the slave trade as equal partners with the slave traders, or they could themselves— their families and the inhabitants of their villages—be captured and sold as slaves. Few of us today are forced to make such dehumanizing decisions. The slave traders, however, faced no such stark reality, motivated instead by enormous profits, thinly veiled as "God's will." Eventually, some of the native nations and rulers adopted Western attitudes. One chief, when told in 1807 of Britain's new law forbidding the slave trade, said, "We think that this trade must go on. That is the verdict of our oracle and the priests. They say that your country, however great, can never stop a trade ordained by God himself."[xvii] Tribal warfare further aided the slave traders because there was lacking a concerted, massive opposition.

During the illegal era, the delta of the Niger River, including the Bonny and Calabar rivers, was a frequent rendezvous of the slavers. Large numbers of slaves, mostly from the Ibo tribe, were exported from this region. It was estimated that out of the 20,000 slaves that were exported from the Bonny River in 1822 alone, 16,000 were Ibo tribespeople, the tribe of Oji, Ikoro, and most of the slaves in *Voyage of Midnight*. Yet despite the forced exodus of the Ibo people, today they inhabit a large portion of the Niger River delta in Nigeria.[xviii]

Whether we are white, black, in-between, or of another ethnic group, it is vital that we remember and seek to understand this legacy of our collective history. It is a legacy of unimaginable suffering and murder, and it is likewise a legacy of privilege extracted from that very suffering. Together we must see into a future in which all are honored, in which our differences are embraced like different textures and colors of the same fabric. And together we must covenant to never let this happen again.

I dream of a day when every child has a home and food and fresh water, when every child is beloved, when every child has a sense of worth, of oneness and equality with all of humanity.

In such dreams, peace is born.

i. When I first read *Revelations of a Slave Smuggler*, it seemed to have too many coincidences, too many incidents that could not possibly be true. A little research revealed that, although it was published as a true autobiography, it is believed by many scholars to be a work of fiction written by an abolitionist to inflame public opinion against the slave trade.

ii. Sir Henry Huntley, *Seven Years' Service on the Slave Coast of Western Africa* (London: Thomas Cautley Newby, Publisher, 1850), 219.

iii. Herman Melville, *Moby-Dick; or, The Whale* (New York: Harper & Brothers, 1851; reprint, Mortimer J. Adler, ed., Great Books of the Western World, No. 48, Chicago: Encyclopaedia Britannica, Inc., 1991), 135.

iv. M. McGrouther, "Find a Fish: Bull Shark—*Carcharhinus leucas* Valenciennes" [information online] (Sydney, Australia: Australian Museum, 2004 [accessed 28 June 2005]); available from www.austmus.gov.au/fishes/fishfacts/fish/cleucas.htm.

v. Rick Crist, "Corwin's Carnival of Creatures: Bull Shark" [information online] (Silver Spring, MD: Discovery Communications, Inc., 2006 [accessed 28 June 2005]); available from http://animal.discovery.com/fansites/jeffcorwin/carnival/waterbeast/bullshark.html.

vi. Christopher Lloyd, *The Navy and the Slave Trade: The Suppression of the African Slave Trade in the Nineteenth Century*, Slavery Series No. 4 (London: Frank Cass and Co., Ltd., 1968), 46–47.

vii. W.E.F. Ward, *The Royal Navy and the Slavers: The Suppression of the Atlantic Slave Trade* (New York: Pantheon Books, 1969), 38.

viii. *Ibid.*, 221–222.

ix. *Ibid.*, 231.

x. *Ibid.*, 115.

xi. Basil Lubbock, *Cruisers, Corsairs & Slavers: An Account of the Suppression of the Picaroon, Pirate & Slaver by the Royal Navy During the 19th Century* (Glasgow: Brown, Son & Ferguson, Ltd., 1922), 120.

xii. Lloyd, *The Navy and the Slave Trade*, 51.

xiii. Ward, *The Royal Navy and the Slavers*, 59.

xiv. BBC News, "Focus on the Slave Trade" [article online] (London: BBC News Online, 3 September 2001 [accessed 10 May 2006]); available from http://news.bbc.co.uk/1/hi/world/africa/1523100.stm.

xv. Olaudah Equiano, *Equiano's Travels: His Autobiography—The Interesting Narrative of the Life of Olaudah Equiano or Gustavus Vassa the African* (1789; reprint, London: Heinemann Educational Books, Ltd., 1967), 24.

xvi. Lloyd, *The Navy and the Slave Trade*, 118.

xvii. Hugh Thomas, *The Slave Trade: The Story of the Atlantic Slave Trade, 1440–1870* (New York: Simon & Schuster, 1997), 556.

xviii. Kalu E. Ume, *The Rise of British Colonialism in Southern Nigeria, 1700–1900: A Study of the Bights of Benin and Bonny* (Smithtown, NY: Exposition Press, 1980), 24–25.

GLOSSARY
of
SEA TERMS

❧

aft—toward the stern of a vessel.

America's Second War of Independence—War of 1812.

amidships—in the center of a ship.

apothecary—a pharmacist or druggist; also a pharmacy or drugstore.

atoll—a ring-shaped coral reef or a string of closely spaced small coral islands.

banquette—Coastal Louisiana word for a sidewalk, especially a raised one of bricks or planks.

bar—a hidden or partially submerged bank of land or sand.

barracoon—a building or enclosure used for keeping slaves in confinement.

batten—to make something secure, such as battening down in preparation for foul weather.

beaver hat—a hat commonly made of felt, silk, or even beaver fur. They were similar to top hats and were fashionable for over two hundred years.

bend—to join two ropes together, or to join a rope and an object together. New sails are bent (joined) to the yards.

bilge—an enclosed section at the bottom of a ship where seawater collects.

binnacle—the housing of a ship's compass and lamp.

block—a rounded wooden case that houses a pulley, used for lowering and lifting heavy loads. A line through a block forms a tackle.

bo'sun—a petty officer on a merchant vessel or a warrant officer on a warship, in charge of equipment and crew. (*Bo'sun* is short for *boatswain* and is pronounced BO-sun.)

bow—the front of a ship (rhymes with "cow").

bowsprit—a large wooden pole (spar) extending off the bow.

brig—traditionally a two-masted vessel, square-rigged on both masts.

brogans—heavy hobnailed shoes, sometimes reaching above the ankle.

brogue—an Irish accent in the pronunciation of English.

bulkhead—a wall-like structure in a ship. It separates a vessel into cabins and compartments.

bulwarks—the built-up side walls above the deck of a ship.

capstan—a barrel-like mechanism designed for hauling in heavy loads such as an anchor. The capstan is rotated by pushing the long handles that extend like spokes out of the top.

carbine—a short-barreled, lightweight rifle.

carronade—a wide-mouthed, short-barreled cannon, capable of firing heavy shot. Accurate only at close range.

cat-o'-nine-tails—a short whip having nine knotted cords, each cord fixed to a larger rope that was then used as a handle. Sailors were flogged with a cat-o'-nine-tails, a frequent punishment usually carried out by the bo'sun.

caulk—to plug the seams of a boat with waterproof materials; to make the ship watertight.

clipper—a term meaning any fast sailing ship.

companionway—a stairway or ladder leading from one deck to another.

cruiser—a ship employed to monitor a specific tract of sea, with the intention of finding and engaging enemy vessels believed to be in the area. The name comes from the cruiser's activity of "cruising" back and forth.

cutwater—the portion of the bow of the ship that "cuts" through the water.

ebb tide—the flowing of water back into the sea, resulting in a low tide onshore (the opposite of flood, which results in a high tide).

fathom—a nautical unit of measure equaling six feet.

flood tide—the flowing of water toward land, resulting in a high tide onshore (the opposite of ebb, which results in a low tide).

fob—a pocket intended to hold a watch.

fo'c'sle—the forward area of a ship, directly behind the bow and in front of the foremast. (*Fo'c'sle* is short for *forecastle* and is pronounced FOKE-sul.)

footrope—the horizontal rope suspended under a yard, upon which sailors stand while reefing or furling the sails.

fore, forward—toward the bow of a ship. The foremast would be the mast closest to the bow.

fortnight—a period of two weeks.

furl—to roll a sail to a yard.

galley—the cooking area, or kitchen, of a vessel.

gangway—an opening at a ship's side where people embark and disembark.

gunwale—the upper edge of a ship's side (pronounced GUN-ul).

halyard—a rope or line used to hoist sails, yards, flags, etc.

hatch—an opening in a ship's deck.

hatchway—the vertical space between one hatch and another, for passage between the decks of a vessel.

head—to set the course of a vessel (e.g., to head a ship southward).

heading—the particular direction in which a vessel is sailing. (e.g., "The vessel sailed on a heading of west northwest.")

helm—the steering apparatus of a vessel.

hogshead—a large barrel or cask.

hull—the main body of a ship.

inboard—inside a vessel's bulwarks.

jibboom—an additional spar that extends beyond the bowsprit.

keel—a timber that acts as the "spine" of the ship, running fore and aft (from bow to stern). The frame of the ship is attached to the keel, much as ribs are attached to the spine.

knightheads—two large timbers that help support the bowsprit.

knot—a measure of speed equal to one nautical mile per hour. One nautical mile equals 1.1508 land miles.

larder—the food supply.

lines—the ropes of a vessel, used for various purposes.

longboat—the largest boat carried by a sailing ship. Longboats could carry many men and be propelled by oars or sail.

long guns—cannon.

lubber's hole—a hole in the *top* through which one could climb rather than going out and over it. (A landlubber is someone who has never shipped before and has yet to learn his duties.)

luff—to turn a ship close to the wind so that the sails shake and momentum is slowed.

main—the principal or most important part in a three-masted vessel; thus, the center mast is called the *mainmast,* the center hatch is the *main hatch,* and so on.

marine—a naval soldier.

masthead—the top of a mast.

mess—the place where meals are regularly served; also the group of people with whom one regularly eats (messmates); also the meal itself (the afternoon mess).

midships—approximately halfway between the bow and the stern.

oakum—a fiber obtained by untwisting old ropes. Used in caulking a ship's timbers.

packet ship—a passenger boat originally employed by the government, also carrying mail and goods.

pinrail—a rail usually mounted on the inside of the bulwarks. The pinrail holds the belaying pins, which are used to secure the lines.

port—the left side of a vessel when facing forward.

privateer—a vessel with governmental authority to attack and pillage ships of enemy nations, including merchant ships. Privateers were used during wartime.

quarter—a word with many meanings in nautical terminology, but in this context it refers to the sides of the vessel aft of amidships.

quarterdeck—the deck aft of the mainmast.

quid—one pound sterling.

rakish—describing when the masts are not purely vertical but lean aft. Gives the appearance of speed.

reef—to reduce the amount of sail in operation.

rigging—the lines and ropes of a vessel, used to support the masts and work the yards and sails.

schooner—in this instance, a two-masted vessel with the mainmast being taller. Both masts were rigged differently than on a square-rigged vessel, allowing for a smaller crew and enabling the ship to sail closer to the wind.

sextant—a navigational instrument used to determine latitude and longitude.

sheets—lines connected to the lower corners of the sails, used to control the sails.

shoal—a sandbar that projects near or above the surface of the water.

shroud—a rope, usually one of a pair, that stretches from the top of the mast (the masthead) to the sides of a vessel. Sailors climbed the shrouds if they needed to go aloft. The shrouds had horizontal rope rungs called *ratlines* (pronounced RAT-lunz).

slack tide—the transitional tide between ebb and flood, where the water is neither going in nor going out. There is high-water slack and low-water slack.

sounding lead—a lead weight attached to a rope, used to determine depth.

spar—a beam or pole, such as a mast or yard, that supports rigging.

squall—a sudden, violent wind sometimes accompanied by rain or snow.

starboard—the right side of a vessel when facing forward.

stay—a line that supports the masts or spars.

stays'l—a smaller, triangular sail set between the square sails. Intended to maximize wind power and used only in moderate weather and light winds. (*Stays'l* is short for *staysail* and is pronounced STAY-sul.)

steerage—a large space belowdecks. On packet ships, it was usually reserved for passengers who could not afford a private cabin.

stern—the back of a ship.

top—the semicircular platform located just above the lowest yard of each mast. Tops are named after the mast to which they belong: foretop, maintop, mizzentop.

topgallant—the sail above the topsail (pronounced tuh-GAL-unt).

topsail—the sail immediately above the lowest sail on a square-rigged vessel (pronounced TOP-sul).

trick—a period of time in which a crewman is on duty at the helm.

yard—a horizontal beam attached to a mast to support a sail.

yardarm—the end of a yard.

BIBLIOGRAPHY

Bancroft, Frederic. *Slave Trading in the Old South*. Baltimore: J. H. Furst, 1931. Reprint, Columbia: University of South Carolina Press, 1996.

Basden, G. T. *Niger Ibos: A Description of the Primitive Life, Customs, and Animistic Beliefs, &c., of the Ibo People of Nigeria by One Who, for Thirty-five Years, Enjoyed the Privilege of Their Intimate Confidence and Friendship*, 2nd ed. London: Frank Cass & Co. Ltd., 1966.

BBC News. "Focus on the Slave Trade" [article online]. London: BBC News Online, 3 September 2001 [accessed 10 May 2006]; available from http://news.bbc.co.uk/1/hi/world/africa/1523100.stm.

Blake, Nicholas, and Richard Lawrence. *The Illustrated Companion to Nelson's Navy*. Mechanicsburg, PA: Stackpole Books, 2000.

Castellanos, Henry C. *New Orleans as It Was: Episodes of Louisiana Life*. New Orleans: L. Graham, 1895. Reprint, Baton Rouge: Louisiana State University Press, 1978.

Chapelle, Howard Irving. *The Baltimore Clipper: Its Origin and Development*. Salem, MA: The Marine Research Society, 1920. Reprint, New York: Dover Publications, Inc., 1988.

Child, Lydia Maria Francis. *The Family Nurse; or Companion of the American Frugal Housewife*. Boston: Charles J. Hendee, 1837. Reprint, Bedford, MA: Applewood Books, 1997.

Conrad, Robert Edgar. *World of Sorrow: The African Slave Trade to Brazil*. Baton Rouge: Louisiana State University Press, 1986.

Cowan, Walter G., and others. *New Orleans Yesterday and Today: A Guide to the City*. Baton Rouge: Louisiana State University Press, 1983.

Crist, Rick. "Corwin's Carnival of Creatures: Bull Shark" [information online]. Silver Spring, MD: Discovery Communications, Inc., 2006 [accessed 28 June 2005]; available from http://animal.discovery.com/fansites/jeffcorwin/carnival/waterbeast/bullshark.html.

Curtis, Nathaniel Cortlandt. *New Orleans: Its Old Houses, Shops and Public Buildings.* Philadelphia: J. B. Lippincott and Co., 1933.

Dana, Richard Henry, Jr. *The Seaman's Friend: A Treatise on Practical Seamanship.* Boston: Thomas Groom & Co., 1879. Reprint, Mineola, NY: Dover Publications, Inc., 1997.

Dow, George Francis. *Slave Ships and Slaving* [CD-ROM]. Salem, MA: Marine Research Society, 1927.

Drake, Richard. *Revelations of a Slave Smuggler* [book online]. New York: R. M. DeWitt, 1860 [accessed 7 July 2004–15 March 2005]; available from www.letrs.indiana.edu/cgi/t/text/text-idx?c=wright2;idno=wright2-0792.

Equiano, Olaudah. *Equiano's Travels: His Autobiography—The Interesting Narrative of the Life of Olaudah Equiano or Gustavus Vassa the African.* First published 1789. Reprint, London: Heinemann Educational Books, Ltd., 1967.

Forde, Daryll, and G. I. Jones. *The Ibo and Ibibio-Speaking Peoples of South-Eastern Nigeria.* Reprint, London: International African Institute, 1967.

Gilliland, C. Herbert. *Voyage to a Thousand Cares: Master's Mate Lawrence with the African Squadron, 1844–1846.* Annapolis: Naval Institute Press, 2004.

Harland, John. *Seamanship in the Age of Sail: An Account of the Shiphandling of the Sailing Man-of-War, 1600–1860.* London: Naval Institute Press, 1984.

Haycock, David Boyd. "Exterminated by the Bloody Flux" [article online]. *Journal for Maritime Research* (London: National Maritime Museum [accessed 15 February 2005]); available from www.jmr.nmm.ac.uk/server.php?show=conJmrArticle.1.

Hogg, Ian V. *An Illustrated History of Firearms.* New York: A & W Publishers, 1980.

Howard, Thomas. *Black Voyage: Eyewitness Accounts of the Atlantic Slave Trade.* Boston: Little, Brown and Company, 1971.

Humble, Richard. *Ships, Sailors, and the Sea.* New York: Franklin Watts, Inc., 1991.

Huntley, Sir Henry. *Seven Years' Service on the Slave Coast of Western Africa.* 2 vols. London: Thomas Cautley Newby, Publisher, 1850.

Hutchinson, Louise Daniel. *Out of Africa: From West African Kingdoms to Colonization*. Washington, D.C.: Smithsonian Institution Press, 1979.

Isichei, Elizabeth. *A History of the Igbo People*. New York: St. Martin's Press, 1976.

Kemp, Peter, ed. *The Oxford Companion to Ships and the Sea*. Oxford: Oxford University Press, 1976.

Lever, Darcy. *The Young Sea Officer's Sheet Anchor: Or a Key to the Leading of Rigging and to Practical Seamanship*. London: John Richardson, 1819. Reprint, Mineola, NY: Dover Publications, Inc., 1998.

Lewis, Michael. *The Navy in Transition, 1814–1864: A Social History*. London: Hodder and Stoughton, Ltd., 1965.

Lloyd, Christopher. *The Navy and the Slave Trade: The Suppression of the African Slave Trade in the Nineteenth Century*. Slavery Series No. 4. London: Frank Cass and Co. Ltd., 1968.

Lubbock, Basil. *Cruisers, Corsairs & Slavers: An Account of the Suppression of the Picaroon, Pirate & Slaver by the Royal Navy During the 19th Century*. Glasgow: Brown, Son & Ferguson, Ltd., 1922.

Madubuike, Ihechukwu. *Structure and Meaning in Igbo Names*. Buffalo: Council on International Studies, State University of New York, 1974.

Maryland Historical Society. "Joseph Despeaux Papers [1778–1933]" [papers online, accessed 28 October 2004]; available from www.mdhs.org/ library/Mss/ms000260.html.

McGrouther, M. "Find a Fish: Bull Shark—*Carcharhinus leucas* Valenciennes" [information online]. Sydney, Australia: Australian Museum, 2004 [accessed 28 June 2005]; available from www.austmus.gov.au/ fishes/fishfacts/fish/cleucas.htm.

McGuane, James P. *Heart of Oak: A Sailor's Life in Nelson's Navy*. New York: W. W. Norton & Co., 2002.

Melville, Herman. *Moby-Dick; or, The Whale*. New York: Harper & Brothers, 1851. Reprint: Adler, Mortimer J., ed. Great Books of the Western World, No. 48. Chicago: Encyclopaedia Britannica, Inc., 1991.

Miller, David. *The World of Jack Aubrey: Twelve-pounders, Frigates, Cutlasses, and Insignia of His Majesty's Royal Navy*. Philadelphia: Courage Books, 2003.

Naish, G.P.B., and Heather Amery. *The Age of Sailing Ships*. London: Usborne Publishing, Ltd., 1976.

New York Bible and Common Prayer Society. *The Book of Common Prayer* [1789], 6th ed. [book online]. Philadelphia: J. B. Lippincott and Co., 1865 [accessed 2 August 2004–March 2006]; available from http://justus.anglican.org/resources/bcp/1789/BCP_1789.htm.

Rediker, Marcus. *Between the Devil and the Deep Blue Sea.* New York: Cambridge University Press, 1987.

Richardson, William. *A Mariner of England: An account of the career of William Richardson from cabin boy in the merchant service to warrant officer in the Royal Navy (1780 to 1819) as told by himself.* London: John Murray, 1908.

Roydon, M. W. "Edward Rushton: Life and Times of an 18th Century Radical and the Foundation of the Blind School in Liverpool" [information online, accessed 12 November 2004]; available from www.btinternet.com/~m.royden/mrlhp/local/rushton/rushton.htm.

Thomas, Hugh. *The Slave Trade: The Story of the Atlantic Slave Trade, 1440–1870.* New York: Simon & Schuster, 1997.

Ume, Kalu E. *The Rise of British Colonialism in Southern Nigeria, 1700–1900: A Study of the Bights of Benin and Bonny.* Smithtown, NY: Exposition Press, 1980.

Umeasiegbu, Rems Nna. *The Way We Lived.* London: Heinemann Educational Books, Ltd., 1969.

Ward, W.E.F. *The Royal Navy and the Slavers: The Suppression of the Atlantic Slave Trade.* New York: Pantheon Books, 1969.

Williams, Guy. *The Age of Miracles: Medicine and Surgery in the Nineteenth Century.* Chicago: Academy Chicago Publishers, 1987.

Williamson, Kay, ed. *Igbo-English Dictionary: Based on the Onitsha Dialect.* Based on the compilation by G. W. Pearman. Revised and expanded by C. N. Madunagu and E. I. Madunagu, and others. Benin City, Nigeria: Ethiope Publishing Corp., 1972.

Wilson, J. Leighton, with notes by Captain H. D. Trotter. *The British Squadron on the Coast of Africa.* London: J. Wilson, 1851. Reprint, York, U.K.: K Book Editions, 1973.

Wood, J. Taylor. "The Capture of a Slaver" [article online]. *Atlantic Monthly* 86 (1900): 451–463 [accessed 12 December 2004]; available from http://etext.lib.virginia.edu/etcbin/toccer-new2?id=WooCapt.sgm&images=images/modeng&data=/texts/english/modeng/parsed&tag=public&part=1&division=div1.